WRITER, SEEKER, KILLER

Writer, Seeker, Killer

Ryan S. Leavitt

Cover art by Mi Enn

Edited by Rogena Mitchell-Jones

Visit my website: www.ryansleavitt.com

Join my e-mail for discounts and updates on books and projects I have coming up. As a thanks, you'll get a free ebook to take home.

Sound good?

Sign up at:
Ryansleavitt.com

Table of Contents

This is for Stephanie, Chris, & Arthur.

"The mind that aims to understand reality can consider itself satisfied only by reducing it to terms of thought."

-Albert Camus

FOREWORD

This story is not for the faint of heart. What you shall soon behold is largely grounded in realism, in spite of your disbelief. It is a search for truth in a place known worldwide as New Orleans. A city that is both a terrible and brilliant place to live.

If you are willing, I'd like to show you a side of New Orleans which may have escaped your notice. This journey is one you may find brutal, challenging, and even perhaps exhausting. When searching for the truth of any matter, one must not exclude the things one considers to be unfavorable or unacceptable. And for a city so young, New Orleans has seen a more vibrant history than most places its age. While the climate is harsh, the people can be seen as easygoing. *Can* be. There is one exception which is fastidiously executed: that which dies or ends in New Orleans is rarely without a boisterous memorial.

And so before we enter the city proper, understand that it is a place where the sacred and the profane dance rather closely together, in a way which has no comparison that I am aware of. What I offer you may seem dark, but I have come to believe by shedding light on the evil that lurks within and beyond us we may expose something we all desperately require to ultimately prevail.

There are terrible acts of violence in this book. As it is in New Orleans. There are things unpleasant and taboo that could not remain obscured. As it is in New Orleans. There is an answer for all that. It is here and now that that answer will be sought after.

May your curiosity of life overcome your destiny for death.

WRITER

"New Orleans and the moon have always seemed to me to have an understanding between them, an intimacy of sisters grown old together, no longer needing more than a speechless look to communicate their feelings to each other. This lunar atmosphere of the city draws me back whenever a time of recession is called for. Each time I have felt some rather profound psychic wound, loss, or failure. I have returned to New Orleans at such periods."

-Tennessee Williams

PROLOGUE

The mail came early. Sasha battled through the unexpected pellets of rain, making her way toward the patio, seeing it tucked at the bottom of her screen door, hardly shielded from the rain. Crouching down to retrieve it, she felt happy to be home from work.

With haste, she entered her apartment, and then she shuffled indifferently through the items addressed to her. First, there was a Canseco's advertisement, then the month's utility bill. However, at the bottom of the pile was something of great interest to Sasha—a letter from Hinanya. She tossed the other mail on the coffee table in the living room. She hadn't lived at the address long, so it was impressive Hinanya hadn't missed a beat.

Making her way to the bathroom, Sasha decided to take a blow-dryer to the letter before opening it. In her eagerness, her fingers dug into the residual moisture on the underside of the envelope's seal. The soggy adhesive gave way. Hinanya was a persistent Luddite. It baffled Sasha as writing letters were becoming so uncommon, a novelty, but Hinanya had relegated them as her primary means of their communication, a decision held firm for six years since they were children in school together. Despite time and distance, Hinanya consistently wrote to Sasha, devoted to their friendship. Even over the gauntlet of puberty, Sasha would always find that if she wrote to Hinanya, Hinanya would write back in earnest. Although Sasha would have to admit if pressed it was Hinanya who'd kept their friendship alive. If it weren't for Hinanya's letters, Sasha understood she would have purged Hinanya from her mind entirely as time went on.

Before reading the letter, now safely unfolded, Sasha turned on her A/C and removed her drenched shirt and her shoes. Sasha was on her couch before her clothes hit the floor.

With nothing else to do that day, she began reading the letter, a hint of Hinanya's vanilla perfume surfaced from her memory. It was in her nostrils, so Sasha wafted the paper to her nose to see if the scent perceived was in the letter she held. It was not.

Dear Sasha,

Hello, dear. What a long time it's been. How do you feel? I can't believe things, how it's occurring all at once. I'm returning. I think it will be an interesting race to see if I can beat this letter to see you in person before you receive it. I leave Mankato tomorrow. To live on my own. My family still objects. But forget that. I seriously cannot wait to see you again. Think of what you want to do. I'll take you out to eat. Anything you want. I recall you had an affinity for nachos? I hope it's still true. I apologize for my consistent declining of those Skype videos you are so fond of. I'm sure it's a lovely time.

     The preparations for moving out have been challenging. You know Taylor is taking it harder than I am, though. I don't know what that's supposed to mean. Remember how Taylor tried to persuade my parents that we should all move back to New Orleans when I made my announcement? My parents refused with such vehemence. Her reaction was violent, to say the least. But since then, it's been quiet. This bare countryside understands, but I don't.

     Oh, and you won't believe this, but my parents don't remember you. I keep to myself as they say, so they're surprised I've kept in touch with anyone from New Orleans for so long. It's going to be really nice to be out of their control.

Surfacing from the letter, Sasha paused as if on the verge of realizing something. Before it fully formed in her head, Sasha caught sight of her poster hung by her window, a reprint of the painting *To Fallen* by the Renaissance artist Juche. It made her resonate with Hinanya's words. Sasha's parents were staunch Catholics who hated the art without understanding it. Now that Sasha had a place of her own, she was free to display it wherever she pleased.

Juche's piece depicted a very controversial image for his time. It was one of a large, nude female angel lying still on the ground with splayed wings and a visibly mangled right leg. Above this broken immaculation was a man descending into the fallen angel, a sexual violation implicit amid the background of distant Eden. The man's face was looking up dejectedly to paradise and not at the angel.

It was weird Sasha couldn't respond until Hinanya contacted her. Hinanya was disconnected from her parent's cell phone plan. She would need to set up alternative arrangements for a house phone when she arrived. Until then, Sasha would just have to wait. It wouldn't be much longer, Sasha supposed. Hinanya was sweet to offer to take her out for something to eat. Sasha resumed reading the letter as Hinanya covered a few other little things before the salutation, which read:

     Love,
     Hinanya

Sasha put the letter down, unsure of how she felt. There were some reservations on Sasha's part, but all in all, she was, like Hinanya, looking forward to rekindling their old friendship. The problem was there was no way to gauge how exactly Hinanya had changed over the years.

Yet the letter felt so honest. Sasha herself was transitioning from high school to the real world too. There was nothing to be done but do her best with her steadfast friend. With no misgivings, Sasha relaxed on her couch to take in the cool air spreading around her, a touch of tranquility before Hinanya's arrival.

1. THE BUS ROUTE

Objects moved past Hinanya in a blended blur. There were buildings and shrubs which served no practical function in the context of the space they occupied. No amenities or enterprise to speak of. No, Hinanya saw mostly disrepair and then ramshackle homes with portions of their roofs scraped away. Or blotches of tar spilled accidentally on the pavement. Her desire to focus on any particular spot or color was out of the question due to the bus's lumbering velocity. Only when the driver applied the brakes had its pace stuttered and offered her a clear view of things. Hinanya truly wanted to be still. Yet even as the bus became stationary, Hinanya's original city was still only visible through the veil of the summer's heat screen. And so her desire was unfounded.

She thought to become still would mean it would be easier to process the information she was taking in. Instances elapsed where what Hinanya saw moved outside of her sight. And within her, people and places scant in her earliest memories were conjured. While those in the present outside walked over jagged sidewalks. Most of them appeared to her as wretched. Though it had been over five years since Hurricane Katrina, their gait seemed to have an air of struggle against some storm currently taking place.

It was harsh, but that was the price of freedom, to no longer be solely a product of her mother or father, a child unable to make independent choices for herself. They had chosen to stay in Minnesota, exiles by choice after Katrina had condemned their home in Metairie. For a long time, Hinanya shared her parent's opinion on New Orleans, how any hypothetical return would leave them at the mercy of another Katrina down the line. This deviation, in their view, was her first bit of freedom. It had occurred recently, less than a year ago.

Sunlight was temporarily cut off as the bus rode under an interstate bridge, and Hinanya was horrified to see her reflection. She shut her eyes and tried to imagine things other than her face. Her hair, like always, was set in a ponytail. Its texture was wavy, black, but graying in some areas around the crown of her head.

She was nineteen.

The graying didn't bother her so much. It was her body as a whole that irked her. She was overweight. In anguish, she clasped her hands around her thighs. Her blue bandanna fashioned as a wristband brushed against the gap of exposed skin between her leggings and her top. Hinanya shuttered in feeling it touch her skin.

Hinanya was an oddity on the bus of mostly black New Orleanian, due to her mixed-race skin tone. The bus route was becoming a habit for the girl.

The faces of the others were becoming familiar as they seemed to size her up as something different from them, some counterfeit that wasn't truly part of the ruined city. The feeling made her think she should get to running or biking to school, but the bus was just so easy. Besides, she'd suffered the same as they had, and it had hardly been her choice to remain away, to not return for so long.

The route took them up Elysian Fields and became more of a residential area where driveways had boats in them. Some pieces of the city she saw were bereft of damage, while other scars seemed untouched and permanent. Like the section of sidewalk that had split and jutted out a foot above the rest.

A young boy who had come onto the bus put some music on. Its jumbled beat consisted of Bounce yet was mashed with jazz elements. As it played, Hinanya felt at home, though she had no love for either type of music. In fact, she felt the song itself was terrible. It beckoned her to be aware of her surroundings. The danger around the corner she'd had no awareness of as a child.

"Turn that music off on this bus," the driver instructed to the youth abruptly.

The boy in turn resisted, but Hinanya gave turned her focus from the exchange. Instead, she resumed her vigil of New Orleans. They were approaching their destination. The argument ramped up, and Hinanya felt the passengers casting their attention away from her. She was invisible once more. It was great. She loved to be left alone, to be unseen. It gave her time to figure things out clearly. There was no arrogance in this. It was merely the optimal mode of her being, a barrier erected from a gracious pragmatism.

A serene field unfolded before her—the center of the university. A half-smile appeared on her face.

Stepping off of the bus with an eager stride, she was impeded by people in front of and behind her, a calamity between the people waiting for the bus too impatient for the other passengers to get off. As Hinanya stepped onto the sidewalk, someone asked her something.

"No," she said without hearing what was said or looking directly at the person, who was standing a few inches to her right.

The bus pulled away once the new passengers had boarded, and the people who'd exited went in separate directions.

Anticipating further dialogue from the questioner, Hinanya left the bus stop, hoping she wouldn't be followed. She wasn't and presumed the questioner waited for a more receptive person to come along.

2. SEEKING TO PART

What was sought could always be understood in regard to what was lacked. And yet what people sought could so very often be different from what was lacking.

Each face Hinanya locked onto while they passed her by from the concrete table she sat on was in the process of reacting to their respective deficiencies, and thus an array of somber expressions. For Hinanya, it seemed to be the case that what she sought could be apprehended in a particular face of these passersby. Not anybody she knew, but instead, an expression telling her she was in the right place, or at least close.

It wasn't the most efficient way to realize her goal, but it did reduce the number of people she would have to interact with.

As a group of three girls walked by, Hinanya turned to see a banner hanging from a building that housed the university cafeteria. In bold hand-painted letters, there was an invitation to a group prayer session, sponsored by the Christian Club in response to the recent mayhem on campus. On the second night of the semester, a girl was walking to her dormitory, apparently quite carefree and in no hurry. She turned a corner into a swinging machete wielded by some deranged character. They brandished a hoodie tied tight around their face and also, according to the girl, had on some dark mask concealing their facial features. The surprise of this was amplified throughout subsequent stories since there was no one around to help her as the blade struck against her left arm and split open skin and muscle. The assailant kept hacking away at her, the action continuing to concentrate on the same spot.

This was when a rushing determination met the monstrous being—as both hands came around the machete to the force of hitting her arm once more. Then once the force was sufficiently distributed, and even more blood displaced itself from veins onto the sidewalk. The machete fell to the ground, its welder stomping the girl on the pavement before darting away into a nearby vehicle.

By the time the girl's projected agony was registered by others, the vehicle was gone, unidentified.

The incident was unprecedented on campus. Even for New Orleans it was especially gruesome. For the university's placement on the outskirts of the city, it had typically achieved a kind of amnesty against such senselessness.

The authorities immediately assumed the girl was intractably linked to some unscrupulous piece of that part of New Orleans. However, an investigation only yielded the fact that she was a budding marketing major from Myrtle Beach was by all accounts an innocent victim, targeted for haphazard savagery that left her arm irrevocably damaged.

What happened had spurred everyone on campus to band together. Complete strangers now looked out for one another to ensure safety, tempered with a contrary quiet paranoia that anyone could have been the attacker. So a subtle implication came that anyone on campus who was alone fell into two categories—a person begging for the girl's fate or one persistent enough to will that fate onto another.

No one on campus felt safe, not even within the vicinity of others, of a crowd.

What Hinanya wanted to know, content with the supposition that this was a random attack of some psychopath, was what else would the attacker had done? How much more of a devious plot and further purpose would have been expanded on if it weren't for the proximity of others? Had the attacker wished to cleave the arm off entirely? To sever it and leave it as he had the machete or to take it as one would a hanging and cracked branch from a tree as for some accolade or sacrifice of the flesh?

It was amusing to Hinanya how the call to prayer had been posted in the wake of this attack as opposed to any other time. Such atrocities were taking place on a daily basis worldwide, but now that it had taken place right under their noses, solidarity was vital?

Since the attack, campus police were on high alert in anticipation of further instigators poised to wreak havoc at the normally peaceful school. But all and all, it seemed to be an aberration. For all that, Hinanya was unfazed. She continued going there and looking lost.

As even if there was a risk in her presence in this place, it was one worth taking for what she sought here.

3. NO COLLABORATION

"Man, that shouldn't matter, you know? I mean, we jus' tryin' to be out here and have some fun," said Nestor.

"You know Grannie. She thinkin' we up to the worst of it. But I mean really, ain't nothing but us homeys chillin' outdoors." Peb caressed some developing dreadlocks on the side of his head with a grin. It was just a beautiful day. In fact, it was Peb's first free pass to go out with his friends.

The young man had turned thirteen the day before. The overwhelming heat of the day had subsided, and the sun was in decrescendo. Which meant, unfortunately, his time out was almost over. Grannie hadn't given him a specific time to be back, but he was sure she would raise hell if he weren't back in time for dinner. It was embarrassing for him to admit, but Peb had never been able to go out after school or on the weekends with his friends. The hesitation on his Grannie's part was due to the many perils to be found far too close to them. But Peb finally talked Grannie into letting him out because if New Orleans truly was no place to raise a child, then why hadn't they left after all these years? She had grown up there, and she'd raised Peb's mother Joyce there, who had died several years prior. The circumstances had never been sugar-coated. Grannie didn't mourn her daughter. Instead, she used the story of Joyce's life as a morality play. Joyce Stone died of complications during liver surgery. And the need for that surgery stemmed from severe drug and alcohol abuse.

Peb, Nestor, and their friend Sam were sitting on the porch of an abandoned house not far from where Peb lived. They had been free to wander around as long as they stayed away from Washington Square. And Nestor was so right. They hadn't gotten into any trouble, just hung out and had some laughs. It was a special day, and Peb knew he'd remember it for a long time.

Sometimes, he wished he could just live with Nestor, or on darker days, that it had been his Aunt Rhea who'd died instead. After all, his mom and his aunt used to fuck with the worst shit. That way Nestor would be with Grannie instead, and Peb's mom would be alive. Still with him and way less strict. On top of that, Peb really wanted a laptop. Nestor had one, but Grannie just couldn't afford to buy him one. Several birthdays and Christmases had passed with his requesting one to no avail. Grannie didn't like technology, and she especially didn't like the idea of Peb spending his hours on the internet. It was so fucked. No one he knew had such stringent rules on being able to go out, yet he hardly had anything to do inside.

His aunt sympathized with him. Last Easter, she'd bought him a Nook and had also filled it with hundreds of books, hoping he'd get into reading. But it hadn't worked for Nestor, and it didn't work for him. The thing was able to Google shit, but that was the extent of it. It couldn't play YouTube and more importantly, it couldn't play porn. Peb hadn't gotten past page seven of a book called *Things Fall Apart*. In fact, the boy had sold it to raise funds for his brother Caso's bail. Caso had made him pawn it and a few other things.

Auntie Rhea was on his side. He remembered the two women recently debating with about letting Peb go out.

"Ma, if you is going to keep him inside, he'll never learn how to make his own choices."

But Grannie had only frowned. "Boys get into all trouble in this city. If I could know that he'd be safe out there while he was tryin' to have fun, I'd let him. But come on, Rhea. Baby, think of what happened to Joyce."

"Quit bringin' that up every day! Don't let Joyce's mistakes ruin Peb's life too. Let the boy do his thing. He good."

"Yeah, but New Orleans ain't."

Nothing bad happened, so that was good. Then again, there had been a bit of trouble earlier that day, beyond St. Claude. Peb had been sitting on a bench with Nestor and Sam sipping Big Shot sodas. Two older boys sauntered past them and then returned to challenge Peb and his friends to a game of crabs.

"Nah, son, we set," said Nestor.

"You never know that," said one of the boys. He was all the more giant as he stood over Peb on the bench. "On the real, you got as much odds as us."

"It ain't about odds," said Sam. Peb thought Sam was a cool-ass white-boy. "Ask someone else 'cause we ain't interested."

"I see you, kid," said the other boy, shorter but broader than the first. "I can tell you bored too. Y'all poor and that's how you'll stay if you don't try and hustle."

"So if you really hustlin'," said Peb, "go somewhere else, 'cause we said we good, and we serious on that."

The shorter boy pushed both his hands down on the table, and two dice rolled out of his unfurled fists. "This the problem, why we always gettin' pushed to the bottom. No one wanna collaborate." He set his head back and twisted it around, a crack emanating from his neck. "No collaboration. Yo. That's how we all stopped being monkeys in the first place, ya heard?"

Peb began to feel threatened. It might be better to accept the bet, take the L by losing a few dollars than to get his shit kicked in.

Then Sam stood up and said, "Let's go."

"Well, all right!" said the taller one, the hostility in his voice trumpeting into enthusiasm.

"I was talkin' to my boys."

"Next time I see y'all, we playin'. It's fun. Fair enough?"

"If they don't wanna, fuck 'em," said the shorter boy.

14

The two boys walked away, making quiet insults on Peb's possible sexuality as they left. As tempting as it was to turn back and confront those dumb pieces of shits, Peb knew it would most likely be the end of his going out privileges, whether they got a good hit in or not.

Though they'd successfully navigated away from the boys, Nestor and Sam were bucking to fight. They were much more verbal about that point after the older boys had gotten away, though.

Other than that incident, it was a glorious day. Freedom and fun, that's all Peb wanted. As for those two, he thought it best not to tell Grannie about them. He doubted he'd ever see them again.

Peb had no interest in fighting anybody, but at the same time, he knew if the wrong person pushed him, he'd have to defend himself.

4. THE ROBBERY

Hinanya was three buildings away from her apartment when a man approached her. He was tall, with a scruffy face—a shambling vagabond.

"Hey do you gotta dollar?" he asked from her left side.

"Yeah, none for you." She walked past with her back turned to him.

"Nah, come on now. This ain't cool. You got manners somewhere up there? Yo!"

Hinanya continued to disregard him.

"Ah, fuck this. Gimme your wallet." She heard the man coming toward her and side-stepped to see the glimmer of a knife. Its path reoriented in the wake of her evasion to where she stood against a wooden telephone pole. She was invited to survive. As such, there was no begging, no shrugging off responsibility. Hinanya sprang into action.

Letting the man thrust the blade toward her stomach, Hinanya twisted her arms around his until the lock was sufficient to force the man to release his grip on the blade. Now unable to maneuver without the threat of a dislocated shoulder, the man's bearing changed from belligerence to sorrow.

"Okay, okay. We done. Don't hurt me!"

Hinanya did not acknowledge him, only transferred her arms so that her left arm could pop his shoulder out of place and the right could strike at him. As she applied more tension against the man's shoulder, she pulled himself upward and sent a half fist into his sternum. But something went wrong. There was a hard surface which met her blow. Pain loosened her grip.

This gave the man an opportunity to take whatever was in front of his sternum out. It was a gun. Generally, this wouldn't stop Hinanya, but she immediately recognized it not only for its model but as identical to one she'd seen before. One she'd held. The exact same one. There was no mistaking it.

"Dumb bitch don't listen. Gives no mercy, gets no mercy, gives no respect, gets none neither—" Whatever it was that the man had planned to say next was cut off by Hinanya's head colliding with his, as she attempted to coil an arm around his. But he reeled back too quickly, and she so dazed that she missed her chance to lock him in. This left an opening for either side to get the upper hand.

Colors floated in her vision, and she set upon disarming the man with that gun she knew so well. She was able to parry his arm away from her as she slid underneath him, and with a primal groan, she hoisted him into the air to throw him onto the ground. The bum tried to land on his feet, but the inertia overcame him. Toppling over, the gun slid from his hand as he tried to stop the side of his face from being knocked against the curb.

From there, Hinanya kicked him and then made for the gun—yes, the gun. The gun she thought it was. Pocketing it, she enveloped him once more, this time in a sleeper hold.

"Where did you get that gun?"

"Huh? What the fuck?"

"Where?"

"The fuck? You dumb light-skinned round bitch think you can fling me around? If you jus' gave me a dollah! Now you actin' like you police."

"You're out here trying to hurt people."

"Man's gotta eat. These streets is heartless. If you out here and you ain't know that then fuck, you fuckin' dumb."

Hinanya realized how long the struggle had been taking place. The gun was in her pocket. It wasn't that late. If no one had seen this struggle yet, they would soon. Something eerie had happened, and it was best to flee with the gun. If that particular gun hadn't appeared, it would have meant she may have broken his arm and called the police, but something uncanny had taken place. It was enough that she'd been waiting for the moment when she was threatened as a result of her return to New Orleans. She relished the opportunity to fight back, to feel that rush of turning the tables on the man must have believed her to be an easy score. Still, it felt like she was biting off more than she could chew.

Hinanya's arm constricted around the man's throat until the refusal of oxygen forced him to fall into syncope. Though his limp body slid off her and the confrontation was done, she knew his acrid scent and essence would not be parted from her nearly as easily. She made no attempt to place him on the ground with care.

She then finished her sojourn back to her apartment to contemplate that seemingly impossible question. How had that man gained possession of the gun Stefan had used to kill himself?

5. INEXPLICABLE RETURN

Opting not to enter her apartment, Hinanya listened from within the first-floor hallway for any reaction to the commotion she'd been a part of. Shortly after she regarded the item in her hand with trepidation. The neighborhood she had moved into was a chaotic one, and minor crimes were apt to go unreported for want of as little police presence as possible. The gangs had an interest in remaining inconspicuous. There was a tacit understanding to mind one's own business in the area. Hinanya supposed the destitute man didn't value any of that.

The firearm, a Glock 21, had to be Stefan's. Hinanya hadn't faltered in that initial estimation. From the alleyway, a bluish hue from the side bulb offered her light to see the details of the gun, hot and sweaty in her examining fingers.

It was the first time she'd ever touched it, though she'd seen it on numerous occasions and had watched Stefan firing it. Though it was missing its black leather holster she had often seen it housed in, Hinanya knew.

Stefan had been one of her only friends during her time in Minnesota. He'd cherished the piece for recreation but had ultimately used it as an instrument for suicide. It happened not long before she'd committed to going back to New Orleans.

Every label matched what she remembered. The Glock logo. 21. .45. The magazine extender. Even hollow-point bullets in the magazine. Stefan always used hollow-points, even when just shooting at targets.

Hinanya's hands clasped the minute grips along the butt of the gun, twisting it to see the most defining feature—irrefutable evidence despite all sense—there were Stefan's initials in pale gray spray paint stenciled on the right side of the barrel: *S.M.*

The gun had somehow made its way from Mankato to New Orleans. Just like she had. However unlikely it seemed. The reality of it defied all rational thought.

Hinanya was sure she had Stefan's gun—only, it wasn't any longer, was it? It was hers.

From a utilitarian standpoint, it had been a good call to relieve the homeless man of the weapon, as it seemed he was willing to use it for limitless evils. But this transposition, the gun she held, after everything Stefan's suicide had meant—she knew she would not relinquish the gun.

She held the barrel to her nostrils to perceive the scent of gunpowder and metal. It fascinated her. Then she slid the gun across her face, caressing her cheeks and her temple with it, knowing just where it would most likely be lethal. Hinanya was intimidated by the power she held.

This Glock was manufactured with a unique safety feature. Instead of the button on the side, which could be toggled on or off, the safety was set as a part of the trigger. An apex trigger. The implication was that with a Glock, the safety was you.

Moving back out to the alleyway from the back stairwell leading to her apartment, Hinanya pocketed the Glock. She saw the man crawling to his feet with the pace of slow-motion video manipulation. Once up, he wasted no time getting as far away from the sight of his defeat as possible, still spouting some inane diatribe against her.

The feeling of power returned then. Hinanya could shoot the man. She imagined doing so in her head, the act of aiming at his body, lining up the white dot above the cylinder between the sights, and emptying the magazine into him. That gravity tensed her only for a moment, then she made a point to loosen her grip on the gun and put it away once more, alarmed that she'd unconsciously taken it out again.

What a ridiculous notion, she thought as the man-made for beyond the range of what the gun could muster. There was no returning it.

Hinanya knew he must have stolen it somehow, so why should she have any sympathy for him?

And a bigger question still: *Did* she really intend to keep it? Better yet, could she keep it without using it to kill herself? Before those thoughts germinated into a definitive answer, a red Volvo pulled up to her apartment building from the street and beeped four times. Sasha. Hinanya was forced to shelf this new development to yield to her social obligation.

6. NOTHING TO KNOW

By the time their food was ready, Hinanya and Sasha were steeped in conversation sourced from their missing years together. The exchange was going better than either of them had anticipated, yet there was a slight tension that resided in unsaid aspects of their conversation.

They were in Sasha's car outside the sushi shop, which was poorly lit. Behind them was a vacant field, scattered with litter.

The area they were relatively close to was where Hinanya had grown up along Lake Pontchartrain. The flooding during Hurricane Katrina had been severe. Incidentally, the university was nearby too, giving Hinanya dread at her failures. She didn't voice those, however.

Sasha's face curled into a goofy expression as she pulled back the lid of her dinner with insuppressible delight. They looked at one and other, laughing. Then Hinanya realized how short Sasha's hair was. Shorter than she'd ever seen it during their childhood. Such a length would have invited ridicule from their peers and perhaps even Hinanya herself. But now, it seemed to be a crime against fashion not to adopt the hairstyle Sasha had.

The thought collided with the summation of Sasha's passionate anthem to her pursuit of becoming a zoologist. "Most of my family is still in Bogota, I could have such a dazzling life down there, but not until I'm done with my things here."

"So I come back to New Orleans, and you're on your way out, eh?" Hinanya teased.

"It'll still be a few years yet. I mean, you're back, and I still haven't figured out why or if you plan to stay."

"Then maybe I'll tell you," Hinanya said, not entirely meaning it. Sasha's strapless blue dress upstaged Hinanya's gray hoodie and black pants as if each participant in the night's plans had proceeded with differing expectations for their reunion. "I mean, whatever you want to know."

"I want to know it all," Sasha insisted eagerly.

"What if it's boring?"

"Come on, Hinanya. Quit being fidgety." Sasha's voice rose in pitch to add, "I'm curious!"

Curious. Yes, there was no doubt about that. Sasha had recently been recognized as a grown-up by the former generation, whose own youth was wasted for a pearl of ambiguous wisdom. She was at a point where it was expected of her to explain her plan to the world. It could feel like interrogations, ceaseless and unexpected. Such a constant bombardment turned a simple question into a rehearsed answer, like the hollow rhetoric of an ineffective politician. But that was fundamental in the arena of dealing with others—the price of conversation.

"Not to deny you even longer," Hinanya deliberated, "but I just think it's incredible that you still want to be a zoologist. It's something you've wanted since we were girls." Sasha had taken a love for animals to an extreme. Though she wasn't a vegetarian, she wouldn't kill bugs she saw in her apartment and condemned people who hunted for sport.

"Yeah, I know. I guess it's just always stuck with me. Some things do, you know what I mean?"

"I definitely do," Hinanya assented mildly.

"I remember you wanted to be a cop?" Sasha asked.

"Policewoman," said Hinanya, cracking up. It was not fake laughter. Hinanya was genuinely amused. A rarity. What a fool she'd been in her youth. There was nothing about working in law enforcement that she would be able to stomach. There was not enough space between the laws to improve things. Indeed, her role would be to enforce things she found to be reprehensible now. "That was a fleeting thought brought on from too much *Buffy the Vampire Slayer*."

Sasha smirked and nodded. "Damn, so what now?"

"I'm in school here."

"But here as opposed to elsewhere? It's not like Louisiana is the greatest place to go to school, you know?"

Sasha, by examining the structure of what Hinanya was not telling her, was able to ascertain it. Hinanya didn't come to New Orleans solely for school. "No, Sasha. You're right." A quick pause, the time it took for a light to switch from on to off, then Hinanya asked, "Do you remember the last time we saw each other?"

Hinanya saw Sasha's forehead crease underneath the thin layer of her bangs. After swallowing another piece of her sushi, Sasha said, "I can't say I do. Just a general image of us around Lawson's in those despicable polyester outfits selling chocolate."

"It was a Tuesday. The evacuation was a rumor. It was an otherwise typical day... I recall having a conversation about Ingrid. You know, her accent."

"Oh. Wow. I haven't thought of her in years."

"We both knew it would be a little while before we saw each other again. We had lobbied to leave New Orleans together, have both of our families head to the same place. But yours was going to Arkansas, and mine was refusing to leave at all."

"It's kind of coming back to me," Sasha said solemnly.

"Sasha, it was very hard leaving you behind. Not understanding how things were going to turn out, I wish I had said goodbye. But we didn't know. Then the storm came, all my stuff was ruined. We fled to the Superdome."

"It was bad. But I think it's a miracle we were able to stay in touch. And now look at you. You're back!"

Hinanya couldn't help but internally disagree with Sasha.

Once their food was done, Sasha drove them to the courts at City Park where they used to play tennis. Hinanya considered telling Sasha more, but all she could see was irreparable consequences.

They exited the car, and Hinanya basked in the surrounding trees with a nostalgic grin. Then the joy Hinanya had felt was exhausted as Sasha said, "You still didn't answer my question."

"I'll let you know when I've figured it all that out," Hinanya said. "Honestly, right now, it's just really something special not to be living with my family. Maybe I'm taking that in."

They sat down in the grass to bask in the comfortable breeze of the summer evening.

"Since we've been writing, there's always something I've wanted to ask you," said Sasha.

"Go for it," said Hinanya.

"So, you never mentioned boys. I don't mean to make you uncomfortable. I'm sorry if I do, but are you gay?"

Hinanya could sense the delicacy of the words. Sasha, after everything still clung to prominent remnants of a Catholic upbringing, and Hinanya had no doubt in her mind that Sasha had wanted to phrase the question more like, "You're not *gay*, are you?"

"It's okay, Sasha. It's a fair question."

But Sasha then blurted out, "I'm sorry. I didn't mean it like that," before Hinanya could respond.

"I'm not gay. I'm not straight. I don't date people."

"Then what are you?"

"I don't think I'm anything. Some people may refer to it as asexual. Really, I stay alone, and I deal with it. I don't have any interest in that stuff. It seems like an illusion to me."

"So you're a..." Sasha delayed the last word for some time as if it was a killing blow from an unwilling murderer.

"A virgin. Yes."

"We don't have to talk about this."

Hinanya set a goal in her mind to alleviate the strain of her remaining time with Sasha. It was a challenge to her, one she sought to conquer. "Nonsense! Like I said, it's a fair thing to ask. I mean, how do I put this?" She paused before articulating, "I don't want things like that because these desires, as much as they are inherent, are also compounded by the outside world. I don't like that, you know?" To ease up on things, Hinanya knew the best course of action was to relate to Sasha. "What about you, Sasha? Are you a virgin?" Hinanya was wondering mainly because it would indicate how much of Sasha's upbringing still had her indoctrinated.

"No, I'm not. In fact, I had a pretty real pregnancy scare last year."

"Oh. You could have told me about it." Hinanya didn't look over to her old friend. Instead, she watched a squirrel shimmy its way up a willow tree.

"It was happening for about a month between letters. It was over by the time I got one of your responses, and I was really embarrassed by it."

"I see."

They lay there in relaxation of there being nothing more to know to gaze for a time into that darkly orange patch of Louisiana sky so far beyond either of them.

7. BEGGAR

On his porch waiting for dinner, Peb was laying down in a white net hammock. Darkness had entirely enveloped the night, and he heard police sirens nearby. Maybe even the next block over. Another shooting. Though he felt it might be interesting to go check it out, he'd been told not to leave the house. Tonight, Grannie was making shrimp tasso pasta, and the aroma spread in the breeze from the locked screen door that led directly to the kitchen. It was an old contraption lined with thin black steel bars, most of them bent and distorted from years of slamming and swinging.

Caso was over for dinner, doing his laundry in the backroom. Peb loved Caso, but Caso kept him at a distance. There was no doubt in Peb's mind it had been Grannie's doing. Caso was involved with something drug-related. Hustlin', as those older boys had put it earlier. His arrest and conviction had landed him into some trouble, so lately, Caso was lying low. The only problem there was no way of knowing that for sure, as Caso kept that part of his life as far away from Peb as possible. And Peb hated not knowing what his own flesh and blood was getting into.

There came a rustling from the side alley that led to the backyard. Peb rose cautiously as his throat stiffened with apprehension. His mind thought of some criminal running from the police, in hot pursuit and making his way toward Peb. Thankfully, once he stuck his head out past the porch, he saw it was just Diggy, a poor man who did small things for his brother in exchange for food. Diggy was hobbling, making his way slowly. Peb stepped down and followed the man, eager for any possible excitement or information related to his brother's affairs. Peb sidled along the alleyway until he reached the edge of the house.

Caso sounded startled to see the man. "Yo, what you doin' over here, man?"

"Somethin' strange happenin' tonight, Caso," Diggy said.

"Yeah? Well, keep it away from me. I'm having a very routine evening, aite?"

"No, we needa talk right now, got it?"

"What choo want?"

Peb felt the hair on his arms prickle at his brother's curtness.

Diggy began stammering something entirely incoherent.

"Fuck, did you get high and come to my Grannie's house? Get the fuck outta here," Caso said, his curtness turning into a threatening ferocity. Peb could sense the air of violence that so commonly surrounded his brother, though he was at a distance.

"No, Caso. I'm jus'... shook. Look, so, saw this big biddy strollin' around Spain and Marais, real distinct walk if you know what I mean."

"Not quite. But go on, Diggy. Ain't got all night, and if Grannie sees you, she'll beat yo ass. So if you need somethin', skip the story."

"I don't need nothin'. I came at her for some change. She was like, on it or something, I don't know. Some kind of Kill Bill bitch. Beat me senseless."

"I like it. S'how suppose to go."

"You ain't gonna like this. The light-skinned bitch found that fifth gun... I was carrying it for safety. She took it."

Caso's composure shifted. Where he'd been briefly amused, the ferocity returned. "No, no, no. Diggy, this some irreparable shit. Who the fuck is this girl?"

"Well, the walk—don't that tell us enough?"

"Walk? Man, anyone could be walking any way they do. I don't know what you tryna say, Diggy. That gun is hot. Diggy, we got to find it."

"Maybe she the police, I don't know."

"What, she look like a cop?" Caso pressed.

"Nah. She actin' like one."

"Then I doubt she was a cop, else she woulda taken you in for whatever dumb shit that led to her getting that gun."

"Then I'm right. She gotta be one of them 8IL people!"

"Fuck, yo' dumbass stupid. I straight up feel like killin' right now." Caso paused and Peb heard something crash onto the concrete. "You really this dumb?"

Peb stepped out from the corner of the house where the two men stood, propelled by the panic his brother exhibited. "What she look like then? Some Airbnb tourist?"

Diggy regarded Peb with hesitation then looked down. He looked over to Caso, and Caso nodded in consent. "Like I said, kind of pudgy, light-skinned. Lookin' nothin' like how she is."

"This ain't good, Diggy," said Caso. "Dawg, I told you 'bout how to keep that gun. How could you let that shit go?"

"She got somethin' in her. More than I got. You gotta help me, man. When I be fuckin' up, well, that don't happen so often now, do it? Nah. We got this."

"You're whole life fucked-up, what you even mean?" Caso turned to look down at Peb. "Get outta here. If we both standin' wit' this piece of shit, Grannie will be heated. That's what you needa do, not worry about some fat ninja chick."

"It sound serious, Caso," Peb countered.

"Peb, fuck off for now." Caso moved in front of Peb and shoved him through the backdoor. Peb regarded the veins in Caso's forehead as he turned away, and the glass door shut behind Peb. Peb went through the house on the way back to the front porch, bound by the force of his brother's will.

26

8. Past the Defense

"Hello," a young man said to Hinanya in the breezeway. Regarding him, she saw he was sunburnt, a tall boy with a tame undercut, and a shirt that hosted an innocuous penguin posturing over its offspring.

She considered him, not caring that her indifference was causing him to writhe and regret his action. There was more he had in mind, but he wouldn't say it until she returned a greeting in kind.

"Hi," she said sheepishly, fully lifting her head from her notebook. She looked to his right and saw the area they were in like a cage. There was a cleverness to his maneuvering, and in feeling cornered, Hinanya wished she could harm him and have that be the right thing to do.

"I'm Kurt. Really sorry to bother you, but I was on my way out, and I thought you seemed really cool, like, your style. I like your earrings." He gestured to his ears, and she noticed the side of his left palm was smudged with ink.

"My name is Intah. Thank you for your compliment." Hinanya offered a genial smile and sank her head back down to her notebook.

Before she locked onto the words she'd just been writing, Kurt said, "So, I'm really new here, and I wanted to ask if you had lunch yet. It's a real challenge, you know?"

"How do you mean?" she inquired.

"I'm not from around here at all. I'm from Orlando, and I don't know. I don't know anybody here. Lately, I've been feeling in over my head and realizing I don't know why I left home if it's such a... hard thing for me to talk to strangers, clearly."

Hinanya looked him over. "I see."

Kurt stammered over her to say, "I'm sorry. I really didn't want to bother you."

"It's okay. In a sense, I'm new to New Orleans myself, and I don't know a lot of people either. I've already eaten lunch, but perhaps we could help each other out another time."

Kurt nodded but didn't say anything else.

"I'll leave you my number, and we'll chat at a more suitable time?" Hinanya suggested. "How's that?"

"Oh, sure!" Kurt fumbled in his pocket to get his phone. Handing it to Hinanya, she typed in her number, then mentioned as a cautionary note to him that it was her house number, but she did have an active answering machine. She half expected him to ask if she had a cell phone, but he didn't. "Thank you so much, Intah. I'll see you around." Then Kurt walked away from her, seemingly in a hurry.

About fifteen minutes after he'd left, Hinanya was seated outside the library on the steps. She took a plastic sandwich bag out of her purse. The lies she'd told Kurt were entirely justified in her mind, especially since she had given him her real number.

Incidents such as Kurt were ones that Hinanya felt she could handle very well. It was her burden as a female, to be approached. Perhaps Kurt wasn't interested in fucking her, but even if that wasn't the case, Hinanya had very little to offer him. It was hard enough keeping up the facade in front of people like Sasha. And everyone was so gentle about approaching one another, given the machete incident.

Hinanya slipped her fingers inside the bag, after having rolled the hard-boiled egg, and removed the shell for consumption. There was no enjoyment in her meal, only fuel to allow her to fill the ends of her day. Some days, she'd scan the crowd in anticipation of a destiny while others, like today, were for the notebook where she'd scribble unfiltered thoughts pouring out from her mind like an open wound. The page she had open was heavily decorated with meaningless doodles, idolatries she'd use to focus a pattern of thoughts sufficiently chaotic enough to bring her further from the present, a pattern wanting never to return.

Kurt was doomed. There was no nicer way to put it if he desired Hinanya. How sad it was for him to muster up so much courage to approach her only to be sent down a path that would prove Hinanya to be utterly useless to him. It was only the dead Hinanya truly regarded. They alone were given her devotion, her time.

Hinanya suddenly felt a stark incompatibility to all things material, the page that lay molested by her large hands before her, feeble attempts for her mind to sort out steps to whatever else there was besides this. A diagram crafted with echelons of being and knowing where the tapestries of reality were stretched until penetrated, and she was beyond them. If such a passage was even possible, was it limited to those who had died?

These beckoning calls to dismiss her body and brain as the total sum of her being came from one of those departed others, Uncle Rawls. The spastic man bent on ushering a younger Hinanya away from the temporary inhospitality of New Orleans during Hurricane Katrina.

She had been a witness to the death of his identity.

Soon there would be other things she would have to do, so she set her task to a second egg. She noticed her right knee was twitching. Then she returned to her notebook. The page she had been writing in was filled with scribbles and symbols utterly to capacity. Hinanya carefully tore it out (there were no perforated edges as it was a composition notebook) and she started a new page, but with essentially the same contents as the last. The scribbles revolved around the word *Wenin.*

9. PROFILE

There came an infallible call to end her life. It happened on the way up the stairs to her apartment, a resumption of what Sasha had interrupted a few nights prior.

It presented itself as casually as an old friend seen in passing from time to time. The question shaped itself into the form of all existence. Hinanya wanted to rid the world of what she was, to become, if such a thing was possible, a nothingness of her own accord.

But never before had she possessed such a convenient and tantalizing means as the Glock.

As morbid as it was, Hinanya relished these moments. She felt her hollowness her worthlessness. While marveling at what an incredible energy a firearm was, she collapsed against her front door, a dilapidated thing with chipped paints and cigarette stains.

She wished for a greater degree of ignorance, which was the only place where solace could possibly reside. The finding of the gun would be a paltry occurrence, not one to be questioned ad infinitum.

Life to Hinanya was not solely about knowledge. A prodigious intellect on its own couldn't stop a speeding train. Train? Yes, the sound pacified her. That ever so faint sound of the train rolling down the tracks beyond New Orleans, progressing on its tracks. As a child, she'd hear it from various parts of the city, sometimes enough to wake her up. Some slamming would emanate from that track, an unknown collision early every morning. Being a thing occurring most every day, Hinanya imagined the slam was routine, something meant to happen. Still, she couldn't account for what could make such a destructive racket and yet be part of its progress.

If it weren't for the gun, her death would be a more intangible desire. But with the question of this shifting reality so persistent, Hinanya didn't go into her apartment. The sleek weapon on her person paralyzed her, that being who so often contemplated her own ending. Where an abundance of options had once been, now the Glock came as the definitive means to her death. Should she will it, of course. As Stefan had. To die as Stefan had would be foolish. At least if she did not figure out how she had really found herself with the gun in the first place.

What had seemed a mystical course of events, Hinanya realized, was more likely a terrible happenstance. However it happened was irrelevant. What would she do with this weapon? What was she?

Hinanya was miserable, but why? There was no love for the mystery of life in her. What she sought was the comprehensive answer or explanation of existence. Such a quest results in a peculiar dread. A denseness forms which can permanently dislocated a person from their sense true and false, real and unreal. The conscious mind must spites operations the autonomic nervous system, all the while still trying to project itself toward a purpose, a greater picture beyond that which it is. This same air was clasped around Hinanya while her arms snapped out in front of her. Where before her fingers were splayed and rubbing the filthy floor she sat on, an anxious resistance dissolved as she loosed the gun from her side to once more feel the barrel against her temple in what was becoming a daily ritual. The oxygen in her lungs was stifled yet affirming, and when it was replaced in short huffs from panicked exhalation, it felt like penetration, a glimpse of her true self, who didn't want breath so much as ecstasy. Rapture. Transcendence.

Hinanya had always kept her true self locked away. Her struggle was hers, the recluse who must search inner space deeper than anyone living ever had. She felt able to conceal this fact from others, for they would think such a thing was not her responsibility, but it was. She knew nothing more than that. Once there had been a yearning within to disclosure herself to others unapologetically, and those who remained in her life were those who mattered, those who would set her right and stop her from killing herself, or bring her to a juncture where she didn't want to die. But that had taken mental powers away from alternative routes, all in all, excuses.

Hinanya was the safety. Only she could stop herself from pulling the trigger of the Glock she had her hands curled around. Only she could pop this facticity.

How many times had Stefan held this same gun to his own head before its load could no longer be contained as separate from him? What series of thoughts led to that final drive to death? Was Hinanya closing in on the proper sequence of thoughts required to do it tonight?

No, she was compelled to stop. Her mission, though unbearable, needed to be complete.

The gun went away from her head in a trembling motion as she brought her arm out back to the floor. The decision had all taken place in the span of seconds between the train whistling twice, sounding off to be heeded. Hinanya closed her eyes and heard the beat of blood inside of her. Then, in conjunction with that, she clawed her way to her feet and found each step more reassuring. She ventured outside. All commotion quelled in an uncommon lapse to the placid suburbia around her.

10. NIGHTSCAPE

The stillness was a deception in her mind. There was so much happening within her—had she not been only moments away from self-immolation? Then there was the matter of the city she resided in. All around her, people struggled in mounting misery. Murders, rape, and theft, things even worse beyond her imagination. Yet where she stood in front of her apartment building, there were only parked cars on the street carved up by elements common to this region. The streetlights spilled out onto the sidewalks sloppily, two of the six she could see were out. In the wake of the train, such a nostalgic fixture for Hinanya, she wanted only to survey New Orleans in a way she had never been able to as a child—however she pleased.

The most peculiar thing to Hinanya was how accurate her theory had been back in Minnesota. Hinanya was subject to periodic lashings out, mental ripples that demanded an expiration of life. These episodes began in the drawl farmlands where her family had fled following Hurricane Katrina. When envisioning the environment of New Orleans, the anticipation of going there and meeting her purposes, she was spared from doing irreparable harm to herself. Something about the peace of Minnesota didn't sit with her. It seemed... artificial. Not where she belonged. For too long, her purpose lay outside of her bounds.

New Orleans was better suited for her because even though properties of silence were the same absence of noise wherever one went, New Orleans's nightscape was like a thrilling fantasy. Around any corner Hinanya turned could come another meaning to subjugate her. The further she paced from her apartment, the closer a life clung to a drug for sustenance. It was this feeling of peril in waiting that gave the girl her will back.

Hinanya's mind was frequently focused on death. When it sometimes became out of control, she considered it an awful rush. In Hinanya's awful rush, all five of her senses were thrown off. Standing, she was compelled to hunch over, to be off her feet in favor of holding onto herself as her mind proceeded to travel at a speed she could not fathom. It was the burden of the awful rush that had piloted Hinanya to New Orleans. There was no apparent trigger, and Hinanya's experiences were confined to her alone. No matter how unbearable the awful rush became, she waited each of them out. Sure they would pass as always. But if not...

The city she took in seemed to be pushing against itself. Wild vegetation grew unimpeded on the front lawns of abandoned homes where spray-painted signs warned squatters away with the threat of poison spread throughout the domiciles. She found herself in the Bywater, a gentrified district which was rather quaint to her. Though a mostly African American population, cheap rent attracted all types of people, particularly artists and transplants. Those who'd started coming in droves with the influx of volunteers looking to help the city after Hurricane Katrina was done. Some of them never left.

Katrina's scar on New Orleans appealed to Hinanya. Walking down a neighborhood in the Bywater, it was much like Elysian Fields. Some houses were in good repair, some were built from scratch after Katrina, and some were still abandoned and untouched after the storm had hit.

As the street she strolled down formed into the wide berth of St. Claude Avenue, Hinanya felt even more venerable than before. Hinanya was reminded of how quickly she had been approached by the man who'd had Stefan's gun, and she wished to come upon him again in hopes of being led to an explanation for everything. How plainly it would all turned out if she'd fallen victim to him. She began to notice more spray painted areas like highlighted words on a page. It was as if nowhere but the sky itself was exempt from some form of graffiti. Most of it was illicit, but there were some municipal markings by sewer openings and electrical boxes. Some of those surfaces were tastefully painted over with New Orleans aesthetic, a paltry attempt for the city to compromise its graffiti problem with flavors and shades it sanctioned. But those boxes were scant in comparison to the walls tagged, the bridges covered in that strange language encompassing freedom of speech, gang territory, and anonymous secrets of the collective human unconscious.

Restless, nearly an hour had passed for Hinanya in this fashion as she became more and more fascinated by each tag she saw, realizing that what she sought was hidden in plain sight, needing only to be decoded for meaning by one such as herself. Though Hinanya knew she was alone, there was most certainly a feeling of being perceived from the darkness, just behind her or to her side.

Still, she strolled past in confident steps. Some stories came from New Orleans of bikers being attacked by someone jumping out with a bat from behind a parked car. Or the robbery wherein the victim did not have his wallet, so the thief forced the man to take off his shoes and pants, then ran off with them.

It all felt so contradictory, where Hinanya had been outside of her apartment, barely able to stand what she was, and now she couldn't feel any signs of fatigue despite the constant pace for the incredible duration. Nor did she believe wherever she walked would lead her into a danger she would be unable to handle, a sign of either a guardian angel or total lack of situational awareness.

It was the part of Uncle Rawls she had had such adulation for. What he had passed down to Hinanya. This search for knowledge to the question, as he'd told her countless times, could only be found here. And each tag seemed to beg its own urgent issue, how people so ostracized were cornered and restricted, sentenced to ignorance, and not even aware of it. Where others in New Orleans grew up to become commissioners of great buildings or naval ships, the tags were useful mostly to serve as defacement to those buildings erected, a blank canvas on which to identify themselves to all who passed. What those writers contributed, Hinanya mused, was all they could contribute to a society that had long ago designated them as a liability. They molded and became what was assumed, and thus Hinanya felt disgusted at the cycle of poverty and ignorance, yet also serenity at the notion that these graffiti artists did something about it. Or perhaps these tags were not at all social critiques, but personal expression. Yes. That was the overwhelming majority of the tags she saw. Monikers rendered in innumerable fonts or anagrams stretching across the width of entire buildings.

There was so much vandalism to be seen, but was the intent of these so-called criminals really so bad if their objective was an alleviation of the suffering they were forcefully subjected to?

By and large, the people of New Orleans considered their graffiti a problem. Even the word itself seemed to twist grossly off the tongue. It appeared to be a matter of poverty. After all, any person with a modicum of artistic talent doing graffiti could become a greater artist of repute to boast about having come from New Orleans. But the clandestine and illicit nature of tagging must be what made it so appealing in the first place.

Hinanya herself doodled in her notebooks. Sometimes there were words for what she had to write down, but other times, it became a necessity to craft a diagram on that material page to something immaterial, beyond itself, steps to whatever else there was besides this if such an outer boundary to reality existed. The very point of those doodles was that they were private. That no one could voice their opinion on them but her. And all she could say about them was that they'd steadily improved over the years. If there was a way out of herself, she had to be getting closer.

And yet with graffiti, talent was nothing compared to the passion. Anyone with a can of spray paint could squiggle some ugly lines or sketch out the face of divinity itself. That was the point.

Indeed, as miraculous as her nights in New Orleans had become, this night was perhaps the most significant, for Hinanya spotted a writer at work.

There was, at first, no distinguishing the entity's gender, being clad in dark clothing on top of a billboard. Frightened of startling the writer as if the figure was a timid animal, she sat down, relinquishing her guard to pay all her attention to a tag being born. More details made themselves known as he turned and she saw the skin as a flash of white with masculine features over the billboard lights. She guessed her query was a boy. He crouched to his side to access a canister of spray paint, dropping the one he'd been using. It fell the distance from the billboard walkway to the sidewalk where it clattered with reverberation. Hinanya was ready for him to scatter, and the boy didn't react to what must have been intentional, he only went on with his work. The waves of his arms showed a flow path Hinanya assumed was indicative of an experienced writer.

Though too far away to tell what the tag was, the process of observing gave Hinanya a new aspiration, one she believed would combine well with her others to the point of completion.

Hinanya wanted to tag. Could it slow the awful rush and the turning of the world? That's what she sometimes attributed the awful rush to, even though it was irrational. To be still—could such a thing even be conceived?

No cars drove by, and thus Hinanya felt the boy was safe enough from discovery. He was the first person she'd seen in a long while since leaving her apartment.

And that was the impression that remained with her as his daring streaks of color blended together with a thoughtfulness that seemed threatened that turbulent neighborhood. Hinanya dubbed him Felix.

She was still far too fearful of interrupting his tag and having him flee to make her presence known, but by giving the artist a name, she could only guess what the piece he foraged was. She was still too far away.

A car cruised down the street, offering even the uninterested the crunching bass of some rap songs. Felix continued his work. Hinanya was amazed. He was really out in the open. It wouldn't have been hard for the driver of the vehicle to see him up there on the billboard. In tandem with that observation, Hinanya looked back at the billboard, and for the first time, saw it as a whole. It was a movie poster for some Hollywood remake.

When Felix was done, he seemed to vanish. Hinanya tried to follow his movements down the ladder in hopes of seeing how to get up there, but he was gone.

Yet his tag remained. This part of Felix that could not be contained was now marking the city.

Hinanya approached it, with no intentions of locating Felix, but only wishing to get a better look at what had been produced. She saw the components must have been letters, but upon closer inspection, she noticed they didn't spell any word she knew but something indecipherable to her. Hinanya could tell that much, even from a distance. The letter ran vertically at first, then diagonally right until they hit the corner of the poster. Then even more letters bounced away from the corner to the left some ways. The tag transfixed her and reminded her why she'd come to New Orleans. If the city were a body, it would be plagued with lesions and holes, something to be escaped, even in the most ideal circumstances. What better place then to overcome oneself?

Attempts to get up to the billboard were futile, but Hinanya was able to surmount a fire escape adjacent to it. The elevation granted her a new view of the city, where Felix's tag was an inextricable part of the whole.

Hinanya would become a writer. It may not be exactly what she needed, but one portion of that unintelligible tag was. The striations of two letters communicated something more by how they looked than what they spelled out. Astonished, she believed what was there. She had to get a picture of the tag.

The eagerness she felt was halted when she heard noises from below her, some pair bound for a convenient store in need of blunt wraps and candy. They were well past her while she still marveled at Felix's tag.

Before departing, Hinanya noted another tag on the opposite end of the billboard from Felix's tag and made out, amongst more illegible tags, the words "doesn't return."

11. INCLUSION

As hard as Peb tried to crane his neck, he couldn't see the Mississippi River from where Caso had parked the car. They were across the street from Crescent City Park. Caso was breathing heavily between muddy wheezes. Peb didn't question it. He simply waited to hear what his brother had to say to him. He'd called Peb earlier that day, right after Peb was out of school, and asked to meet up with him. Meetings of this nature were few and far between. Most of the time, Peb only saw his older brother when he needed to do laundry. As such, Peb's mind had been contemplating what this could be about.

"Have a good day, Peb?" Caso asked, also trying to get a glimpse of the water.

"It was whatever, you know?"

"Sure do." Caso dug into a pocket on his gray-collared shirt. He took out a pack of cigarettes and began to the ritual of smoking one. "You don't smoke?"

"I have, a couple of times."

"Nasty," said Caso. He lit himself one. "You so young. Don't even know shit."

Peb's body tensed as Caso's free hand flung out to grip the boy's right shoulder. "If anyone givin' you trouble, why ain't choo say nothin' to me?"

"Who said anyone givin' me trouble?"

"My boys. I sent them out the day you was out, 'member a few weeks back? They asked you to play a game of crabs?"

Peb was startled. "You playin'. You really set me up?"

"I needed to know what kind of person you was. It ain't right for me knowin' you be out now and not keep an eye on you when I can."

"Yo, I took care of it."

"Yeah, you walked away. All right. But if you got beef wit' someone, I need to know, Peb. If you let people step on you—"

"Caso, I woulda stomped those bitches if they came at me. But they was all talk."

"Nah, that wouldn't have been a good idea. Peb, what I'm tryna say is I'm your brother 'n I can protect you, but not if I don't know what kind of trouble you in."

"Aite. I see what you sayin'." Actually, Peb was not sure where this was going. Caso was typically so detached from his life.

Caso squeezed his brother's shoulder harder. "So who givin' you trouble at school?"

"No one, bro! Damn."

"How am I gonna trust you when you didn't tell me 'bout those crabs boys? Huh?" Caso's hand swung up and smacked the side of Peb's head. It was fucked that Caso would hurt him in order to figure out if he needed help. Which he didn't.

"You can trust me 'cause I'm your brother. You know I trust you."

"You ain't tryna break my trust, right?" Caso asked, leering into Peb's eyes.

"Mhm." Peb regarded the veins in his brother's forehead as Caso flicked his cigarette out. Then Caso's hands went to the steering wheel.

"This city ain't friendly. You got to be someone who people know not to fuck wit'. I became that, Peb. I didn't want it, but you gotta have it. It was a necessity out here. We got hotshots tryna to take me down again. I know you 'member when Diggy came crawling over to Grannie's that night."

"Yeah." Peb remembered everything that had been said, too.

"I ain't got that gun back yet. It's life or death kid."

"You ain't find her yet? Maybe she gone, man."

"Nah, she here. We seen her around."

Peb was flabbergasted. "What the fuck?"

"Yeah. My boys been keepin' an eye on her."

"Why you can't jus' jump her?"

"Couple reasons. First, I needed some information on her. Her habits, where she stay. Don't know that yet, and that's the problem. If I knew that, I could jus' send someone to jump her and someone to rob her place. One of them will find the gun, depending on if she has it on her or not. But you know, based on how she walks around at any hour of the fuckin' night, she got it on her. She's provocative."

"That mean sexy?"

"Uh, she ain't no kind of sexy. Get that shit out your head and lemme talk, shithead."

Peb murmured an apology.

"Thing is, I don't think she's goin' anywhere. You know what she been up to? Tagging. She's a writer. She ain't bad. Thing is, she writin' some off shit. Not jus' some pussy tagger alias messages. But more than that. I think Diggy had it, he wasn't jus' tripping out. This girl's a fighter. I don't know. She a good fighter like DBZ or somethin', I can feel it, Peb. She overpowered Diggy. Now, it ain't like she can fight off five off our crew that know what they doin'. But she ain't given up the gun to the police. She holdin' it. And if I didn't know any better, she lookin' for somethin'. In the tags out here. Like it's a fuckin' forum or some shit, see?" Caso gestured to the abandoned crawfish shack a few doors down from where they were parked. It was so severely tagged up that it seemed more canvas than building. "She informed. Dangerous. I can't get it. Yet."

Peb felt his phone chirp, which meant he'd gotten a text or a Facebook notification. He reached down to check it, but Caso smacked it out of the boy's hands, and it fell onto the floor.

"Don't be disrespectful. I'm explainin' shit. Either you don't care or you about to gossip. Don't do nothin' but listen right now."

Peb nodded.

"It's like we comin' at her slowly, from a distance, and she onto it. It's insane, to be real wit' choo. I need help on this one thing."

"Anything, bro," Peb said.

Caso jabbed him. "Shut the fuck up and listen I said! This bitch, going 'round tagging weird shit like we don't even know what, walking around wit' my gun, and she making things unbalanced."

"Huh?" Peb asked, his curiosity overtaking his imperative to be silent until Caso was finished.

Surprisingly, Caso didn't strike at him again, but said, "Someone told me she actually tripped a guy who had jus' robbed Henry's. He was runnin' outta there wit' some cash and blunt wraps, and she tripped him. On some real shit. His gun went flyin', and his face got bashed on the pavement. From there, one of the clerks held him down, and some other people called the police. By the time the cops were there, she was gone."

"So she... what?"

"This weird, I know. But all this activity of hers is gonna catch her. I ain't wanna kill her. I jus' need that gun. Maybe if you were out there, you could spot her."

"What she look like?"

"That's the thing. I ain't wanna tell you. It's all dangerous. I will say, when you see her, you'll know. She kinda fat, right? Like, Blasian or some shit. Dressed dark, loose-fitting, except for yoga pants on occasion. You spot her, don't approach, don't follow, jus' make a note where you saw her. How we doin' this is we mark on a map where she is. Eventually, we can construct a rough estimate of where she stay, maybe even spot her going back there. I think we already close. We get this gun back, I'll be good, Peb. All straight?"

"You say she go out at any hour of the night, though?"

"That's true. Late."

"Grannie don't want me out like that."

"I can cover for you, dawg. You know, now and then. You young though, you can sneak out. It ain't hard. But let me reiterate. Do not jump at her jus' to get the gun."

Peb nodded. There was a certain degree of excitement that he was at last involved in his brother's activities. He understood the stakes and wanted to do whatever he could to keep his brother from going back to jail. It wasn't until much later that he wondered what he wasn't being told.

"We find this bitch, I'ma get you a laptop."

41

Dumbstruck, Peb asked, "Huh?"

"I know. It's why you get up in the morning. What keeps you goin'. You want a computer. Grannie's poor, so that ain't been happening. I ain't quite as poor, don't you worry. We jus' goin' work together to find out where she lives and we goin' to Best Buy brah! I'm not talkin' about them Wal-Mart shits, okay?"

"No you ain't," Peb said, a rising smirk on his face.

12. THE JOY

For the majority of Hinanya's life, she'd been unable to process joy. To recognize something like happiness, take it in, and feel *good*. This culminated in the failed attempt to take her life at the age of thirteen, several years after New Orleans at her relocated home in Mankato. She had been standing alone on the balcony of her parent's bedroom, gazing at the gate leading to the driveway (beyond that a snow-blind wasteland), certain that most ways she jumped would result in her being impaled upon the Fleur-De-Lis pieces adorning the gate. Imagining the fall many times, this was the time she'd brought a kitchen knife with her. She ran it up her chest with more and more pressure, wanting to follow through. That was what she'd thought she wanted. Joy would be somewhere within the cut or the fall. Had her interest been really the experience of the fall that precluded the impact? No, even then she wanted to know. To find out if there was another side.

The knife had faltered then. Still, she felt a thin line of blood come forth, and it streaked through her top.

Hinanya pelted the knife from the roof, her right arm flinging it in mimicry of the jump she had almost willed her body to make. It hit against the gate, then landed in the snow.

Hinanya let herself bleed out of the shallow cut above her breasts.

Later that night, she cut herself in shallow lines again, ashamed of her weakness.

For all the times she contemplated tumbling from the balcony, this was the closest she'd come to death. After that evening, the numbness had subsequently set in for Hinanya, years transpired like the vast distance to the stars. It evaporated when she decided on New Orleans.

Her arm tingled onto numb, and Hinanya felt only genuine joy in her graffiti. She made to trail Felix's tags while making her own. Being a writer opened up an unprecedented zest in her being. The means and the ends of it were equally worthy of her time. Hinanya fancied herself as the opposite of the evils in New Orleans, the machete welder and the muggers.

Though both she and the villain concealed themselves, Hinanya wanted to embody hope and safety. There were places where the police wouldn't willingly tread. Hinanya tagged freely in those locations and had gotten into some minor scuffles with some would-be robbers. She'd stopped a man on his way out of a convenience store, tired of the injustice. Then she'd gone on to tag. The tags were primarily questions, codes she'd wished she'd remember better from Uncle Rawls. He'd been the one who incubated the idea of being a writer in the first place. A seed at last brought to maturity.

A new artist made her mark on the city. And there was joy. A found emotion after many years of searching. So it is no surprise that complications arose.

It began one night while she was tagging the side of a laundromat's wall some ways from her apartment. She wore dark clothing and concealed her face with her bandanna. An SUV appeared, then pulled over long enough to make Hinanya want to leave. From inside the vehicle, they sang that ridiculous "Bed Intruders Song."

"Uh-oh," they said between the chorus. "You done, bitch?" The car inched closer to her as Hinanya abandoned the tag. She discerned three people, and when the car was across the street from her, air horns appeared, and the individuals in the SUV pressed them, startling Hinanya. Lamenting her incomplete tag, she knew she was in for trouble. What did they want? She hoped not to find out, but as she darted away from the scene, they pursued her.

In a hurry, she hurtled herself around a corner only pinned by a sedan. Once more, air horns. They let off the sound.

"Where you goin', babe?" one of them asked.

"Pow-pow, you the bitch who jacked the gun? Uh, interesting. I think you is."

Two females exited the sedan and started following her. Hinanya bolted away as quickly as she could. The passengers outside of the car didn't pursue her on foot, but hopped back into the van, instead.

Something was very strange to her about the air horns, as well as the volume of people after her. If they were intent on simply harming or robbing her, the air horns were a detriment to their efforts, as it would no doubt arouse the slumbering neighborhood. One of the women had said something about a gun. The stolen gun that she herself had taken. Someone most likely didn't want it in her possession, for fear she would discover the circumstances surrounding how it had arrived in New Orleans as she had. It didn't add up. Whether random or intentional, they had made their presence known and forced her to leave a tag incomplete.

Outnumbered, Hinanya fled through several backyards and alleyways. After she was a mile from the laundromat, she relished the thrill and decided to call it a night shortly after the train's whistle, despite the fear of being alone in her apartment with Stefan's gun.

13. PUDDLES

"School's fine. I've got a professor who's a jerk," Hinanya said into her phone to her father. She was perched against the nook leading up to the roof of her apartment building. She wasn't supposed to be up there, but no one would give her any trouble, she knew. The night had not yet begun, but when it did, it would be another chance for Hinanya to wander New Orleans for her answers. Before that, though, she had to successfully navigate a conversation with her family.

"What do you mean?" her father wondered impatiently. "Are you being subversive? You'd better adjust your attitude toward this teacher. It's his style. You've got to try and jive with it."

Hinanya hadn't been devoting enough attention to her father and had accidentally let that part about the professor slip out. "No, Dad. I'm taking it in strides, doing what I'm responsible for and keeping my mouth shut. I just consider him unconsciously incompetent."

"That will show up clearly in your assignments. Your feelings will show through."

"Hopefully, if Hinanya is right, the man will not notice," Hinanya's mother countered.

"It's just, sometimes it feels like he's after me in particular," noted Hinanya.

"No question about it," her mother responded aptly. "He sees your potential. But remember, Hinanya, if you ever change your mind and return here until you find a place more suitable to your intellect, we will be happy to have you back."

"Thanks, Mom."

"I'm going to put your sister on now," her father said. "Have a good night, dear. And continue working hard. It will pay off. Hold on. I need to find her."

Hinanya waited, looking at the buildings below her. None of them were exactly the same height. Some were colored in pink, purple, orange, any color imaginable. On the ground below her, she saw a puddle that had formed, a small deposit of rainwater mixed with grime from the roof. Hinanya imagined that as the measure of her investment in the concept of family.

Every interaction with them made her wonder if she actually loved them, and just what exactly that meant, or if it was just what was expected because of society. And yet she knew those who didn't have a family, such as orphans, longed for it. What propelled a person to love besides chemicals masquerading as a selfish need to be doted on? What did family really mean in comparison to a non-relative on the cosmic scale? It was accurate that, as mammals, care and attention were essential pieces of a person's existence, but wouldn't it be more genuine to form a family based on those who actually valued and shared your beliefs? What, then, would that be, though? Hinanya was as lost as ever, but she was left thinking of a humanity stricken of its sexuality. What form would families take if reproduction was something independent of sex? Better put, if the whole world was like Hinanya herself. The girl didn't feel she had the biological imperative. Her desires curved to form things that were contrary to it. Theories of what else humanity was capable of. There were some others in the world like her, probably more motivated, but she wasn't able to tell if that would make it a better place. Most likely, even if it were, it wouldn't last, for to take away sexuality meant no natural reproduction. A world like that would bear no children and thus, eventually, deem itself pointless. Still, Hinanya longed for an alternative purpose to humanity besides reproduction, or the amassing of knowledge that each generation seemed to value less and less. For their species to move past that issue would be such a boon, to do more than simply sustaining a race to another chapter. Another chapter that evolved but did so with a greater disregard for nature. Could it be this very tinge against life be used to defeat mortality itself?

Really, what it boiled down to was her wonderment at what humanity would be capable of if they were able to dial back their sexual drives and distractions. The removal of the passion could beckon the cessation of war. It was all about possession, taking more than one needed because it had the power to. It was all no more than a drive to have an orgasm or build a security career to impress someone else enough to get them to give them an orgasm.

Reaching that point, considering the way the world was, seemed, just as ludicrous to Hinanya. She hoped there would come a better way in her wake, should she decide to die without seeing that problem resolved—because, due to her issues, she couldn't will those in the world to control themselves or have mastery of their desires in order to accomplish something greater. Were Hinanya free of her damaged mind and abhorrent shell of a body, she might have dreams of revolution, of making humanity better.

But Hinanya might never fix herself, so how could she be expected to fix others?

Some blocks away, presumably on St. Claude, Hinanya heard a loud collision, most likely an accident between several vehicles.

On the other end of the line, it seemed like they had finally found Taylor. Hinanya didn't mind, she supposed—her mind was busy.

"Hey, Hinanya," said Taylor.

Hinanya heard her and took a few seconds to respond. When she did, it was quick. "What were you up to? I don't want to take your time away."

"No, it's okay. I was just playing a game."

"Hope you weren't on a raid." Raids were Taylor's time not to be disturbed. They could last for hours and required her undivided attention.

"No, of course not. Just an old platformer."

"How's it been with one less person in the house?"

"I hardly notice a difference, to be honest," Taylor said. Hinanya knew this was a lie. Taylor had been devastated to see Hinanya leave. "How's New Orleans?"

"I love it, Taylor. It's where I belong."

"Good to hear." Hinanya understood that Taylor meant it was good Hinanya had found a place where she belonged, and it was to be taken spitefully. She itched to go out and became irritated with Taylor.

"Hope you're doing okay, Taylor. I really don't want to hold you up. Anything else on your mind?" Hinanya didn't like it when Taylor held onto pretense as she was. Hinanya preferred honesty out of people, no matter how gruesome it became.

"Not that I can think of. Thanks, Hinanya. I'll talk to you later though. I love you."

"Okay, I love you too, Taylor. Sorry I won't be there for Christmas." The girl was so stubborn. They both shared that trait. At times, Hinanya wondered if her sister suffered from the same thoughts and afflictions Hinanya had at that age, or if it was merely a product of experiences that had spoiled her will to live. It was known suicide and depression existed somewhat in the genes, yet Hinanya wondered about the role of the world. How it eroded all things. In dealing with Taylor, Hinanya tried to be sociable, to be whatever the girl saw in her. But often, Hinanya was too preoccupied with herself. Her parents had never known of Hinanya's proclivities, so the same might be true of Taylor.

Still, if there was one difference between Hinanya and Taylor, it was that Hinanya could pretend. Taylor, on the other hand, was transparent. Fortunately, it might save the girl's life one day.

14. CONVERSION

Finally. It was done. Not a moment too soon, as Hinanya's left arm was burning. It seemed like more pain than she could ever remember. Still, she held fast to the side of the stationary truck bed. Removing the bandanna from around her neck and dropped the empty spray can along with her tote bag. While both fell, she shimmied down and swung to slide into the opening between the ramp and the truck.

The longer she remained at the sight of the tag, the more likely it was she'd be discovered. Hinanya had yet to interact with any other writers and still hadn't found Felix. There had been a recent cracking-down against the writers of the city. She'd seen a lot of incomplete tags. Some force was uniting against them as they tried to make their mark. Though no security patrolled the back of the Rouses, Hinanya knew a cop could swing around to where she was at any moment, surely looking for someone like her.

An urge came to her, and she decided, instead of dismounting from the ramp, she would climb it once more to lay on top of the truck bed, a feat she accomplished with a calculated effort. There she felt safe. Truthfully, she needed time to recoup, safety or not. Once she'd made up her mind to tag the truck bed, an ostensibly mobile piece of art that would provide the advantage of being paraded around the streets of the French Quarter, it felt like such a good move.

Hinanya took issue with the fact that she had yet to experience a response to her tags in full. Though she wrote over others and displayed curiosity in code to the New Orleans underworld, no signals had come to her.

It began to feel like she was only doing it to handle her life between tags, as it was unbearable. Before she rose from the truck bed, the awful rush began once more. Disregarding her physical discomfort was impossible. She tried to focus on her creations, all the tags she'd produced in full all over the cities. Then the ones she'd been unable to finish came to mind, stopped by passersby.

Hinanya's consciousness traversed to places unknown even to her and the call to pull the trigger on the gun on her side flared up again, a forceful pull elapsed that engulfed her entire body and seemed to increase as she hesitated.

Hinanya desperately tried to focus on creation once more, not destruction. Creation for a little longer, yes. The dimensions of her first tag, five by seven. Green ink upon the black paint of a restaurant. A keyboard, with each key substituting a feeling instead of letters. It had taken two hours, the task split between two nights, but once it was complete, it was so evocative to her. She'd even left some keys blank, for others to fill in other emotions, no matter how vulgar additions would be. It would be their freedom to contribute. That was how Hinanya wanted graffiti to be. Welcome to anyone. Not some secretive code or territorial pissings that alienated others.

The girl breathed in deeply as an urge from her body transferred wholly to her upper arm. Her art was out there, and no matter what her fate, it would outlast her, even as the expandable canvas of another.

Hinanya grumbled in response to thoughts of doubt, and her eyes fluttered between open and closed to see the sky. The memory of her tags might remain in another's mind beyond her. And still, she was producing. An even greater impression could be made. It was not over, no, no it wasn't. Production, expression, creation. All in the form of a release. That was what felt so very right. The pain no longer bothered her as it should have. At some point, it would return, but she told herself she was making progress.

With what she knew.

Somewhere, someone in her vicinity knew of Wenin.

It was a matter of where she was. That territory. They could welcome her or devour her, but if it was the latter, she had plenty of fight left in her still. That was why art happened. The darkness, the unidentifiable aspects within her screeched in agony for it. To be satiated from nothing more than the production of some silly emotional keyboard on a building. To take the suffering she experienced and to form it into something useful. What had once threatened to end her now compelled her onward. The most valuable conversion that could take place was one of suffering into beauty. That is what art was. It came not as a product of brightness, but a desire to experience brightness.

Typically, Hinanya found the dichotomy between good and evil, light and dark, to be too binary. Darkness was merely the absence of light. There was no need to fear it in itself. It was only the conceit of humans and their inability to see it that made it seem so frightening. That same abyss was where all works of creation began. And her work didn't make her feel frightened. No, they suggested to her that challenging situations produce challenging persons. There didn't have to be anything intrinsically sinister about the unknown.

Hinanya's tags were being judged, or they would be. That suited her fine. She'd likewise been an arbiter to all the graffiti she'd seen. She was just beginning but held an eye for the aesthetics of her environment.

Instead of being too critical of herself, her tags had given her relief. All thanks to Felix. She wanted to pay homage to him. To find him. To ask about Wenin. Yes. It was this clarity that gave her clearance to get off the truck bed and take the long walk home, abandoning her supplies little by little along the way.

Hinanya followed along under the I-10 overpass via North Claiborne to her apartment building. An abandoned vehicle had been fashioned into a bum's home on the underpass. It was relatively early, not long after midnight. She also spotted many tags that impressed her along the way. It struck her as funny that most people who've been up and down these streets probably didn't see the graffiti. They probably overlooked it all. But Hinanya had fresh eyes and an idea of what it might mean. As such, she did not return disappointed, as she had so many days in Minnesota, returning unfulfilled and thinking up all the ways she could kill herself.

Sadly, the foundation of her survival came from the danger of walking through the New Orleans ghettos. Edgework and *risk*. It was how she manifested her petering survival instinct here, by constantly putting it to the test. The gun she now cradled only amplified that. She was as likely to turn it on herself as she was an attacker.

Was that really the case any longer?

As she approached her house without incident, she was reminded of Sasha's most recent request. At first, the idea had annoyed her. Now she saw it as the opportunity it was—as another lead toward Wenin.

If things got bad enough for Hinanya, she always had an escape plan in Stefan's gun. Until then, she would play things out. The next day, she contacted two people. First Kurt, the boy who'd approached her at the university (she'd kept in touch with him, surprisingly), and then Sasha to confirm the day they would all be meeting.

15. BOUNTY

Peb found out that he and his brother weren't the only ones searching for the girl on the morning of his first wake 'n bake. His first time smoking weed at all, in fact.

The morning started out for Peb as routine as could be expected—opening his eyes and fighting his way out of bed to shut off his alarm clock.

After he'd taken a shower and eaten breakfast, he noticed a text from Sam telling him to meet them in the back of the abandoned barber's shop by their school.

He made his way there, steps inhibited by the fog enveloping his thoughts. Ever since Caso had tasked him to spot the girl, Peb had been relentless, yet he'd had no luck in seeing her. Not even once. He still didn't know what she looked like. A few nights he'd been accompanied by Diggy for safety, but the homeless dude bugged Peb, and he preferred to go alone in spite of the risks. Truthfully, he wanted to emulate his brother and be someone not to be fucked with. How else could he build such a reputation?

Still, Peb knew he had to dial things back on going out late. The task was harder than he'd thought it would be. In truth, he'd been clouded by his determination to get the laptop, but it was compromising his daily life. He admitted to himself he'd have to change tactics if he wanted to help his brother retrieve the gun.

Peb slid through the gap in the fence to meet his friends, who were in a circle passing something around.

"It's so early, dawg. What's good?" Peb asked vacantly.

"We got weed," Nestor replied.

"You tryna smoke now?" Peb asked, puzzled. "I mean, I'm all for givin' it a go, fuck yeah, Nestor. But maybe later? After school?"

"Nah, fuck that," said Sam.

"Mhm. He right. We smokin' now, pimp," said Nestor, the joint already lit. "Dude, I can't stand another day of school. I need this for me to cope."

"It's medical," jested Sam.

"What if they figure out we high?" Peb asked.

"Don't be dumb, Peb," Sam chastised. "You don't get high your first time."

"I heard that's jus' some shit they say that ain't necessarily true, though," Nestor countered as he squinted.

"It's true," Sam insisted. "No need to argue. We gonna find out I'm right."

"Aite," said Nestor. He had the joint. With a deep inhalation, Nestor took it in, then let it out several seconds later. Peb thought his friend was about to cough, but Nestor suppressed it.

Nestor passed the joint to Peb. "This gonna be in the history books, son. First time we lit up, ever!" His tone was of jubilation, and Peb tried to see if there was a difference in Nestor after having taken the smoke in.

Peb pressed the joint against his lips. It was uncomfortably soggy. The three of them often talked about wanting to try drugs, but it had been Nestor who was most serious and proactive in actually following through. Peb was more in the camp of letting it come when it did, but Nestor was thirsty. Peb felt that first experience smoking was going to be forever marred by the fact they had to get to school in just a few minutes. Peb didn't like the idea of that, but it was too late. Already, the smoke was in him, and he found it harsh, but he held it in like he'd been told. It jolted his system for a moment, then he felt light-headed as the smoke escape his lungs out into the air. Peb tilted his head back as he passed the joint to Sam, who took it with no hesitation.

After the joint made another complete orbit, Peb punctured the silence and confided in his friends. "Man, I want that laptop so bad, it been fuckin' me up, though. Damn, wish we could skip today."

"We still can," said Nestor.

"Nah, we should have schemed before. When did you get this shit?" Peb asked, gesturing to the joint in his hand.

"Jus' this morning, out the blue. I been askin' Gregory up the street to slink some from his brother, and he finally did."

"So this is stolen weed right now?" asked Sam incredulously.

"Nah, we paid for it. Y'all have to front the funds next time."

"Being broke sucks, man," said Peb with annoyance.

"I bet being rich sucks too," said Sam.

"The fuck you mean?"

"I don't know. Seems like every fake-ass friend wanna piece of you at that point," Sam said, shrugging his shoulders. "You go around with shit, and nobody is real with you no more. They jus' act however they feel will get them some of what you got."

"Still. Poor's worse," said Nestor.

"Yeah," agreed Sam.

Peb couldn't help but change the subject. "If I don't find that girl for Caso, I ain't gettin' that laptop."

"Nah, that ain't the only way. You jus' being narrow," said Nestor. "Dude, all you needa do is boost a couple of bikes and sell them over to my homey Julius in Baton Rouge. He comes once a month and buys stolen bikes, then takes them back. How much for a laptop? Three, four hundred dollars? Man, that's eight bikes *tops*. Get you a lock pick set or keep an eye out for dumb white kids like Sam—"

"Hey," Sam objected.

Nestor groaned. "White people who leave their shit unlocked in their backyards, and you'll be golden. Shit, say that you find this bitch and you get a laptop. You do this bike shit on top of that, and maybe you have enough to get a PlayStation wit' some games. Boom! You set."

"It ain't hard to steal bikes around here, Peb," Sam said. "I heard once that ninety-seven percent of people that live in New Orleans had their bikes stolen. Don't even look at me like it's a bad thing. Peb, if people really don't want their shit taken, they'd take way better care of it. Believe me."

Peb considered it for a moment and thought it might not be such a bad idea. What if he came across a bike he could grab while he was after that girl? All the better. And if not? Whatever, he was still helping his brother out. "Fuck yeah, that's what I'll do. Gimme this dude's number."

Peb lifted his backpack behind and headed to face his school day. The sleep deprivation left him unable to tell if his first foray into marijuana had indeed gotten him high. But there was no doubt that the combination left him entirely disoriented and fearful most of the day.

It all unfolded slowly until his friend Alycia poked him in the computer lab. "Yo, check this," she said, pointing to the screen. Peb saw it was an article from some New Orleans blog, and the more he read, the more his excitement rose until the video feed at the end brought him a grand satisfaction.

LOCAL BUSINESS OWNER OFFERS REWARD FOR NOLA'S GRAFFITI PROBLEM
by Douglas Penner

Ever since George Buckland, owner of the Golden Chicken chain of restaurants (with locations in the Bywater, Mid-city, and the Little Easy) released a statement a few days ago in a bid to stop the New Orleans graffiti problem, the community has been rallying behind him. Buckland has been deeply invested in the past to bringing the neighborhoods of New Orleans up to par with communities such as the ones in Metairie and Kenner.

"Enough is enough with this constant vandalism," he says. "Our city is beleaguered enough as it is. Homes, buildings, even light-posts are being swallowed up with ugly marks. I've had enough. So just the other day, our camera picked up someone tagging our dumpster. As a community, I believe we should track this person down so they can answer for their crimes! To that effect, I am releasing the footage publicly. Any person who has legitimate information that leads to the identity of this individual will be rewarded personally by me, in the form of five hundred chicken po-boys, our best-selling item, to be paid out at the Good Samaritan's discretion."

Buckland has been working in concert with Spencer Ruth, owner of the non-profit organization Spray Away. Some argue that Ruth's cover-ups neuter New Orleans, as the graffiti is painted over in a layer of gray, but others are glad for his continued service in trying to make New Orleans a place that discourages graffiti.

I spoke with Charles Malone, a resident of the Lower Seventh Ward, who is interested in getting Buckland's reward. "Yeah, the police are telling us we need to stop staying out to find this guy. But I don't know, I think since we've all been out, there's been way less graffiti."

This is true, but Chief Barney Jones of the N.O.P.D. is wary of the mad rush to find the culprit.

"We have people looking to take the law into their own hands... They don't care about justice, they just want that free chicken. It's quickly getting carried away, and we anticipate the streets getting rowdier and rowdier until this whole thing gets resolved. We're talking about dozens of people walking or riding around the Bywater and outlying areas confronting anyone who looks remotely suspicious. That's not how we want our citizens to operate."

Whatever the outcome, it seems Buckland will not rescind his offer. "This is why we live in New Orleans. If something bad's happening, we band together to help each other out. It's not about the chicken. It's about putting a stop to all these people defacing our properties. We're tired of it, and I am prepared to do what it takes to help."

You can see the footage in question here, where an unknown person clad in black uses spray paint to tag the dumpster. It appears to spell out the word "apoplexy."

And sure enough, Peb clicked on the footage and saw exactly how he imagined the girl who had stolen the gun from Diggy, how she'd been described to him. The face was shrouded, but Peb felt sure it had to be her. With this proclamation, it meant that the entire community was after her, albeit for a different reason than Peb and Caso.

It concerned Peb, but despite himself, he laughed at how fucked she was.

16. SHUT-EYE ANGEL

Things began with Sasha proposing a toast before Hinanya and Kurt had even sat down.

"To our first double date ever!" Sasha announced with pride.

"Why of course," Kurt said, raising his glass of Merlot.

"I think she was talking to me," Hinanya said, casting a sideways glance to Kurt.

"I was," Sasha said, raising her eyebrow then playfully shoving Kurt. Sasha's date, Bradley, looked left out already.

And Sasha, though she liked Bradley, mostly wanted Hinanya and Kurt there to help ease the friction of meeting someone from the Internet. Hinanya put her fake smile on and did her part. Hinanya found that there was some fun to be had with Kurt. After talking on the phone with him (letting him do most of the talking), she admitted she'd given him a fake name and told him her real name. The truth was he wasn't too difficult to talk to. She was even considering taking him shooting.

As they sat, Hinanya made eye contact with Bradley, and then they both looked away. Bradley's dark brown curly hair was receding prematurely, though he was not yet of the legal age to drink. Sasha sensed his burgeoning sexual advances and had been trying to steer them into something more sustainable. Men were so unruly. It was because, for the most part, they got away with it. Give them the Internet, a keyboard to hide behind, and they were practically beyond redemption. Despite Sasha's futile attempts to temper Bradley's longing, somehow the girl thought there was potential in him. Hinanya supposed her friend must have been very lonely indeed to come to such a conclusion. What struck Hinanya as odd was, even though she offered her apartment as a venue for the double date, Sasha had insisted they do it at hers.

Following the toast, Sasha informed the group to dig into the meal she'd cooked for them. It was homemade a veggie pizza topped with buffalo tempeh bacon. Hinanya was impressed but made a note not to overeat.

The conversation was stilted at first. Sasha and Kurt went back and forth until Bradley grumbled something in line with what the two had been talking about. Religion reared its ugly head as the primary discourse from then on.

"I believe the evidence speaks for itself, sure," Kurt said, agreeing with Bradley. "But no sum of evidence, no matter how resounding, could possibly ever account for the questions we ask on a daily basis without admitting God."

"But it's been shown. We could have come from nothing," Bradley pointed out. "That's a possibility now. It hadn't always been. The assumption, and yes, I must say it's a good one, has been that we necessarily must have been created from something. For most of humanity's history, it was a thing to believe. Now I think people are finally adjusting. We are uncaused. Eventually, God will be known as a joke, and humans will unite in laughing at their ancestor's foolishness."

"Mmhm," Sasha hummed tentatively. "So you are convinced there is no God?"

"I am," said Bradley.

"Because you've never had any experience besides your brain and your body, is that about right?" Hinanya added, her first genuine contribution to the conversation.

"That's a good way to put it, yes."

"But if you did?"

"Then I would be convinced in the other direction."

"You are telling me you've never felt God?" Sasha asked.

"Right," said Bradley.

"I'm with him, to be honest," said Hinanya.

"Interesting," said Kurt, clearly at a loss for what to say. The table was split in two regarding the existence of God. Hinanya did not relish the inevitable disputes that were sure to follow.

"If you two have had some divine experience or encounter with something metaphysical, that's wonderful," Hinanya said unabashedly. "It's just unfortunate because it is impossible to give me anything more than an account of the experience, not the experience itself."

"But anyone can have it," Sasha said. "It's about faith."

Hinanya nearly scoffed, but she held it in. "There is an element of the unknowable here. Some things, indeed, we cannot explain as mortal beings bound here. Thus it is perhaps best to assume that this here," she gestured all around her, "is all that there is. I'd like to tell a story, actually, if you don't mind."

"Please, go ahead," Kurt urged her.

"Oh, I have one after!" Sasha realized.

"Maybe we can go in a circle," suggested Bradley. He nodded to Hinanya. "But in the meantime, you go first, Hinanya."

"Yes. Of course. So my mother's side of the family comes from a village called Bandung in Java. I spent a few summers there. The islands of Java and Bali, border one and other. Given their proximity, they should be very similar places. However, they differ significantly. Java, when compared with Bali, doesn't receive as much attention. It's just not quite as much of a go-to place as Bali. Some Islamic terrorists went to the hub of Bali's tourist area, Kuta and detonated several bombs, killing hundreds. It was an outcry against what happened in East Timor.

"A few years later, one of the largest earthquakes ever recorded on a seismograph caused a tsunami that hit the region. Java was hit, but Bali was largely spared in comparison. The inhabitants of Bali, the Hindu ones at least, quietly contented themselves in their karma, feeling that was the justice they needed after being hit by those Islamic terrorists. What that tells me is people find the divinity in coincidences. Many people like to cite the Noah's Ark tale and make comparisons to Hurricane Katrina. It is sad how people were able to invoke the concept of karma yet wash their hands entirely of the tsunami as it was a judicious force of a holy nature to them. I do think that's wrong."

"The world should be able to accept the possibility that this human lifespan is all that they get," Bradley said. "Just like I am willing to accept that God might exist."

"But opening up that possibility for disbelief means some people believe they are damned," said Kurt.

"Exactly the problem," said Sasha. "No one should be eternally damned. I never liked that idea."

"Maybe because all it's really been good for is controlling people," Hinanya purposed. "If religions didn't have threats attached to them, they wouldn't be so prevalent."

"But I believe in grace and redemption for all who seek it," said Sasha. "I see the world, and sometimes, I've even witnessed some miracles."

"Sasha, tell us your story now," Kurt said.

She nodded, pleased with the request. "Oh, it's just a silly little tale my grandmother used to tell me when I persisted in asking why the whole God and Heaven bit were so one-sided and immaterial. She explained that direct contact with real angels was dangerous for one reason or another. Proximity would boil your blood or make you go deaf. But an angel's gaze was the most dangerous, for if one chose to look at you, to make eye contact, they could see into the depths of your soul. This troubled the angels because they wanted to help man, but at the same time, they knew God had designed this clear divide. They weren't content to simply judge. They wanted to have a more active role in things. So instead of the angels observing and waiting for men to do right or wrong, they instead opted to assume the form of man as their friends and family. She told me if you have such a hard time imagining winged beings with ethereal powers, simply consider those around you. Those who love you. That's what angels are to me. Or how I see them, at least. Those who'll shut their eyes in blind faith for you."

"That's beautiful, Sasha," said Kurt.

"Actually, I do like that idea," said Bradley. "It allows a person to embrace bliss and grace without a subscription to all the fucked-up facets of religion."

The conversation died down peacefully, and Hinanya realized a modicum of truth in Sasha's words. Felix was an angel to her.

Hinanya and Sasha made for the bathroom after dinner was finished.

"You've so got the right idea, Hinanya," she said with a firm hand on her shoulder as she looked into the mirror to check her makeup.

"Huh?" Hinanya asked.

"I need to be like you and not give a shit who is interested in me."

"Oh. I'd just say to be patient if Bradley isn't working out. I'm sure someone decent will come and bother you as Kurt did me."

"It's obvious he likes you. But I remember all that stuff we talked about at City Park. What gives?"

Hinanya sighed. "I was trying to oblige you." She deliberately avoided looking at herself in the mirror, but even so, she caught a glimpse of herself and cringed.

"He wants you in the best possible way, though. He's sweet and wholesome. I'm jealous."

"You shouldn't be. I bet he'd drop his little gentlemen act and stick it in me in a heartbeat."

"Hinanya, what the hell? Just... wow, I can't believe you just said that. Look, you're in complete control of that situation, is all I meant. Be nice to him."

"I am. He wanted to hang out with me, so I let him."

"But does he understand you... aren't interested?"

"I've explained my views on dating and relationships."

"Right, but... does he understand?"

That was something Hinanya hadn't considered. She assumed because she explained it, it was evident. But that might not have been clear enough. Still, Hinanya filled in the gap. "He's totally content just hanging out. He doesn't have any friends anyway."

"I'll bet he's just trying to make a long-term investment for when you finally realize you want someone in your life."

"I hope he's patient then because he'll be balder than Bradley."

"Hey! Don't be mean," Sasha defended. "Bradley's not *so* bad himself." She picked up her hairbrush and started making small swipes even though her hair was orderly.

"Yeah, the other day you told him to screw himself. So eloquent."

"Oh, Hinanya, just try things out with Kurt," Sasha said abruptly.

"No. I just don't have a sexual drive. Attraction's a lie. Take out the sense of sight, and it doesn't matter. Drug someone enough, and as long as they feel pleasure, they don't care if a boy or a girl is sucking them off. Plus, I really don't feel anything down there."

"When's the last time you checked?" Sasha asked.

Hinanya, not taking the question seriously, ignored it with an anxious jolt. "I don't need someone else to validate my existence. I believe it can come from within me. Although, admittedly, it doesn't right now." This statement was enough to shake Hinanya on the spot, as this fact was secretive and not something she liked to share.

Sasha smiled and looked at Hinanya in the mirror. "Well, I love you. And I appreciate you for coming out today. Thank you. I wish we hung out more often. I guess school's just got us out of sorts, huh?"

"Yeah, exactly. Tests and stuff," said Hinanya.

"Maybe you can join me for church sometime." Sasha put down her brush. "Are we ready or what?"

"I'd say so."

Sasha slept with Bradley that night. According to what she had told Hinanya, it was a disappointing experience.

17. REALIZATION

It was the banner on Buckland's which ultimately led Hinanya to discover she was being hunted. In shock, she evaluated herself, thought back to the past few months of being a writer. How her obsession with peeling back the truth of the universe had been somewhat sated. Upon following the link to Buckland's footage, which was printed on a sign offering a reward, Hinanya knew it was time to stop tagging. There was no way around it. And thus, the awful rush came shortly after, and she redoubled her efforts to complete the project of escaping herself. Of course, tagging had been a way to track down what she'd been seeking at the university, but even so, she felt so much closer, no matter what she did. Uncle Rawls had left behind many leads for Wenin. Hinanya would find him.

Weeks passed with no developments. Hinanya wandered those New Orleans streets still, Stefan's gun by her side, trying to devote her attention to that oddity in her pocket. She tried to track Felix, though she still hadn't seen him since that initial night at the billboard. She thought she may have spotted some of his work around though. It seemed as though something he'd made could be found on any given city block. Looking for any recent work of his had been how she'd found out about Buckland's.

The people with the air horns made sense. All of the watchers in the streets that had been making it so hard for her to find a good place to tag. And there were also the forces that had been responsible for the transfer of Stefan's gun from Minnesota to New Orleans. Clearly they were aware of her, yet they hadn't quite gone so far as a direct confrontation. Were she to tote it or have to use it, the police might become involved. So Hinanya assumed they'd strike in secret when she wasn't expecting it.

That's why, when one of the people tailing her was just a boy, Hinanya relished the opportunity. First, she confirmed the scrawny boy with dreadlocks was indeed following her, which she determined quickly enough as an hour after she'd noticed him, he was still watching her, though she'd gone in an erratic direction through the streets of the Bywater. Soon after, the boy was the one being followed. Hinanya had turned the tables on him in hopes of finding out what she could. It proved to be very enlightening. The boy, upon losing her, wandered around late into the night until he found a bike to steal. It was a black mountain bike with red brake lines and a red basket above the rear tire. The reflectors on the pedals shimmered as he made off with the bicycle.

This greatly upset her. Hinanya hated to see someone so young stealing. With such a callous illusion of power, the boy was in danger. Especially considering he seemed linked to whoever wanted the gun back from her. She realized she'd seen the boy around before on another bike recently. They'd made eye contact. Taking note of where the bike had been stolen, she tried to figure out where he was taking it. Though Hinanya couldn't follow him once he pedaled off, she was able to tell in which direction he went.

18. CLASS

It was the last class of the semester. Hinanya's stomach was feeling inflamed. There was no final, only a lecture. The professor stood before a half-empty room of at least seventy desks, and most of those in attendance were as absent as if they had not shown up at all, between ducked heads with smartphones or peeking out of the window behind them to figure out if it was still raining. But Hinanya was transfixed upon the professor, even though she could not remember what class she was in.

The professor had a high-pitched voice with a depth that didn't seem to match the body at all. He regularly referred to notes on his desk. It was evident the lecture hadn't been memorized much at all. The man's hair was a sandy brown, fading and with a few gray strands apparent. Though he was tall, it was hard to tell exactly how tall as he slouched. Hinanya watched his eyes as they seemed to regard every face in the classroom but her own.

The tan button-up he wore jutted out around the waist, a sloppy tuck job.

Hinanya relished his words, and she seemed alone in that. But that was the entire point. The man's enthusiasm and cadence were not dimmed by the inhospitable reception.

"Language is actually a feeble kind of thing. It is unable to express what we might consider the actual reality. It is merely a representation, a substitution our brains have adopted because it was the best thing at our disposal in the course of our evolution at the time. However, there are severe problems with language. Take for instance the diversity of languages, which most certainly contribute to stark nationalism and endless confusion, dividing up the human race into hundreds of categories where you're excluded from each one unless you happen to know certain languages. Some people propose the solution of a one-world language, but I don't think it is that simple because even if everyone spoke one language and things were better, we would still be dealing with the problem of language itself.

"Language, as the model of our existence in expressing itself, our oral and written method of expression, stands in opposition to being and awareness. Where there is no language, there is awareness. Language springs up when awareness dissipates in anticipation of representing something with a word. Knowledge, for instance. It is a word. If you did not know language, you still can know things.

"But awareness has no representation. Yeah, yeah, I know awareness itself too can be rendered into language as I am doing right now, but before man developed language, it had awareness. Now we have both. Language dominates awareness, but it is a foolhardy enterprise. It is so hard to be aware when our thoughts bound into a miasma of words cascading in our minds. It's quite relentless as I'm sure you know.

"Language has time-bending properties, as we can now successfully transmit information across time," the professor looked down at his papers. Then he rose up again. "We transmit signals across generations, and though there seems to be a positive trend in the evolution of man, I beg the question of if the paradigm of language won't be a contributing factor in our own destruction? We created it to make things easier, no doubt, but now we can use language to lie, to deceive, and to hide who and what we are. Man can use language as a tool for good or for evil, depending on his bearing.

"So my question to you, as we wrap the semester up, is language something to be abolished? We certainly would be hard-pressed to be done with now, considering, but I imagine the potential for transcendence." He closed his eyes for a moment and nodded. "I can see it. Given the proper developments and conditions, man as a collective species developing technology sufficient to communicate direct thoughts to one another, not in language, but under a more genuine transmission. Bodily cues known best by infants before cultural imprints dilute range. Telepathy, yes. Aided by the technology, of course. No more lies, but no more individuality either. Just being. A being of many bodies in concert. Could we separate the consciousness from the body, back and forth with ease? Stretching out even further, perhaps this being could approach divinity? Given once more, the conditional proof that it was allowed to refine and develop itself indefinitely. I ask you to wonder, what are the limits of humanity if humanity is able to actually unite? To cast off poverty, ignorance, and the sickening effects of religion to create itself as a non-dualistic form in the universe?"

The man seemed to have more subsequent musings despite the conclusion. But his time was up. Hinanya sat riveted while the class gathered their things and prepared for the winter break. Eventually, she exited the class, pleased that the professor either hadn't noticed or didn't make mention of the fact that she wasn't among his roster of students.

19. GATHERING

For five blocks of St. Bernard, there were motorcycles and vehicles parked on the neutral grounds of the streets. People were milling around, enjoying a warm winter night in New Orleans. Peb saw a long line with dozens of bikers, the wheels and frames of their bikes lit up with vibrant string lights. There was more litter tossed on the ground than people, mostly plastic bags from the bodega nearby or paper bags and boxes from the Rally's where the contingent of revelers had congregated around.

At each intersection, people were selling various foods out of their cars and vans, and there were even a few grills on the backs of truck beds.

The gathering itself had been precipitated against any would-be writer interested in tagging that area. One of the gatherings a few days before, sadly, had ended in gunfire. But the people were determined to continue. The police were at the edges of the gathering having yet to intervene, though they waited tensely at either edge of the outdoor celebration diverting traffic looking to go up St. Bernard.

Each time, officers would catch a splinter of the gathering clad in backpacks, flashlights, and baseball bats only to discourage them from seeking out graffiti artists.

Peb, on the other hand, walked into the gathering, nodding dutifully to the officers, even though they were both crackers. His interest in the gathering lay only in seeing his friend Tressina, who worked at Rally's. The euphoria he'd felt when he heard of Buckland's reward for the graffiti had been deflated when his brother snapped.

"This is fuckin' madness, goddamn!" he'd groaned each word with a continuous struggle.

"What's the problem?"

"If someone else catch her, police'll end up gettin' involved. If she stops, then we can't find her as easy. Either way, I'm fucked. Fucked, Peb. You don't even get what that means."

"You gotta know I been trying," Peb said with an attempt at comfort. "No, actually, wait. I been doin' legit everything you said. We coulda had her by now." Peb and some others had been following her around at night. "Now you trippin' 'cause she pissed off other people?"

Peb prepared to be throttled, cursing his bravado. But his brother walked off. Before he was gone, he said, "You tell every person you see after her out there that I'll fuckin' triple that free chicken reward if they bring the bitch to me and not Buckland or the cops."

"Got it."

Peb wished he could be the one to get all those chicken po-boys. Literally, everyone was talking about it.

The boy made his way past the crowd and waited in line for a burger and a milkshake, and minutes later, he was excited to see Tressina was working the walk-up booth. Though he harbored feelings for her, Peb was shy, feeling the girl was out of his league for now. At least until he got some scratch. She had a real job, after all. He was just a little hustler with big ideas.

Tressina working at Rally's worked out well for Peb, as he fucking loved Rally's and imagined an even greater love for Tressina. He spotted her, wearing her uniform. He stole a glimpse of her chest. She also had on those rectangular glasses. Peb often fantasized taking off while stroking her curly afro as she went down on him. It wasn't like he didn't think she looked sexy when she wore them. He just assumed it might be easier to suck his dick without them on, though he had no real grasp of the physical reality of such an act yet.

She smiled at him as he approached the booth. "Yo, what up, Peb?"

"Ey. What's good?"

"I'm aite. What choo want? You know I ain't got no milkshakes right now."

"You fuckin' up then. Like I came here jus' to see you. Bitch, I wanna milkshake!" He spoke in jest, but she waved a finger to caution him all the same.

"Chill with dat, my manager out here. Sorry. But hurry up. Look at all these people out here. It's crazy."

Peb turned around to see he was the only one in line. "You serious? I think I'm the last customer."

"Jus' wait 'til someone comes and you still ain't ordered, then I'll be pissed."

"Nah, I don't want none of that. Jus' gimme a burger with them funny fries."

"Sure. You don't want ketchup, right?"

"No, I don't. I hate those fuckin' packets. Once I got a piece of them in my teeth. Now I'd rather eat it without ketchup than put that weird plastic tube in my mouth to open it."

"I'll open 'em for you."

"If you want," Peb said, not knowing if she was joking or not.

"I'll open two packets for you."

"Appreciate ya."

"You sure do." Tressina paused to punch his order in, then sunk with a sigh. When she surfaced to look up at him, Peb thought she looked like a wounded animal. "So, not that it's contagious or anything, but I gotta tell someone. I think I'm pregnant."

It felt like his chest was shrinking. Crestfallen, he attempted to mask it by casually asking, "That ain't necessarily a bad thing though, right?"

"I don't know, Peb. Been off the wall. Sissy's still at that medical internship in South Korea, and I might be a mother before I turn sixteen. My mamma... well, let's jus' say I'm not eager to have this conversation wit' her."

As Tressina gave him the details surrounding her pregnancy, Peb felt she was suddenly farther beyond his reach than before. Like, further than he could ever get to. Peb was a virgin, and Tressina was clearly not. The more she spoke, the more Peb wished someone would come to the counter. Tressina believed she could have a baby and still become a rapper, and Peb thought she might be right.

Eventually, someone did come, and Peb used it as an excuse to check his phone. It had been on silent, to his detriment, as his brother had been blowing it up with calls and texts. All the texts said to call him, so Peb did.

Peb knew he had to leave and waved Tressina goodbye, as the first thing his brother said was, "You need to do me somethin' important right now."

"What up?" Peb asked.

"We needa find some fuckin' hoodrat to take the heat for this Buckland shit, Peb. I need the heat off this girl so I can nab her without consequences. Maybe this whole witch hunt bustin' my whole way up."

"Okay, what's the plan?"

"You and my boys find someone tagging who resembles the body frame of the bitch. Then..." As Caso went on with his plan, Peb understood the urgency of things. It had to happen soon. So Peb left the Rally's gathering to get back to his house.

By the time Caso's instructions were clear, Peb was in his backyard, only to find the bikes he had stolen gone. He'd have to walk to meet Caso's people, which meant he probably wouldn't be able to help them in time. The bikes had been chained. Someone had bypassed the locks. A chill went down Peb's spine as he thought of the police confiscating them, but as he walked through the house and greeted Grannie by lifting the bag of Rally's, he knew no police had taken them. Remembering the time he'd locked eyes with that Blasian bitch, Peb supposed he understood things just fine.

20. LIMINAL SPACE

Dreams are a dose of fancy permitted by consciousness, facilitated by a body in need of replenishment. The senses diminish, and the mind slows down to a focal point. One so fine it can occasionally be comparable to waking life. And it was with a high certainty that the dream Hinanya was having was the most lucid she'd ever had. So much so that at times, upon recollecting it as a whole afterward, she would have sworn her slumbering consciousness was more cogent than any time in waking.

The aura of clairvoyance that pervaded her episode mystified things, and try she as might, it was hard to chalk it up to a mere dream. But she was forced to, citing the hard bite of being she was, at the limits of her brain and body.

It began and remained a peculiar thing. The passage of time seemed off while her surroundings became a hospital room, manifesting with such ferocity that Hinanya perceived a chalky scent in the air and the feel of a cold metallic chair.

A bed was at the center of all things, and in it laid Felix, bruised, swollen, and scratched up. All of his skin was tumbling away like sand falling through an open palm. Yet it didn't completely part from him, only shifted for a time until the motion surpassed him and became a fog in the room. His image became steady, if only between the ripples in the fog that spread out. Though it was foggy, she knew they were in the Bywater, by a shipyard.

Hinanya nodded to Felix with a fierce look. She'd never before seen his face, and it was blanked out. But he nodded in return, and in his eyes, she was pulled elsewhere as a nocturnal scene took over the hospital room. They were outside on some street corner, where the boy who'd stolen the bikes and his friends were attacking Felix, laying punches into him with no mercy, kicking and stomping him as he collapsed onto the pavement, then running off as Felix's blood pooled out all around him. It expanded under Hinanya, and she began sinking through the fluid. Out of the corner of her eye, she saw Felix's incomplete tag, and Felix himself looking down on her.

No creator should have to suffer these indignities, she surmised. *The self is an impediment enough for creation.*

Hinanya had the desire to finish the incomplete tag, to make it whole, but in fear of ruining it, she—no. No. The truth was that she was unable to return. The sinking into the blood was out of her control, though she wanted to rise.

Hinanya pieced things together based on the news following Buckland's reward announcement. The city no longer had any patience or appreciation for graffiti, and it was clamping down, looking for a scapegoat that would mollify the fallen of their city.

Another thought came, but it formed more like an impression than the of the word itself.

RETRIBUTION.

That would have to be her reality. Felix had been jumped and accused of being the writer on Buckland's camera.

Felix's suffering must be paid back in full. Hinanya had established that suffering could be converted into beauty, but could it also be translated into justice? Justice, it seemed, came much harder than beauty. And even more, justice was never beauty itself. Only equalization. Neutrality. Balance. The apprehension of beauty was recognition of something greater than what the *self* possessed, otherwise how could the *self* appreciate what it apprehended as beauty? At the same time, though the drive for justice could rival that of beauty, the pursuit of justice was not one of something greater but something equal. Naturally, the same pain reciprocated.

And she didn't know Felix. His pain was greater than hers.

Her sister came into the dream. Yes, she remembered Taylor, in the room next to Felix's, separated through time. When the girl was three, she'd gotten into the cabinets and drank a toxic level of bleach. They never understood how the girl could withstand taking so much of the burning liquid in, but she had.

Hinanya dropped the book she'd been reading in the den to race to the kitchen to find Taylor there and raced immediately to her mother in tears. Taylor was vomiting and screeching, she had been in danger, and their mother had been unaware. Hinanya remembered choosing to intervene then. She'd saved Taylor. She didn't have to, but she did.

Back in the hospital room, Hinanya began hearing her old nun teachers from Catholic school preaching on eternity. It frightened her greatly, perhaps more than the alternative prospect of nothingness. Time continuing on and on. Eternal existence and awareness would eventually lead to one to contemplate an end. But there would be no finality in eternity. No beginning either.

Hinanya had become discontent with the concepts of both non-existence and eternity in heaven in her youth. Both were horrible. That's when her mother had told her about reincarnation. The eternal recurrence of things was something that could never be fully grasped. And so she would never have to understand. Having those questions freed us from the full burden of life after death.

Was that also the hospital where she'd been born? She figured she must have been born in some hospital around New Orleans. That infant memory was in her mind somewhere, yet nowhere to be found, buried under all the existential junk.

Were the answers to the actual nature of existence in there somewhere too? Could her *being* actually touch them, in contrast to what her mother thought?

No, she had to focus. She was here for Felix. They saw one another but shared no further information. How strange. Felix was fine. Those boys hadn't really tried to hurt him. Just rough him up a little bit. Make him bleed while they ran away.

Doctors came shuffling in. Besides their name tags they were silhouettes.

Dr. Franklyn, her old neighbor in Minnesota, who'd espoused about the wonders of apple cider vinegar.

After the doctors were there, Felix stopped noticing Hinanya. That was all right. That's how Hinanya liked it, and she assumed that's how Felix liked it too. They must have been of the same kind. He was just a little more put together than she was. Not perfect by any means, otherwise he'd never have become a writer like her. All this suffering from the synthesis; when reality meets self. She wanted to talk *to* him, not *for* him. Why didn't she?

Perhaps it had something to do with the fact Hinanya wasn't sure if he was real. Real or a speck her mind had manufactured upon her arrival to New Orleans to survive long enough to find herself and transcend her being.

Felix was part of a greater untouchable presence that had drawn Hinanya back to New Orleans, so she had to strike out against the people who'd put him out of commission, even if it was only a dream. Even if Felix didn't actually exist.

They could have taken his eyes... how would Felix write without his eyes? What would he become if he couldn't be a writer? What would he do if he knew he couldn't be anything any longer?

Felix was seemingly ambivalent to it all. If there were such a thing as a metaphysical substructure to the universe, then no doubt interaction between the physical and spiritual would be dicey, perhaps impossible. Hinanya knew such a conjecture to be valid. It was the difference between two fundamentally different types of matter.

And so Felix had communicated to her in a form beyond language? His graffiti?

How could he leave marks on those urban walls? How could he be attacked?

Angels, as Sasha had said, are just those who'll see you.

How do I see you?

With that, the dream she was having ended, and she was greeted by the awful rush. The sudden jolting became even more disorienting when Hinanya realized she was not in her apartment but some abandoned building under complete darkness with no recollection how she'd gotten there.

21. ALL MIST

A New Orleans downpour could bring all plans to a standstill. When people raced inside from a storm, all intentions were put on hold. Meetings rescheduled, activities postponed, all for a ubiquitous act of nature. No one wanted to be out, whether in a car or walking as if the rain itself could be more dangerous than any other aspect of New Orleans life. Crime and nefarious incidents were likewise postponed or canceled until a dryer time.

It was such a storm which had taken Hinanya out of her mad dream. Droplets pelted against the breached roof above her, and she rose up from her uncomfortable position on the floor. In addition to not knowing how she'd gotten to where she was, she also was at a loss as to where that was. A staircase led her down toward what seemed to be a large opening in the building. Everything besides the aperture was absolute darkness. Coupled with bleary eyes, Hinanya held her body tightly against the wall and examined the steadiness of each step as she descended. In trying to remember how she had gotten to where she was, she found herself growing nauseous. The last thing she could remember was going to sleep in her apartment. Then that dream. It had seemed to transport her to—

The train.

Walking outside of the decrepit building, Hinanya caught sight of it, the intermittent chain of carts to either side of her down the tracks.

That was exactly when it moved from where it had been sitting, it's clanging percussion soon extinguished by the din of the whistle and the bells at each street's railroad crossing. It moved off, and for a time, Hinanya observed each cart. It took some time, so she took stock of herself. She was dressed in the clothes she'd fallen asleep in, the only problem was she was sure she hadn't worn the gun on the inside of her jeans when she'd slept, yet there it was.

That word, the theme of her dream came to her: Retribution.

Whatever she'd seen, whatever it meant, she pieced it together as a metaphor. The boy who'd taken the bikes, which made victims out of his own ignorance, needed to be shown.

Hinanya turned around to see the building she'd walked out of, and the soreness of sleeping on its floor had just begun to register. She'd passed by the buildings many nights in her exploits but had never gone in. It was a two-story brick building with five windowpanes on each of its four sides, most of which were either busted in or boarded up. Below the windows, the structure was held up by six round, rusty pillars. It stood adjacent to the railroad, a parking lot on one side and a vacant lot on that other. Devon Riley Dixon, the old funeral parlor that had been open for business when she was younger.

There was also a dense mist that percolated when the rain was abruptly cut off. Her imagination still held sway over her.

The train continued rolling past her. Then all of a sudden she felt a sharp pain in her chest. Swirling colors overtook her, and they coalesced into a physical representation of nausea, which then toppled her over as she vomited onto the drab ground.

After that, Hinanya was all right. The train kept rolling past. Hinanya wondered where it was going. She didn't begin the short trek home until the train finally disappeared, off to another place.

Felix was most likely fine as well. Or nonexistent. But she had not literally witnessed those boys attacking him. It was a dream. Dreams aren't reality.

Still, she didn't know how to prove that notion wrong. At least not until she spotted Felix again after this ridiculous writer hunt was settled. But would it ever, if she didn't turn herself in? No, more likely than not, it wouldn't blow over. Hinanya supposed there was potential to write somewhere else if it was actually helping her. And it had been. Just not as much as finding Wenin would, and she knew that time was near. Everything was in motion.

As for the boy who needed retribution, Hinanya considered it from as many perspectives as possible as she made her way home. It still seemed early, perhaps before ten o'clock at night.

Hinanya held a deep well of hatred for ignorance. For the boy, who was not stealing the bicycles to survive. That's why she'd recovered the bicycles and arranged for them to be returned to their owners through the police station.

New Orleans spouted an extreme ignorance, which insulted her to her core and made her act out to attack it. Yet to attack it could be considered ignorant in itself. In some ways, she knew that her method was flawed. The best way to deal with ignorance was knowledge.

And what about her madness? Her drive to suicide. What if that was ignorance? How would they know if she was quiet about it to everyone who cared for her? If the only time she reflected upon it was to herself? Then there was her own graffiti, classified by society as an illustrated ignorance. Buckland saw the problem in such a myopic manner. She needed to do better against ignorance.

The hefty thoughts consumed her until, at last, by the time Hinanya had gotten to the parking lot of her apartment building, she had a plan for the bicycle theft. Under the steps leading to her floor, she had hidden her supplies under a tarp in a milk crate. Creeping under the steps, she took it all out, only to turn around to see someone appearing several feet in front of her, the only thing between them the mist shrouding the figure's identity.

Hinanya was alarmed and prepared to unholster the gun, only to recognize that it was Kurt.

76

"Hey!" he said with enthusiasm. "Sorry for the surprise pop-in. I hope I'm not interrupting anything. I was just passing by and wanted to see if you were around."

Kurt had given her a ride home from the double date, and they had tentative plans to go shooting soon.

"Hiya!" she said. "Yeah, you scared me."

Holding the milk crate for him to see brought her anxiety, to be on that slippery slope of revealing her writer persona to Kurt. Trying not to seem jumpy, she returned the milk crate to where it had been under the steps.

"Want to get something to eat?" he asked.

For some reason, being there in front of Kurt after her fugue made her think of Taylor. Kurt and Taylor. Maybe because Hinanya had the desire to push Kurt away, as she had Taylor many times. Tell-tale signs illuminated that she was not interested in him. It was a feat she wanted to take care of gradually, as not to inspire him to think she was playing hard to get or something.

"That is something I'm not up for right now."

"I left a message on your machine first," Kurt clarified. "I was going this way anyway, see—"

"It's fine," Hinanya said, cutting him off.

Kurt seemed relieved, and then Hinanya understood he'd probably been more nervous approaching her than she'd been in the surprise of seeing him. Hinanya suspected Kurt considered her to be his primary objective. Why her? He must be utterly demoralized at his prospects.

"I'd let you in, but my house isn't presentable."

"Ah, but we're going shooting soon, right?" he asked, lifting his shoulders and arms up.

"Definitely. Just have something to take care of over the next few days, and then we'll be good to go. Say Monday?"

"Works for me."

Instead of heading upstairs and wishing him a good night, she asked him, "Have you ever fired a gun before?"

"No."

"Hmm."

"In fact, I've never seen a gun in person before."

Hinanya laughed, tempted to show the Glock to him now, but she thought better of it.

"You're freaking intense, Hinanya," he said.

"I'm sorry," Hinanya said with feigned remorse.

"No, you're not the one who should be sorry. Whoever fucks with you will be. I like that part of you. A lot."

Hinanya took the compliment. It was as if Kurt knew she was having all sorts of conflicts in those New Orleans streets. With nothing better to say, she responded with, "You're right. Why should anyone be sorry?"

22. CONVERGENCE

The boy's path was so predictable that once she had him tailing her yet another night, she lost him again, turning him around six blocks from where she hoped to end things.

Intentionally popping up again, Hinanya paced quickly through a driveway into a backyard, and the boy followed. But it was not her house, and she hopped up the fire escape to wait for him. The boy looked around, walking forward with a shiver brought on by the late night's wind.

Hinanya tackled the boy. He thrashed and tried to fight back, but it was useless.

"Why have you been following me?!" she demanded, snarling into his left ear while bending his right arm back.

"Dumb bitch."

"Gotta wonder why," she said. "I'm just trying to mind my own business."

The boy snorted. "Bull fuckin' shit. If you haven't caught me by surprise. I woulda got you."

"That's quite a bold claim." She loosened her grip on him. "I'm the one who took those bikes. I've seen what you do same as you've seen me. A piece of shit."

"Fuck *off*. Runnin' around here. Takin' people's shit. Stoppin' us from doing our thing. As if you know what any of it means."

"Your people want the gun back, don't they?"

The boy didn't answer her. Hinanya assumed that was a yes.

"You know that gun was stolen in the first place, don't you? You ever think maybe I'm charged with retrieving it?"

"Diggy says you ain't no fuckin' cop."

"Well, you're just a stupid kid. And I think you need help if you want to stop me."

"My brother's got his whole crew pulsin' down on you." The boy tried to squirm away but to no avail. He just couldn't accept being stuck. "You can't hold me down all night. I'll shout to wake all these houses up, and you'll look bad."

"If you did that, then the cops would get the gun back when they came."

"So then you really ain't police. Jus' a dumb bitch."

"What's your name and who's your brother?" Hinanya asked.

"Suck dick and ride out."

Hinanya formed a fist, ready to strike at him.

"You hit me, and my brother will kill your ass."

"What's the name Wenin mean to you?"

The boy looked up at her, perplexed. "Fuckin' 'hood legends."

"What will you do if I let you go?"

"Call my boys and fuck you the hell up."

"Thought you could take me if you weren't caught by surprise," she mocked.

"Bitch." He spat on her face. Hinanya wiped it off.

"I know you need to be tough growing up around here. Faulting you for it is wrong. Still, I wish I could make you understand you could be more." At that, Hinanya got off of the boy.

"You want a shot at me? What's goin' on?" the boy wondered. His veneer went away. "Peb. They call me Peb."

At first, the boy simply got on his feet, staring her down. Then, all of the sudden, she ran off.

For several blocks, Peb followed her until they reached the train tracks. Peb was furious and wanted to put the bitch down. He'd already called Caso to tell him what was happening. Caso told him to back down, and that help was coming, but Peb didn't want to lose her.

He watched the girl go into the old Devon Riley Dixon building, pleased she was cornered.

He heard her taunting him once he was inside. "Come and get it, kid."

The provocation enraged him, and he went stomping in, turning on the flashlight on his cell phone. "This jus' like earlier, you thinkin' you can be sneaky on some Batman shit."

He heard some shuffling but couldn't tell where she was. Perhaps above him." Remember tonight, no matter what. What I'm telling you right now— you don't have to be afraid. You don't have to make others afraid. We can all live together. There is plenty to go around. Did you know that? There's no need to fight over things. I just need to know how y'all got this gun."

"It don't matter. I don't know, and I don't care. It ain't yours either 'cause you stole it." Peb whipped his flashlight around to try and catch some movement. In stepping toward the sound of her voice, he began to feel venerable, so he stopped.

"No. You don't understand. This gun, I'm sure of it, belonged to a friend of mine. He used it to kill himself all the way up in Minnesota. Now it's here."

"How?" Peb asked into the gutted pitch black lobby.

"I was trying to figure that out."

"You crazy. Ain't no way that's the same gun. You know what? I actually don't give a fuck. Come out. My boys are on their way, so you ain't going anywhere anyway. This done. Over."

Peb heard sniffling and realized the girl must have been crying. "His name was Stefan. I was told he killed himself, now I don't even know. Maybe someone made it look like a suicide, which makes no sense to me, but here I am. Delusional. What if I used this gun on myself? What then, huh, kid?"

Peb was caught off guard. The situation had shifted on him in a direction he hadn't anticipated. Where he'd been ready to pummel her, now he had to try to stop her from shooting herself. Thinking on his feet, he said, "They call me Peb. If you shoot yourself with that gun, the cops will come and find it. And my brother will be in big fuckin' trouble. Don't do that."

"I don't want your brother to get in trouble. I just wanted to know what the fuck happened to my friend and how it is that a homeless man tried to pull that friend's gun on me. The police should have it. It doesn't belong here."

He heard a creaking noise above him. Still no sight of Hinanya with his flashlight as he waved it to and fro.

"Well, he do what he need to to survive!"

"My friend didn't have to die."

"We didn't kill your friend."

"You didn't."

In the silence that elapsed, Peb felt he was in way over his head. Not only was he trying to talk her down, he realized in her deranged state, but she could also just as easily turn the gun on him. A desire to flee overwhelmed him. "So we wait 'til my brother comes out and ask him."

"They can't have this gun back."

"We going to get it sooner or later."

"Not if I kill myself right here!" she screamed.

"Then I grab the gun and run off."

"Hah. Little black boy running off with a weapon? You'll get charged with murder if you're not careful."

That was when Peb realized something strange was happening around him. The pure darkness began to glow in a few select spots above him. Something was burning.

As Peb tried to get out of the building, Hinanya appeared in front of him. Thankfully, the gun not in her hands.

"You want a chance at me. A fair shot to bring me down, right? That's why you've been following me?"

"Well, yeah. You stole from Diggy."

"He was trying to steal from me. If people had just left me alone, Peb."

But Peb couldn't do that. Though he knew he was outmatched, he launched a fist at Hinanya's face. It landed, and she fell. He prepared to hit her more as she lay on the floor, but she rebounded and advanced, chopping his neck. Peb was nearly knocked off his feet himself from having the air in his throat fussed with. What followed was a short trade of blows.

Now that Peb was so close to the girl, he understood that even without her martial arts skills, her greater size made his offensive pointless. Hinanya delivered an upper elbow to Peb's jaw, and he fell back, slamming to the floor of the building on his back. When he opened his eyes again, he saw the building was catching fire. She wasn't letting him leave.

"What the fuck!?" he asked.

"You wanted to fight me? Here we are, Peb!" she said hysterically.

"Nah, we gotta go!" Peb tried to get up, but Hinanya held him down with her right knee on his chest.

"Your boys, they'll find us."

Peb's head rolled back and forth, squirming in disbelief. Did the girl wish to kill them both?

"I asked you a question!" Hinanya hissed. Tackling him, he was once again stuck.

Going limp Peb nodded. "I don't know."

"Good. You don't ever have to find out."

Hinanya curled both the fingers of her right hand together as if in prayer, which disturbed Peb. So much so, he was actually relieved when she brought the two fists down on his nose in a hammer dive. The pain was followed by blood, but all he could feel was the sudden relief on his chest. Hinanya was walking up the steps of the burning building.

"I will find out," she proclaimed before she was gone.

Only for a few seconds did Peb contemplate following after her, then thought better of it. Instead, he hobbled to his feet and limped out of the building before the exit became a flaming arch. "They gonna be looking for you now, bitch!" He spoke with certainty, but in his mind he imagined her unfazed.

Caso and his boys arrived before the police and fire department. Where Peb desperately pleaded for Caso to let them leave, he was dumbstruck when Caso informed Peb they would be staying to talk to the authorities.

"First of all, tell me exactly what happened," said Caso.

Peb did.

"All right," said Caso, not missing a beat. "Second, do not say a fuckin' word to the police. No matter what, Peb. I will not like that. You can't talk."

"Why can't we leave, Caso?" Peb wondered. The old Devon Riley Dixon building slowly caught fire.

"I'm your brother, and you trust me, right?"

Peb nodded.

"So shut the fuck up and let me talk."

And Peb did exactly as he was told. Caso did not mention the graffiti girl once. He deliberately got it twisted in telling the cops. "My brother here, he been talking 'bout doing this a long time. We didn't believe him. We'd cruise by this place, and he'd jus' go on and on 'bout how ugly that parlor be. Maybe even, he mighta been tagging it to his liking. We jus' don't know."

"We got a call earlier about a suspicious boy skulking around over here by himself," said the cop. "Good to have confirmation. Yep, got the idiot red-handed."

As they hoisted Peb into the back of the police car, Peb saw Caso looking at him with malice. It was enough to keep him silent. But there was more to it. Peb never imagined he'd give so much of himself to his brother only to be betrayed. Now he was curious about what it was with that gun. What was so important to Caso that it meant more to him than his own brother. Probably not all that much considering Caso didn't care much about Peb at all. He'd played him the whole time. And try as Peb might, he knew it was better to take the heat for the night's incident than try to contradict his brother's account. Caso was a double-crosser and learning that was worth the price he'd pay.

It was the kind of mistake you only made once.

23. LESSON IMPARTED

Sitting perched on top of a nearby water tower, Hinanya waited for hours as everything blew over.

People came out from their homes to see the building as the firefighters tried to save it, only to see it fall and fold to the ground.

The water tower was the sight of one of the tags she'd been unable to complete because of all of the neighborhood patrols. She hoped to return there one day after she was done doing the right thing.

Her words to Peb had been genuine. In the midst of the awful rush, she'd wanted to die in that abandoned funeral parlor. It was the first time she'd confided in another about her suicidal thoughts. And now he was being, presumably, blamed for the fire.

How was that justice? Perhaps, she supposed, the brush with the law would straighten him out. Or not. Maybe she hadn't made the right decision. She was responsible for what had happened, and the wrong person got caught. Then again, he shouldn't have been after her in the first place.

The men who'd been surrounding Peb remained long after he was taken away. Hinanya got a good look at them and thought one of them must be the brother. The one who would be after her all the more now. He'd given up his brother like a pawn in game of chess.

The train seemed to be delayed by the commotion and bustling down below. The smoke mesmerized Hinanya. It rose and bounced against the other buildings nearby, flirting with the notion of setting them ablaze as well.

The height she found herself at was much higher than her parent's balcony all those times. Most of her life she wanted to know what came after. The choice she hadn't made that day. After such a fall, the end all would know.

Hence the pursuit of Wenin. Another lead to answering her questions. Her journey was nearing its end. Wenin and his 8IL.

Or, if she so desired, this could be it now. Sometimes it seemed like her psyche was falling apart, burning down slowly with combustible thoughts, not unlike the old building she survived. That's why she'd willed it gone. She'd survived it. Hinanya relished that victory, grasping the can of spray paint she held against herself like a child, itching to complete her tag despite the risk of being found out.

A morbid but amusing thought jostled her then—the idea of her family coming to New Orleans to identify her dead body. Telling relatives that they had no idea Hinanya was suicidal. That she had been *sick*. But that was the nature of her sickness. It hid itself well, sometimes even from herself.

In such a world as the one she experienced, there was the possibility that suicide could be a very pragmatic option, even if nothingness followed afterward.

A gunshot first, then a fall. Maybe soon. But not before Wenin. Not before 8IL.

In the meantime, perhaps she'd purged the world of some of its ignorance. Maybe she'd done some good after all, despite being herself.

The girl on the water tower lay back, settling down as best she could. Overhead, the clouds rolled by, separating and joining together in great tufts, going slightly more incandescent in a purpling glow produced by the retreating night. Hinanya accepted all she could see with just her naked eye.

SEEKER

"I don't know which is worse: to learn or not to know"

-Meg & Dia

1. MISSING

Two hands clapped onto the crumbling brick walkway. Arms extended to reveal a shadow collapsing into the hard orange light, making itself known. Hinanya slowly pushed against the bricks with a sour feeling from the abrasions she'd sustained in her impulsive final leap down from the water tower.

The pleasure of viewing the night sky became less attractive as the police presence at the newly burnt down building a block up from her dwindled, and the nature of her circumstances claimed her once more.

Tonight at least, she had done what she'd set out to do. Hinanya knew it was time to head home, for she was exhausted.

Earlier, when she'd been looking down at the firefighters surrendering the building to the smoke and flames, she'd wondered if it was best to simply leave the matter of Stefan's gun alone, and instead, to focus on what she'd actually come to New Orleans for. Everything about the gun felt wrong. It had complicated Hinanya's entire objective in New Orleans. It was time to go a few days without incident—that gun was trouble. And Peb being taken away by the police had left Hinanya baffled. Couldn't she just tell herself it was a slim yet sickening coincidence? That this was no all related somehow?

She'd conducted her life carefully, doing just what she was told, and performing all the tasks that were expected of her until she was able to free herself from the control of others. Perhaps she was abusing her newfound freedom? What a shock it would be for her family to learn their daughter was not the pleasant overachiever, but the maddening paramour of death. No job or function could fulfill the girl's need in life. She wasn't destined to bear any child, or traverse any of the other predictable avenues of society for that matter. No, her endgame was Wenin, and that was all that was important to her.

The answer to the question: was it possible to have an out-of-body experience?

Presented with the possibility of true healing, the idea of curing whatever was wrong with her was out of the question. Hinanya wanted to go beyond the reality she'd known every day, even if it meant never returning.

The thought occupied her completely until she stepped into some fallen fencing and her right pant leg tore. In examining it, Hinanya was prevented from from noticing the three people who stood before her until it was too late.

Hinanya jumped back as they moved toward her. A large woman stood between two men. She felt she'd seen them before somewhere. The woman stood tall, towering over the other men. They increased their stride to flank

Hinanya's left and right.

Hinanya fled.

Her trajectory took her just beyond the Marigny, and she saw the colorful houses blooming like flowers under the glow of the streetlights. Bordering the Bywater, the Marigny had a slightly neater appearance than its neighboring district, brought on by an influx of affluent residents.

Both outnumbered, and certain they would catch up with her, Hinanya whipped around and planted her feet shoulder-width apart. Her legs straightened and she eased tension off of her knees. A shooter's stance. Her pursuers sped up not realizing Hinanya was reaching for Stefan's gun. But when the girl searched for it, it was not there.

The gun was not on her person at all.

2. DIVISION INTACT

Hinanya cut around the corner of an alleyway, losing control of his breath but knowing she had to keep going. Those chasing her were behind her, closing in and calling after her. One of the men stopped in his tracks and said, "I got something for you, bitch. Hinanya decided not to look back. No, she had to find a way out of this.

It had to be close to sunrise, and she thought there had to be some unassuming denizen of the Marigny out walking their dog soon that could deter the pursuit.

Twisting and turning down the streets, she saw a car going down a road several blocks from her, and Hinanya felt she'd lost them.

Being caught was a spreading poison in her mind.

The woman who'd been after her stomped out from behind some bushes and she ran toward Hinanya. She and Hinanya were both winded, but the fight transpired without delay. The blows were forceful, beyond a threshold Hinanya could sustain. One strike to the chest knocked Hinanya back, and she was unable to defend against the next punch to her jawline.

"We could be jus' talkin'," the big lady began, "but you needed to be wreckin' shit. We know who you is, come on, babe. You ain't right now. We got a way of doin' things out here, okay? All right?"

Hinanya spit up blood as she tumbled to the ground, only to be struck once more in the back of the head. Her scraped hands bled fresh as she crashed onto the pavement. The woman kicked Hinanya in the face, sending her onto her back. But Hinanya, despite her pain, rolled away and slowly rose up to launch into a desperate assault: a half-fist to the woman's sternum. The woman tripped on her feet for several paces, gripping her chest.

"The gun doesn't belong to any of you!" Hinanya protested as loud as she could. The others appeared at each end of the street. Having just barely gained ground against one opponent, Hinanya was now being boxed in as the group flocked to surround her. A car came down the street from her left side slowly, a pure menace. The headlights were shut out as they parked but the engine remained running. More people exited for her.

Six people in all, enclosing the perimeter around her. Hinanya got as far as a playground parking lot before she saw the flash of silver. The ones who'd started chasing Hinanya finally had her at gunpoint.

"You good," said the one holding the gun. The man smirked at the sight of her vulnerability. "Damn we've been looking hard for you. Lemme introduce myself. My name Caso, 'cause I'm cheesy." He stretched out that last word for emphasis. "And I know you good. So good." Caso brought his gun closer to her face, poking repeatedly at her left cheek. "But you ain't better than me. Yeah, you woke and all, but you done. As for me? I ain't even had breakfast yet."

3. THE TRAIN

By the time Hinanya figured out that Caso and his friends weren't going to shoot her, she was in tears. Her life was in their hands, and she despised that lack of control. Hinanya needed to be the cause of her own death, no one else.

Though the others were surely armed, only Caso had a weapon trained on her.

"We helped you by havin' Peb take the L for tonight's little show. You'd be in a lot of trouble right now if it hadn't been for me. Been lookin' for you a long time now, girl. What they call you?"

Hinanya was on her knees behind a dumpster in some back alley by the playground. Five people, including the girl she struck stood all around her. The first hints of a new day were unfolding above her, a partly cloudy overcast day by the looks of it.

"I don't have Stefan's gun with me."

Caso's upper lip twitched. "That'd be the one you stole from Diggy?"

"It was my friend's!" Hinanya cried. "He's dead."

"I ain't know any shit 'bout that and I sure don't know nobody named Stefan, but what's a dead guy need with a gun? See, I'm jus' a middleman. Looks like you and I jus' needed some real talk to put it together. I ain't even tryna fuck you up. You'll cross someone else and get it soon enough anyway. You don't belong out here. You know that. Tryna all this and that. Bein' a hero. It's sad. Nah, I mean, it's impressive, but it's sad where it's all headin'." Caso turned to his companions. "Check her pockets, 'cause I hope she's lyin'." He looked back at Hinanya as they approached her. "You realize we goin' to wherever it is to get it right now, yeah? I lost my brother to find you. Our Grannie ain't never goin' let me see him now. But whatever, like you care. I jus' feel like we both worked together to fuck him over tonight. That's how it goes, some sad shit. Only thing useful he did was tell me you had the gun on you."

As one of the men riled through her pockets, Hinanya heard the whistle in the distance. The moment brought a shift in the atmosphere. The captors dropped their guard, so Hinanya twisted her hands around the one searching and got him into an arm lock. She had a shield if Caso changed his mind about firing. Still, with how close together they were, it would be easy for Caso to twist the pistol around his friend's head and ram the muzzle into Hinanya's face. With the same momentum of the swing that Hinanya had used to seize the squealing man in the first place, she fell forward, toppling some of the others over. During the drop, Hinanya released her grip and made for Caso's left hand, which still held the gun. With a precise alignment, her two forearms wrapped around Caso's, and she tilted them with all of her force until she heard the signature cracking of a broken bone.

Writhing, Caso demanded those who'd fallen to get up, and Hinanya fought her way through those left in quick blows, misdirecting fists being sent her way, and made her way back into the street. At one point, she launched a knee into someone's chin as they were trying to regain their footing, and Hinanya's knee was temporarily snagged on the pink beads around the man's neck until they broke apart. She ripped the necklace away from him, pocketing the beads as a trophy.

Frantic for a way out, she recalled the reason she'd dared to make an escape in the first place. Just a block away, the train was coming across the track from the opposite direction in which she was running. Hinanya found little difficulty in leaping onto the steps of a cab and rushing into it. The problem was, she was still being tailed, and she knew Caso's men would follow right behind her. After what she'd done to Caso, they'd probably have no compunction about throwing her off the moving train. Disappearing into the shadows, Hinanya felt around in the darkness of the sidecar for something that would help her.

Moments later, the first man was about to jump in after her. Just before he fully made contact with the steps, Hinanya swung a milk crate out. It was anchored with the pink beads. The rotation of the milk crate she'd began whirling, coupled with the speed of the man just getting onto the cab, sent him flying out. He then pummeled those who had been right behind him.

With that, she relaxed with the comfort of a successful getaway, indifferent as to where the train was going, only glad to have survived. At several intervals, the freight train slowed to a near stop, and Hinanya took the opportunity to get off. Still, she waited, though not looking forward to the unknown distance back to her apartment, as she was too fatigued to move. The fight had left with a swollen jaw and a throbbing temple that was exacerbated by the bumpy train ride.

Caso had said he didn't know from where the gun had come, only that he was charged with its care. There was no use in antagonizing him any longer. Hinanya hadn't suffered so much simply to dwell on Stefan. She had to keep reminding herself of that, even knowing in time Caso would come after her for retribution in kind. By then, she might be gone from New Orleans, achieving transcendence.

She watched in awe as it slid away with haste onto an overpass. In its wake, she discovered an interesting garden of a neighborhood. Trees with long gnarled branches extended themselves parallel to the streets and the road. The neutral grounds at the center of the road were likewise inundated with vegetation, violets, and ivy vines.

As she walked, she tried to gain a sense of where she was, and Hinanya felt safe in the early morning sojourn. She was faraway from where she'd narrowly been defeated in the Bywater, and this place was a haven in itself. A lush community where Hinanya could know tranquility.

Most of all, as she passed block after block of cozy houses and lit porches, and onto a stretch of local restaurants and businesses, she couldn't help but notice a lack of graffiti. A nice part of the city to be sure, but what made it so? In her head, she saw mild-mannered residents, never at a loss for wisdom or money, and so indifferent to the destitute conditions not far beyond them. The illusion faded at N. Broad, where New Orleans showed its true depressed colors: rotted foundations and precarious blocks which suggested a threatening atmosphere.

When doubling back to the garden neighborhood, Hinanya saw potential in those untagged establishments. Far from Caso's domain, Hinanya felt the matter was settled. She could tag again. But first, she needed to find her way back home, (she found she was very thirsty) propagated by the forces that had propelled her to return.

4. THE LIABILITY

Typically, the sight of the unkempt bathroom crossed through Shaun's awareness with indifference. He would look past the mess, trim his scruff, and then do his day. But to return after a time to see the remains of so many separate trimming sessions congealed to the sink with globs of toothpaste and soap scrum prompted him to stop. In desperation, he'd sublet the space to his friend Mickey, who'd taken to heart the sentiment of leaving things as he'd found them.

As Shaun pulled out a wet-wipe from its yellow tube, he felt remorse in seeing just how grungy his profile had become in the mirror. The long, brown husk of a once luscious ponytail drooped beneath what he was able to see, though he could feel the elastics holding things together. The beard he sported brought his face to a level of feral savagery. Then he saw, with great dismay, the region surrounding his eyes, a more drab shade than the rest of his pallor skin. It was easy to see the stark indications of sleep deprivation and unapologetic drug abuse. It wasn't in his eyes but around them. The bags that consolidated from prison nights tormented both by the fleas he'd suffered there and the guards who would do nothing about them.

That punishment on top of the imprisonment, to Shaun, should have somehow earned him a shortened sentence. But that wasn't how the law operated. How the pigs saw it, once you were in prison, all manner of misfortune that befell the prisoner was just part of the fun.

He would cleanse. He was going to wipe it all away.

Shaun's experiences with breaking the law had left him hollow. He'd try and dig himself out of another hole and end up in a larger one. If he didn't find a job soon, he'd be out of his apartment and on some skeevy friend's sweat-stained couch.

Shaun lived in a shotgun apartment just off Saint Roch in the Bywater, across the street from a cemetery. The shotgun apartment was an unusual design common to the South. From a porch there was the common room, utilized economically into a room for Shaun's friend Frank, an aspiring actor in his mid-thirties. Shaun would have to walk through Frank's room to enter into a slim hallway. To its side lay the bathroom and after that, Shaun's room. Beyond Shaun's room was the kitchen, and Frank would in turn have to walk through Shaun's room to get to and from the kitchen. The kitchen led to a final bedroom, where their other roommate Alanna stay. She came and went via the back door, and she also had to transverse through Shaun's room to reach the bathroom. With their lack of self-contained rooms, shotgun apartments required a certain kind of person, one who didn't mind seen and being seen at any possible time. Privacy was somewhat diminished for no remarkable advantage, saving the cost of construction—fewer walls to erect. Consequently, Shaun had grown entirely used to his living arrangement on Saint Roch. Despite it being in a bad neighborhood, it was where he wanted to be. To serve his house arrest and then be free.

As Shaun finished cleaning the bathroom, Frank informed him that Ciara was waiting in the smoke pit for him. That was what they called their tiny fenced-in yard shared with the adjoining shotgun apartment to their left. The smoke pit consisted of a circular glass table and a few chairs long past their prime from the consistent exposure of the torrential downpours that soaked the region. It was aptly named, as Shaun and others frequently used the area to smoke everything that could be smoked—marijuana, salvia, DMT, PCP, and last but not least, meth. But with a bi-monthly drug test as one condition of his house arrest, Shaun was forced to stay far away from the smoke pit most of the time, as the synthetic urine sold at the gas station near his house was marked for fetish purposes only. Too much of a risk.

Shaun made straight for the smoke pit to see Ciara. He was relieved. She was working her way down a short cigarette he was certain she'd been saving. When he'd last seen the girl, she'd been rationing the things as if there was going to be an oncoming shortage.

"Shaun, what up, my guy?" Ciara asked. Ciara was tall, hailing from San Antonio, and wore jean shorts that showed off the entire length of her legs no matter what the weather. Shaun appreciated the decision, considering how one glimpse of them could jump-start his heart rate like a line of coke.

"I got no clue. I mean, good to see you or whatever, but I think I'm just going to skip the 'my life sucks' bit and ask you the same question."

Ciara pursed her lips, telling Shaun she was here for a professional not social matter. "8IL."

"Huh?" Shaun asked, feigning an oblivious air.

"It wasn't a question. You need to get some to somebody."

"Nah."

"Once again, not a question. It's your responsibility."

Shaun relinquished all pretenses. "Fuck no. Fuck you for fuckin' askin' about drugs while I'm on house arrest! I'm getting some lame-ass job, watchin' *The Walking Dead,* and jackin'-off. That's *it* for me for like, the next two years."

"You know no matter what you say, you're still obligated. Even if you weren't, you realize how hard it's going to be to stay straight now that you've been through the system? Look, whatever angel boy bullshit you need to pull for your halfway Hank officer is fine with me. But I'm sure you don't want to turn your back on this. 'Cause it'll be so bad for you if you don't. Shaun, you're not smart. You do what you do, sure. But you aren't dumb either.

Backing out of your commitment, I, that'd be... I'd really miss you, you know?"

Shaun tried to keep his composure at that, but he was unable to mask what he knew to be a true threat. "I thought I was square with him."

"You're close. And after, you can go straight as fuck."

"Fuck you, bitch. If he starts grilling me, I'll out him on it all. I'll be famous for it. No one else is willing, but you know me."

"Shaun, call me whatever you want. You're gringo to me any day. But get that, in reality, we've still got you. Always have. You don't know his name, where he lives. What he looks or sounds like. He's an urban fucking legend that most hardcore druggies here have never even heard of. He's every fucking shadow in his town. The best thing you can do is do what he tells you."

"Ciara, look, I may sound out of line, but if I get nabbed for anything again, I'm in big trouble. I just got on this ankle bracelet. And I never want to go to jail again. And here I am stuck up in this place." Shaun gestured to his apartment. "Have you ever been set-up like this?"

"All my life," she said stoically. "Look, you will help us." She paused to regard him with what seemed to be sympathetic eyes. "When you're free to."

"Fuck off. My point is... I'm too afraid. The whole reason why I got busted is messin' with you assholes."

"Hey, what happens out here isn't anything but a storm. You check the weather and prepare, but a rain slicker isn't going to save anybody from drowning. As our man says, 'Don't live below sea level if you aren't ready to drown'."

"Ciara... I'm a liability now."

"I understand. Just as I know that you understand too. If you thought prison was bad, just think of what happened to those boys from the bunker..." She looked away from him for the first time as she trailed off. As her words sank in, a breeze came through to jostle the folded umbrella at the center of the table. "Really, think of yourself as a former and future asset. I mean, don't you know how close you are to getting your hands on 8IL yourself? I mean, there's no drug test in the world for that yet."

It was with that Shaun begrudgingly accepted his lot. Shaun stood up to ask Ciara what Wenin needed of him.

5. BEEN

While others Hinanya's age deluded themselves with relationships, Netflix, or any other of the many distractions, Hinanya knew it was all to force away internal suffering. A true reality of bliss had to beyond these thoughts, these illusions. That was why Hinanya didn't desire any lifestyles her culture mindlessly doled out. None of them truly reconciled suffering. They only attempted to. Calls to love, faith, and servitude were all failures.

After the Devon Riley Dixon episode, Hinanya reminded herself of where her path had started: Uncle Rawls.

Sixteen months before Hinanya and her family evacuated New Orleans over Hurricane Katrina, Hinanya became interested in taking martial arts lessons. Her parents indulged the notion, enrolling her in a dojo. That was where she first met Rawls. At the time, he was a junior instructor, a 1st Degree Black Belt who'd been teaching classes there in lieu of the establishment's tuition fee.

Every now and then, two people bond instantaneously with no clear connection. Hinanya and Rawls had little in common. He was a rambunctious twenty-two-year-old man with a thin afro and a gangly frame, owner to several reptiles. She was a quiet child, prim and trying whatever she could to lose her excess weight. They never truly managed to right their flaws, but when they became spending time together that was the goal.

As the months went on, a mentorship blossomed into a facsimile of siblings. Hinanya would Rawls between school and karate lessons in the park. Though Rawls typically annoyed her with his tangents, she began to learn that certain topics lent more lucidity in his speech. Specifically, he was enamored with thoughts reality and consciousness.

"But what does that mean?" Hinanya had asked sincerely.

"Like when we meditate in class," Rawls explained. "But other stuff too. You and I, right now, are at the level of normal consciousness, undiluted by any sensory deprivation or chemical interference. Some believe it's possible to achieve a state of consciousness, which exists entirely independent from our body and brain. But no one in the world can agree on what consciousness is, see and—" Rawls paused, biting his lip. "Never mind."

"No, keep going," Hinanya insisted with a push. Rawls mockingly defended himself from her, deflecting the move.

"I mean it. I don't know if it is possible to be... beyond what you are. But if so, then our bodies are only representatives of what that is. Call it a soul. That's why a lot of people mess around with drugs. That's why I have," he added with an unapologetic shrug. "Because if there's any chance and we ignore it, then we're fools. Indisputable proof to the question may end all religious warfare, the greatest of all the human contradictions. Imagine if science could conclude the nature of an afterlife or a soul that extended past our mortal lives. Walk back from that notion, assume it may be true, and you see how the government is closing off the possibility of investigating the truth."

In an honest exchange of information based on his experiences, Rawls periodically went on in that manner. Though he was often hesitant to share this point of view with a child, he persisted, on the condition she kept it to herself.

"Modern day public opinion on drug culture has been morphed into a black and white spectrum of recreation or abuse. The government has peddled this to the people and despite the contrary evidence. Forbidding access to drugs which have empirically demonstrated benefits is the true crime."

"I'm sure that wasn't done on a whim," the young Hinanya pointed out. "Drugs are linked to crime and violence."

"You're absolutely right. There were many reasons, only a few of them good. There *is* a lot of potential to harm oneself. There's the negative stigma. Consider the Manson family. They took LSD from time to time and became venerable to brainwashing. People started associating it all with insanity, immorality. The government backed it all up. So in the name of safety they closed a way for the population to cultivate independent thinking. It was no surprise the government felt the need to put censures and penalties on that. Now people inquiring about fundamental questions about reality are automatically criminals. Over the years it has been about money. For a government to forbid proper use sabotages the reason why we have a government in the first place."

As soon as Hinanya was sold on the potential benefits of recreational drug use, Rawls would use counterarguments and support the War on Drugs, leaving Hinanya flabbergasted as to what the truth was. Rawls didn't see a child, only a voracious intelligence deserving of knowledge.

"You can't just want to try drugs because of the things I've said," he told her one day after karate class.

"But you said we all suffer, and drugs help!"

"But drugs aren't a blanket solution. Drugs numb. They melt language, reinterpret sensation. They need to be placed in the proper context too. Stuff like cocaine and heroin are synthetic nightmares which have no call to be used in a recreational way. I've tried most all drugs. Sensory deprivation tanks, meditations. Failed astral projections led to suicide attempts," he spoke with an increasingly severe tone. "Any course to altered states of consciousness imaginable. Despite all of that, nothing has swayed me to believe there is a way out of this representation of myself." He pointed down and swooped an arm around his body.

"That's sad," said the young Hinanya with a solemn nod. "But why does it matter?"

"It is just another manifestation of the search man has had since the beginning. To summon a part of ourselves that is always there, sprinkling delicately over our mundane lives. Our time so unnatural and far from our purpose, if we do have one. We don't like that this might be all there is. With drugs, we are given the option to explore if there is more beyond this realm. Even if there isn't any beyond."

"Oh."

"In these trips, these altered states, I've done battle with my consciousness as if it were a monster. I've admitted truths to myself I'd been denying for years. Drugs aren't a comprehensive solution by any means, as I've said. But when done in the proper way, they may yield therapeutic benefits under specific conditions. That's why it makes me so mad to think people stay thinking drugs are pure evil."

It was about a year after Hinanya met Rawls that she began to refer to him as 'Uncle' Rawls.

"You're so lucky," he mused one day. "You're not all black. The world is going to treat you way better than if you were my color. All people see when they see me is some black body who belongs in jail. I just want to be, Hinanya. I want to seek and find a way to show the world there is an essence beyond the skin that transcends hatred. Wouldn't it be something if it was a drug? Man could still develop a substance that provides the answer to the question we've had all along." Rawls let out a deep sigh. "I think that's why we do it. Ultimately. To find an answer to relinquish all of these surface labels. Maybe someone will figure something out. I've heard a rumor to that effect." That was all he would say on the matter. The man subsequently vanished shortly after that ambiguous declaration, no longer frequenting the dojo.

The sudden change permanently devastated Hinanya.

6. ENVIRONMENT

Hinanya crested the steps and unlocked the door to her building. There were innumerable moths swimming around the light. She quickly slid through the door in hopes of keeping the bugs outside. They swarmed each lamppost around her neighborhood, breeding in droves.

One of the windows by the door was busted. Great. From that observation, Hinanya made for the second floor where her apartment was. The main room had only a bed and a bookshelf. There were also several books askew on the floor in various positions—half-opened or upside down. In the corner was her closet. Besides the books, the place was tidy. Hinanya kept all of her clothes, dirty and clean, in the closet. The kitchen consisted of an oven, a few cabinets, a fridge, and the countertop with a home phone set-up. Hanging over the bathroom door was a large blue tarp.

Hinanya went to the kitchen. It was meticulously clean. No stains on the oven, no dishes in the sink. It even smelled good, a faint hint of lemon. She had no other choice but to keep her apartment pristine, as the building was plagued with German cockroaches. There was one scuttling away from the top of the stove as she approached. Hinanya hit play on her answering machine and started making hot cocoa.

"You have one new message," the robotic female voice of her answering machine told her. "Received yesterday at 7:16PM."

A tiny pause elapsed. Hinanya set a pot of water on the stove.

"You are almost there," a voice said. It hadn't been who Hinanya had expected, not at all. It was a girl's voice with fine diction, slightly monotone. For too long, the voice didn't say anything more. Hinanya thought the message had ended—it hadn't. "There's a series of tags recently done. One will lead you to the next. The last one will point you to where you've gotta go. You've *gotta* go."

Hinanya rushed to the side of the answering machine and summoned a pen and paper hastily from a drawer to mark down any further information, but the message ended. So she was on the right track after all.

Since her run-in with Caso, Hinanya had been cautiously approaching other writers, asking for more information on the codes which Wenin used throughout the city. She couldn't believe someone relevant had found her so soon.

Hinanya tried playing it again, her head pressed against the machine to hear any other sound playing in the background or subtle feature, but there was nothing.

As the water boiled, Hinanya saw the caller ID had it designated as private. Knowing everything she did, Hinanya didn't bother with *69. The message, as far as they were concerned, contained all the information she needed to find them. She was on the right track.

After she turned the water off and mixed the cocoa, anger and duty guided Hinanya. She ripped the telephone charger off the wall and used it to smash the answering machine. She had no use for either anymore.

Vacating the kitchen, Hinanya picked up the books from the floor. It seemed that she spent so little time here. Hinanya sank into a lawn chair she'd salvaged from a street corner. Overall, it wasn't in bad shape, though one arm was missing. That's when it hit the sleep-deprived Hinanya—Stefan's gun was still missing.

Halfway through a delicate sip of the cocoa, Hinanya went into a frenzy through the apartment in search of the gun. Then it hit her. Why was she tearing her space apart? If the gun was anywhere, it was on top of that water tower. She had it when she was at the abandoned funeral parlor! Didn't she? So what if someone found it since she'd fled? Hinanya decided she would go back to look for it, despite the risk. Unless, against all odds, she'd just left the gun here. Had her apartment been broken into? Someone had smashed that window outside, but there was no sign of her apartment itself being penetrated. Five minutes into the search for the gun in her apartment, an overwhelming weariness overtook Hinanya. She tried to fight it, ashamed she'd lost something so important. Most of her possessions meant nothing to her, but that gun was a symbol of her will to live—even if it was also simultaneously an instrument by which to die. The girl retreated into her bed and her eyelids fluttered until she couldn't keep them open any longer. Her beleaguered mind tumbled into a most rejuvenating slumber.

7. THE MOST ADAPTABLE

"Try it again," Hinanya said with a harsh breath. She once again helped Kurt level the rifle.

"Oh, okay," Kurt said.

"Kurt, are you ready to shoot yet?"

"No."

"Don't put your finger on the trigger until you're entirely ready."

"Jeez, Hinanya," he responded. "You're a tough teacher." The two were at an indoor shooting range near where Kurt lived in Uptown.

"It's serious," she insisted.

"Can you show me again?" he asked.

Kurt handed the rifle over to her, and she held it expertly while getting into position. Hinanya fired off the last four rounds.

Kurt looked downrange with wide eyes to see she'd shot the paper effigy of the shooter in the head, heart, and lungs. "You're so good."

"Reload it," she said, handing it back to him.

"Oh, not this again."

"It's easy." But Kurt found it too difficult. Hinanya ejected the clip, set the rounds in, and aimed the weapon at the target. "Maybe I'm just stronger than you, huh?" Hinanya suggested, taunting him.

"Possibly."

He fired once more with her help, ultimately disappointing Hinanya. Kurt wouldn't shoot to kill, not even if the targets were inanimate. Each admonishment she gave came straight from Uncle Rawls. Little did Kurt know, Hinanya wasn't nearly as cruel to him as Uncle Rawls had been to her.

Those bleak summer days following Uncle Rawl's separation with the dojo were spent in a secluded outdoor range some miles north of New Orleans across Lake Pontchartrain. She was still a little girl then, but if Hinanya failed to mark her fake human targets in fatal places, Uncle Rawls would make her feel terrible about it.

Eventually, her aim was impeccable and unerringly lethal.

At first, Hinanya questioned Uncle Rawls as to why he favored firearms over martial arts. "Isn't the whole point of karate that we have empty hands?"

Uncle Rawls nodded. "But the bad guys want to take advantage of that. They have guns, and we don't. So what happens if they pull one on us? We need to know how to use them, Hinanya. To kill. If someone wants to hurt you and pulls out such a weapon, they deserve to die. They have crossed a line I don't think they should be allowed to return from."

"But, our sensei, our school. Uncle Rawls, it's all about mercy, forgiveness. The precious value of all life."

"Yes. But those lessons don't account for life in New Orleans one bit. Guns are not my—and should not be your weapon of choice. You should always try to disarm a person. But in a world like this, people don't care about the value of life like you. They'll shoot you with your back turned. That's why we're here, so tell me," Uncle Rawls sniffed and used his chin to itch his right shoulder, "could you kill another human being?"

"Not after everything I've been taught. I would try to find another way."

Uncle Rawls shook his head. "No. You're a smart person. I'm sure you can imagine a situation in which there was no other way. Where it's him or you. So?"

"Maybe," said Hinanya, setting the gun down staring at it. Maybe I'd freeze up at that moment."

"Then there's no point in you learning self-defense. Your subscription to mercy puts you in more danger than anything else will. Let me clarify. Say someone comes at you and you have to resort to shooting them, so not wanting to kill them, you take out their leg. What if this person is on some kind of insane drug and can't feel the pain? So they keep going after you like some kind of zombie? No. If you really want to defend yourself, you *need* to be ready to kill. If you want to carry a gun, you need to understand that it can and should take a life—when it's necessary. Because someday, it might be."

Hinanya felt stressed from hearing all this. She knew Uncle Rawls wanted her to be safe. But she never wanted to have to carry a gun. "You still haven't told me what made you change so much."

Uncle Rawls never wished to be specific about that. "There are scum in this world. Scum that will kill you unless you kill them. Then think of the consequences of leaving a creature that slimy alive. With a dead body, there's no evidence on their side. All you say is, I was trained to kill when I knew my life was in danger, and that's what I did. Maybe, maybe you end up in jail for manslaughter. But at least that fuck who came for you doesn't harm anyone else. If you're going to shoot, it's to kill. Become what the horrors of the world are afraid of. I'm not telling you to look for trouble or go on the offensive. All I'm saying is it's all a legitimate part of our nature. When people say survival of the fittest, they mean to say survival of the most adaptable. That's what *fittest* really means. Those who are able to become what is needed like *that*." Uncle Rawls snapped his fingers. "There are times where our society's theatrics breaks down, and it's up to you to decide what's right or wrong for yourself."

"Uncle Rawls, but I—"

"No fencing! What were you about to say?" He seized her shoulders, standing above her with a grizzly intensity.

"What has happened to you? You took self-defense seriously, but you never went on about killing like this."

"I'm—"

"...in a bind here, Hinanya," Kurt said.

Hinanya was thrust from those days of shooting with Uncle Rawls into the present moment. Kurt was driving her back to her apartment. It had been an entire month since she'd received the voicemail with the obscure instructions on finding Wenin. Hinanya had had no progress whatsoever, sufficing to tag up the garden neighborhood she'd come across. Perhaps she needed to return to the Bywater.

"Hinanya?"

Hinanya tilted her head to look at him. "Hmm? Yes, sorry."

"I'm in an awful bind here," Kurt said again. Wasn't that exactly what Uncle Rawls had said, the phrase he'd used word-for-word that day she was remembering at the shooting range?

"What's a matter?" Hinanya asked.

"To be honest, a lot of things. Principally, I enjoyed spending time with you but exploring your hobby seems to be a challenging task."

"I'm sorry. It's just... you hear all about these accidents with guns. Two kids playing and one shoots the other one inadvertently. You kept pointing that rifle in all directions. It was loaded. I got frustrated. I hate when people take these things lightly."

"Yeah," Kurt said. "How'd you get so good at it?"

"I had a... teacher who taught me. Before we parted ways, he treated me like a soldier preparing for war."

"Who was he?" Kurt asked with a raised eyebrow, watching her expression from the corner of his eye.

"Family."

"He sounds hard."

"He was real."

"Was the war?"

Hinanya hurried to correct herself. "No, no. I mean, there was no war. Not the one he went on about at least. It's just he... he was real. He genuinely was looking out for my safety. He had my best interest at heart. And for everything he did, I stand by him."

As Kurt droned on in a passive-aggressive manner regarding his feelings for her, Hinanya remembered how she'd tried to get to the bottom of what had caused Uncle Rawls to change so drastically. It was what she sought now.

"If you can take my words to heart from here on out for yourself, it might save you," Uncle Rawls had said during one of their shooting lessons.

"From what?" she wondered in frustration.

Hurricane Katrina hit the Gulf Coast shortly after that unanswered question.

8. TOTALLY HARMLESS

The last vestige of the Louisiana winter assailed Shaun with a wind that whipped his face and fingers. He was taking a long trek from Saint Roch to the edge of the Bywater, nearly where the Industrial Canal cloistered off the Ninth Ward and the East Bank from the city proper. Eight bridges were pinned apart along the approximately five-and-a-half miles of water, which merged Lake Pontchartrain and the Mississippi. Shaun found himself under the Bywater side of the Claiborne Avenue Bridge, a four-lane passageway of Louisiana Highway 39.

The bridge rose with sequential pillars that grew higher and higher above Shaun in an arc. But the spectacle of man's ability to erect structures that overcame natural obstacles that didn't impress him. All he could think about was the cold.

Tonight, Shaun was meant to pick up the 8IL from one of Wenin's liaisons. Some time had passed since Ciara had come to his house, and she hadn't appeared in person to him since. He knew the game well enough to know to wait. And he had.

Ciara was a righteous cunt. Finding a decent job was more challenging now that he'd been to prison, however brief his incarceration was.

By the second row of pillars, there was a construction platform that rose up roughly a third of the way up the underside of the bridge. Despite the set-up, it was well known as a project on hiatus. The pillar itself was showing signs of sinking into the swampy surface at a disproportional rate to the others. Still, the sinking itself was not urgent, and so the city had pulled back immediate care, leaving the remnants of a construction site for an eventual return.

Shaun tried not to walk too quickly, but at the same time, his anxiety to get the 8IL propelled him to hustle before someone spotted him. It really pissed him off that the meeting place was all the way on top of the platform. He felt he could have thought up tons more accessible places. But he was just a peon indentured to Wenin. Fortunately, Shaun knew he was relatively safe. Wenin needed him to get the stuff to someone, and he was known to pull many strings. If the cops intercepted him, it would be through his own fault and not that of Wenin's. The man was power, a professional. And 8IL was his currency. There was no telling what exactly it was—only what it did. Every person he had spoken to had a different description, but Shaun's favorite anecdote was that it converted your thoughts into lights. You *saw* your thoughts in terms of color and intensity.

As for why Wenin had deemed that the rarest and most obscure drug on the planet be transported and carried off by an ex-convict, Shaun couldn't say.

Were he searched, no cop would know what Shaun had. 8IL was still coming out of the prototype stage, becoming more refined yet still scarcely available to anyone. Shaun had heard a rumor that Wenin had been offered a hundred thousand dollars just for a sample of the stuff and the man had declined. Money was of no interest to Wenin. Only the vacation from the binding prison of his own body.

Though Shaun was pretty sure he would not be meeting with Wenin himself tonight, there was a chance, given the few chance encounters he'd had with those in Wenin's association, one of them could have been Wenin himself. Shaun often thought of Wenin in terms of Jigsaw from the *Saw* film franchise. As such, Shaun treated every liaison he encountered with respect, to the exception of Ciara, who he knew couldn't be Wenin—not to say that Wenin wasn't female. Shaun wasn't able to discount that possibility. He'd disqualified Ciara because he'd known her since she was seven. Given that he'd seen her picking her nose, it was unlikely she created the most potent synthetic drug known to man.

The climb up the ladder was done with care as not to rattle the site too much or arouse suspicion.

With any luck, the liaison would already be there, Shaun could receive the parcel with the 8IL for the unknown beneficiary, and he could be home in time to meet that dank piece of ass Bethany.

Shaun had followed the instructions exactly as he had every time before. Don't be early. Don't be late. Be on time. On time is 1:14AM. Get the shit and bounce, no small talk.

He had to grab onto a plastic poly sheet to get onto the platform. Though it was hard to see, the glimmer of the streetlights a few yards away indicated that no one was up there but him—which was bullshit.

Wenin's contact was already supposed to be there. There was no good reason for this fuck-up. To Shaun's reckoning, even if the liaison wasn't able to make it or had been intercepted by the police, Wenin would have let him know way before he hit the drop site.

Wanting to curse, Shaun stifled his expletives in long dragging groans while he took out his phone and turned its built-in flashlight on.

No one was there. No greeting or call sign from anybody. Something was off. He was fucking alone. Shaun wanted to get away, but he was more afraid to leave the platform than trying to figure out what was going on.

Sure enough, Shaun found out as the bright cone of light flew over a dark rounded object on top of a row of wooden pallets.

Making for his .357 Magnum, he relaxed when nothing moved. He strode forward. There was a body up ahead. It had been placed in the shape of an "O". It lay breathless atop wooden pallets.

Shaun walked over to the body, expecting some terrible bullshit to engulf him at any second, but nothing happened. He was just there with the body. Just a harmless *dead* body. When he realized who it was, he fell backward in a jilted stumble that made the platform rock back and forth with a disconcerting creak. Shaun ended up on his hands and knees holding onto the metal surface as if the whole thing would collapse. But it didn't.

Lucky him, now he was just stuck up here with Ciara.

If he fled the scene, perhaps whoever was waiting to do him in too. From what Shaun could tell, she hadn't been shot but bled dry. This was a common Wenin-style execution. He had drained the blood out of several sites along the wretched girl's arms until she passed out from a loss of blood, Wenin's signature method of execution. The "O" shape wherein her arms and legs were wrapped around one another like a rope twined around itself. He thought this might be a puzzle. Then Shaun put it together.

The liaison was here, he just hadn't realized it. On top of that, he was now running late.

As Shaun got closer to the body, he regarded her face. Dreadful. She was long gone, and never coming back. Shaun stifled a whimper and turned off his flashlight. Then he saw a pair of yellow cleaning gloves and understood implicitly. He found the gloves to be tight as he tried to pull them over his hands without tearing them.

First, he checked under her hair and skull for foreign objects, then the pockets of her leather jacket and pants, but as he had anticipated, they were entirely empty. Shaun gave the girl a thorough but respectful frisking until he felt a strange tremor within him as he patted around her legs. There was no room for dignity. Wenin could have easily slid the 8IL down there without a second thought. Shaun *had* to check. Nothing there. Shaun closed his eyes tightly and continued, figuring the worst part was over. What kind of sick fuck would make someone have to check all over a dead body? Or was it Shaun who had been compelled to check the inappropriate area? He hadn't wanted to, it was disgusting.

That was when he got an idea. Hadn't Ciara's mouth been rather stuffed? Sure, she was dead, but...

Before Shaun moved back up, he eliminated any chance that the 8IL was taped along her legs or in her shoes.

Orifices it was. Wonderful. Shaun shivered from more than the cold, then thumbed around in the girl's ears and nostrils to no avail before he tried his idea and slowly pried open her mouth. What had happened? Ciara was, by all accounts, a faithful servant to Wenin. More than Shaun was, and Shaun worshiped the man. How had she become this dead drug mule? Would his parents be asking the same thing tomorrow morning? Was this 8IL just being transported via corpses?

The conspiracy made sense to Shaun but realizing he was fucked in any case, he let it go and remembered Ciara's bit about drowning.

How he wished he was a fish.

In those moments of contemplation, he considered just taking the 8IL from Ciara. Take it from her and administer it to himself—and fly away because 8IL gave you light. And light speed. And freedom.

Screw whoever this was for. Shaun deserved it way more than them. With 8IL, there was so much hype. The thing was, he knew in order to be the least fucked, he'd have to wait his turn. Ciara had said it was almost his turn. He didn't know why he believed Ciara, especially now as he went into her stiff jaw. There it was.

The thing in Ciara's mouth was a transparent plastic container that curved as Shaun pulled it out with his right hand, his left holding just under the girl's chin. When it was out, Shaun felt relief. Shaun crawled away from the body. Though he knew the precarious nature of his situation, and by all rights, should have begun his way back home for the next possible step, two things kept Shaun on the platform a bit longer. First, there was the fear that Ciara's killer was lurking and waiting for him. Second, he just had to behold what he knew to be 8IL for himself. With the ability to apprehend it properly, he saw the container was shaped like a barrel with a sealed metal top and bottom. Within, however, the contents seemed void. As if it was an open flame, he cautiously moved the container closer to his eye line in order to check for punctures. It seemed fine, yet to him, the container still looked empty.

Common sense overtook Shaun as he regarded the operation as botched and resigned himself to the fate of Ciara. It wasn't until he got home that he learned from another of Wenin's liaisons that the night's exchange had, despite Shaun's protestation, gone swimmingly.

9. RESILIENCE

Hinanya thought she had given up trying to find the gun. Coming home to a somewhat fruitful night of decode Wenin's graffiti codes. She did laundry, she was surprised to see some spotting on her panties.

Ever since the trauma she'd experienced in the wake of Stefan's suicide, she'd had irregular menstrual cycles. It got so concerning that she'd gone to a doctor in Minnesota. After Hinanya said she wasn't sexually active, the doctor had told her how stress might affect a hormonal imbalance leading to irregular periods. She'd learned to live with it, as it had been six months since Stefan died.

In doing the laundry, she found herself scouring the machines one last time in case the gun might have been in there. It wasn't missing any longer—it was gone.

The wash cycle began, but Hinanya did not switch the clothes over to the dryer for two hours. She sat in a fetal position on the floor, feeling at a low energy. Most of all, she was disappointed she no longer had an easy way to end her life if she so desired. Because she did. The proximity to the 8IL didn't matter at times. Her thirst didn't matter because no matter how much water she'd drank in the past few days, it never seemed to be enough. It was as if she was dehydrated. She certainly knew she was malnourished, but she stayed away from food as long as she could. It was a form of resilience to her. A tease against a body that wanted to shut itself down.

Why couldn't she recall where that gun had gone?

10. NE

From where did all of today's synthesized drugs come from? The question was one she had come to wonder about long after Uncle Rawls had departed from her life. A lot of what was available on the streets came from amateurs looking to make a buck, adulterating substances and fudging purity. Yet aside from the scammers, there had to be a clandestine community of chemists and activists who provided these drugs to people. Scientists and medical professionals, disobedience citizens so appalled by the War on Drugs that actively fighting it meant bringing more drugs into the world.

Hinanya was speaking to her parents for what she thought could be the final time. The decision was made upon noticing the ancient but operational payphone on a park trail. She was almost in Metairie, a suburban city outside of New Orleans. She was nothing more than a constant financial and moral burden to them. She remembered them always behind, scrambling, but trying not to show it. And just when it had seemed as if they'd achieved a balance, they lost everything in Katrina and moved to Minnesota.

Taylor's birth and Hinanya's mental illness were both products of Hurricane Katrina. Hinanya often wondered what course her life would have taken had the stormed missed them.

Thus came the need to find the truth. In what Uncle Rawls referred to as 8IL. Maybe there were no humans. Maybe humanity was just a fleshy and temporary container. Or maybe there was an alternative purpose.

"Okay, Dad," Hinanya said into the phone, her eyes focused on something written on the walls across the street from her. "I love you. Goodbye."

"Wait, Hinanya—" her father said, stammering his words. They had just been in the middle of a conversation. About how Hinanya was not actually going to university, how the entire time she'd been in New Orleans, she wasn't enrolled. Instead, she was engaged in a spiritual pilgrimage. To healing herself through the graffiti she dared to mark up the streets with.

Her parents were livid. They'd only sought her happiness, yet were ill-equipped to facilitate it. The perfection she sought was only theoretical. An unstable composition of elements that could never hold together, like man-made elements in a laboratory. When her parents had taken Hinanya from New Orleans, they'd altered her. And as she hung up, she knew they had left her behind as they had left New Orleans behind. Hinanya walked on, waiting for liberation to come.

Hinanya stood outside of her childhood home, the blue house now affixed with vinyl siding. The sight of the place, restored after it had flooded, gave Hinanya a peculiar tingling. The place that hosted her oldest memories was still standing after all. This was, apparently, where she to be.

Of all her time spent back in New Orleans, she'd had no reason to return to this place. But the signs were clear. There was something on the lawn she knew was for her. Luckily, it was late, and the neighborhood was placid. The last time she'd been here, she remembered people trapped in their homes. People waited on top of their roofs. Katrina crosses were marked on the doors by FEMA, official government-sanctioned graffiti. Search codes indicating what had been found inside of the house. If people had been found, if they were alive or dead. Each quadrant of the X had separate information. After Hurricane Katrina, Hinanya's family had come to see their broken home.

Now here she stood, remembering the house before her and the "NE" spray-painted to the right of the X, which she knew meant "no entry."

Back then, Hinanya's parents had denied the magnitude of the situation up until the moment where it was irrefutable. She was likewise detached from the reality, her mind using her Game Boy Color to distract from whatever was happening with Uncle Rawls. Trying to become a Pokémon master while her city fell apart around her, not registering the facts until her AA batteries ran out.

Though the X was no longer to the side of the front patio door, the concept of "NE" still applied. The graffiti she'd been told to look out for had appeared near her apartment, and it had led her here. Wenin and Hinanya were corresponding back and forth. She'd done it. With no more hesitation, she retrieved the item on the lawn. Bringing it under the streetlight, she nodded with approval.

Before returning home, she looked out at the black drapes that hung in the window to imagine who lived there now.

Metairie sickened Hinanya. It was composed entirely of dull and elitist breeders, clinging meager comforts and possessions. She wondered what became of the vanished wooden banister that led upstairs, the one she'd never been tall enough to reach. Once she had dreamed only of being tall enough to touch it without reaching her hand up.

Hinanya took out a hundred-dollar bill and slid it into an envelope, which she then put inside the unknown resident's mailbox.

How long ago had Wenin's liaison been there? Were they watching her now?

In any case, Hinanya heeded what she'd just picked up, her way to finding a liaison.

11. THE LEAD

Hinanya hadn't spoken to Kurt or Sasha in a few weeks. And she still had not seen Felix after all this time. Everyone in her life was cut off. Just as Uncle Rawls had done to her. Everything was in alignment, and recalled those last moments with Uncle Rawls. How they led her down this mystical trek up Saint Roch, not so far from where she'd gained possession of Stefan's gun.

When Hurricane Katrina had been on its way, Hinanya's family refused to leave the city. Soon, they were forced to make for the Superdome as the storm began. By the time they got there, the place was packed with people, and Hinanya snuck away. She was still young then, and got into immense trouble for it. Knowing Uncle Rawls lived only three blocks from the Superdome, she had headed to see him. He'd become reclusive, afraid to leave his house. She hadn't realized how deep such a phobia could run until she saw him.

Uncle Rawls opened the door as far as the chain lock would take it with a slow hand. He poked his head out, he was unshaven. He wore no shirt and gray sweatpants. Seeing her, he opened the door all the way. The interior of his apartment was likewise askew, with overturned chairs at the kitchen table. The desktop computer's screen was cracked and covered in some dark stains. In Rawls arms was a shotgun, which he put down.

"Hinanya," he said as if in a trance.

"Uncle Rawls, let's go to the Superdome."

"You need to go back there, not me. Let's go for one last walk."

"What? How could you stay in your house when this thing's supposed to hit?"

But he only threw on a black jacket and walked out into the hall, leaving his door open.

"Uncle Rawls?" Hinanya asked, gesturing to the open door.

"Goddamn it, girl, stop calling me that."

He had consistently offered such a response since his profound change, but this was the first time she asked, "What should I call you then?"

"Look, the rain's calmed down. Let's take advantage of that."

"That will be of no concern to you after today."

"I'm... extremely confused," she admitted, concealing the well of emotions within her. At the time, Hinanya was still young, bereft of a tragedy she knew she was coming. All she could do was try to keep up as he made his way down the long hallway to the stairwell that led to St. Charles Avenue. For some time, they walked, and Hinanya waited patiently.

"Someday, after you've survived this ordeal, you shall not feel as though you should have," Uncle Rawls said. "Your only course will be to ponder the things I have told you. But just in case, know that I am wrong. I am not sure how I could convince you of that, though."

"What?"

"Listen to me now, as it's important. A body apart from a soul. The exits are drugs. Altered states of consciousness. Hinanya, what I took. It's called 8IL. It's brand new. No one knows about it. Hardly anyone's tried it."

"How did you get it then?"

"Hush." Uncle Rawls grasped onto his stomach for a moment, seemingly in pain. His gait was hampered, and then he was able to right himself. "Not relevant. I have left in me, am me... and it was deplorable to return when what I experienced was so much more real and enjoyable."

"It was just getting high!" Hinanya protested. "You can't really tell me you were just a soul floating apart from yourself."

"I'm sorry, but you have no idea. You won't until you're older."

A hard fall of rain came down, drenching them in seconds.

"No." She stepped away from his path and shed a singular tear, feeling the pressure of more coming. "Telling me what's going to happen like some nutty prophet."

"I'm telling you how it's probably going to be for you. You'll want to find out for yourself, and you'll be able. Now not. When you're grown up. If you can withstand the despair of this artificial plain, suffice to remain in your disgusting husk of a body. One day you too can know why."

"You're scaring me," Hinanya said, unable to look at him.

"Fear is a base animal emotion. It is meant to lead to the truth, to those who have *viveka*, keen discernment. Hinanya, follow the signs for Wenin. He is the creator of 8IL. Available later only in New Orleans. Now, and for a long time to come, he will use graffiti as a means of communication." He pulled out a slip of paper. "Some of the ciphers are designed to become obsolete once people have pieced them together. This is an initial guide. Nuances to the graffiti you'll see on the walls will follow a logical progression."

"What?" she asked as she took the paper.

"This will lead you to 8IL. It's only in New Orleans, and that will probably always be the case. Remember 8IL. What it is? Assurance of an after-life, coming out of yourself. It's what man has needed for his entire existence. But you must find it for yourself." He closed the paper into the girl's hands. "Never lost this. Never share it. There is nothing more valuable on this planet than what you have just learned."

12. THE CANDIDATE

Shaun didn't know when the 8IL candidate would come to him. All he was told was to be home and awake every night between 1AM and 4AM, so he was. And when a knock came on the door several weeks after the police had discovered Ciara's body, drained of all of its blood as if a vampire had had its way with her, Shaun eagerly rose to meet Wenin's selection, in wonderment of what kind of lucky bastard was waiting on his porch. As he opened his door, all he saw was a fat chick, actually very similar in his mind to Bethany. Out of shape, homely, but with captivating eyes that met his.

They stood against each other, dealer and buyer.

"Please, come in," he said, swinging his arm to welcome her. The formality was alien to him.

"Thank... you," she said. "But am I in the right place?"

"Did you hear the train whistle?"

"Hasn't everyone?" she asked him.

"No," he said, not really sure. Once she was inside, he locked the door and hoisted a block against the floor and the knob at an acute angle for added security.

"Yeah, this neighborhood's no good," the girl said with a hollow air.

"I won't argue you with you there. But it's where I belong. I spend a long time looking for a place I belong. Too bad it's here, huh?"

The girl let out a secondary *hmmm* as Shaun led her to his room. There were no chairs, only a bed on the floor and a dresser adorned with a small flat screen television and some assorted DVDs.

She sat on the floor, and Shaun chastised himself internally for not offering her to sit.

Though the last thing Shaun wanted to do was admit he was as in the dark about this situation, he did manage to ask, "How did you get picked?"

"Not relevant," she said.

"What's your name?" he asked, not letting the silence set in. "I'm Shaun. Shaun Nichols."

The girl offered no response, only looked at him.

With his most delicate tone, he asked, "Who are you?"

"I'm myself. For a bit longer at least."

"Look, so I was told to ask you a few questions before I gave it to you," Shaun said, a lie he hoped not to be caught in.

"So then ask. Then give me what I've come for. I've come a long way. I've deciphered the graffiti ciphers for months and prepared for this night for years."

125

"What is it you seek?"

"8IL."

"It is yours," Shaun said, proud to be passing it off to her. As he went into his closet to where he had hidden the stuff, a barrage of approaching sirens wailed in the distance, and Shaun's adrenaline spiked, leaving trepidation in its wake. He cocked his head over to look at her, and she shrugged. He froze as the sirens grew louder and louder until finally, he knew they were off to somewhere else.

Comforted, he attempted to relieve the tension. "New Orleans—our lady of perpetual sirens."

"Yes, it is," the girl said.

From the poorly hidden compartment on the ceiling of his closet, he grazed his fingers around the container of 8IL and brought it over to the girl.

"I think I'm next," he said.

"Are there any more questions, Shaun?" Hinanya said impatiently, her attention transfixed on the container in his hands as if she would pounce on him, batter him, and then make off with the stuff in a crazed stampede.

"A few."

"Give me the container. I'm taking it here and then walking home."

"That sounds fuckin' deadly. I heard someone in the know call this shit time-crack once. You ain't gonna be able to operate yourself."

"What's your point?"

"Maybe that's not how Wenin wants you to take it. Some things are experimental. Some things shouldn't be done alone. I think if you needed someone to be there with you, I mean I know you don't know me, but I'm practically contracted by Wenin to make sure you take this and all goes well, you know?"

"Never mind Wenin. That's my 8IL. I've earned it. What I do with it is my choice. I'm taking it as soon as you hand it over. By choice or by force."

It was somewhat refreshing to see such brash honesty in a world of hidden intent and treacherous scumbags. Shaun deserved force if he tried to fuck-up this deal. "No, no. Don't worry. Look here." He passed it to her. Rotating the thing in her hand, she looked complete.

"Are people still looking for that graffiti artist that tagged Buckland's?" the girl asked.

"I work at Buckland's," Shaun said. "They are. I mean, the whole thing's kind of blown over."

"It was me."

"For real? Yeah, I mean, some people are still after you."

She snapped her eyes up from the container to him. "Big fan of chicken, are you?"

"I ain't no snitch."

126

"I don't trust anyone," the girl commented. "The graffiti, it was nice. Something to get me to what I was looking for. Now I have it. I may never tag again. Not if I don't need to."

"I don't think it's a good idea for you to be out around here."

"There's only one way back." She got up to leave. "You seem somewhat full of it."

"Huh?" Shaun asked, taken aback by the observation. "Why?"

"First off, you regard your neighborhood as one not to be in, yet you live here. And then those questions."

"Okay, okay. Look, I just... I'm fuckin' jonesin' for that shit," Shaun said, locking onto the container. "I've done buku shit, right, but... damn, I'd trade it all. It's been my dream."

"As it has been mine."

"How can I be next?"

The girl sighed. "I don't know. All I can say is I know I won't be the last."

"Aite, I can dig that. Where do you live? I can at least make sure you get back safe."

"No. I can assure that alone." Her attention returned to the container. At each end, there were seals, which she peeled off with a strange competence. Once the thin metal wrappings were unveiled, Shaun saw each circle that comprised the top and bottom of the barrel were actually small discs.

"This is the part I do in private," she said. "Is that your bathroom over there?" She pointed toward the hallway.

Shaun scrambled to his feet. "Yeah, you got it," he said, pointing down the hall.

Shaun waited as the girl was in the bathroom behind a closed door for fifteen minutes. When she returned, she said. "Thank you. I've left the container in your bathroom trash. I shall be going now."

Shaun let that gratitude sink in. It had been a sincere but cursory line. The girl didn't even know what he'd gone through just to make sure she got the stuff. "You heard about that body they found a few weeks ago under Claiborne Avenue Bridge?"

"Yeah, some girl."

"Bet she was doin' what you about to do. Look, you're obviously someone important, and I don't want you to get fucked up and go out like this. Let me —"

"No. Stay still, forget about me as I find my way home, then desperately charge into your bathroom to suck out whatever drop or minuscule sum of 8IL remains after I've gone like we both know you want to."

"Fine. Yo, I'd say come to Buckland's and I'd hook you up sometime, but considerin'—"

The girl waved him off.

Then she was gone. It played out just like she'd said it would, but Shaun was disappointed when he went to the top of the trash to see the punctured container, still empty. One disc was there, snapped in half. It was also empty. Shaun smelled it then licked it and began to whimper, a trembling caricature, his knees buckling under the weight of every mistake he'd ever made.

13. BE (I)

"How will I know it's really 8IL?" It was the last thing she'd ever asked Uncle Rawls, as he was walking away from her after her family had fled to the Superdome. He'd answered her then. Then he walked away, failing to say goodbye.

Hinanya never saw him again.

Hinanya made her way home from Shaun's house, likening the sensations of the 8IL to that of a wine drunk. But it would grow worse, she knew, so paced faster toward her apartment.

The city streets were stagnant tonight.

She'd finally gotten what she'd always wanted, so would it be enough? If she did manage to vacate her body and somehow gain the knowledge that her soul would transcend her duration as a human being, she would go on, comforted. However, if not, all she'd known would hold no solace for her. Hinanya was a seeker that night, bent on finding if forever was hers or not.

The 8IL gave her a euphoria, and for the first time in a long time, the girl giggled, uncontrollably so.

The bouts of laughter echoed in her mind until they subsided at the mental image of Stefan's room. She had cleaned it. After the forensic analysis had converted the living space into a crime scene, it was Hinanya who'd gone through her friend's personal effects. She who'd taken all traces of Stefan's essence from the place. Perhaps it was Stefan's ability to make her laugh that bound her in hysterics now. Or perhaps she remembered what a joke it all was.

Stefan had never taken 8IL. She'd never even told him about it. Could that have saved him? They might have gone to New Orleans together, a team.

The streets and homes of St. Claude Avenue began to sparkle as Hinanya experienced preliminarily hallucinations. A gutter set against the roof of a house bent apart only to right itself once more. An old truck sped down the road, and its engine bellowed out as if in torment. Sentience seemed to be presenting itself in inanimate things. Bacteria, that was all. It was all covered in bacteria, so it was alive in a certain sense.

Suddenly anxious, Hinanya rushed down her street in order to reach her apartment. She knew she needed to get behind a locked door, and soon. Yet, at the same time, Hinanya lamented having to separate herself from the New Orleans nightscape she relished so much. Hinanya kept turning her head to different places, becoming suddenly frightened of a portly yellow cat making its way from the curb to the street, appearing to close in on her until it diverted into a hole in the fence. Everything she now saw was like the ocean, the objects around her shifting to and fro.

At last, she made it to her apartment building and challenged herself to make it up the staircase, accomplishing it with concentrated difficulty. It was only after she'd taken the keys into her hands that she realized how twitchy she was. Like the steps, Hinanya had to take her time in opening the door. As she walked through the threshold, she saw with relief that the window by her door had been repaired, and not just with cardboard or a trash bag, but the glass in the windowpane had been replaced.

Once inside, and sure she'd locked her door, Hinanya made straight for the kitchen. The drug was to be taken in two stages. First, a vile silvery liquid was to be swallowed, which she had done in Shaun's bathroom, after cracking one of the circles from the container. Knowing better than to dwell on the taste, Hinanya had taken it into herself quickly. Still, a sensation had come through, one that felt to her like an electric jolt. To alleviate her displeasure, she'd produced saliva to take any remainder of the stuff in, and she felt for a second the brush of some flake or bump against her tongue as it all went down her throat.

Straining to summon the second circle that had been within the barrel container, Hinanya heard a snoring noise. She marveled at the potency of 8IL even as she had not even completed the full dose of the stuff. That excitement was thrown miles away from her when she turned around to what she assumed was another hallucination to behold a slumbering person... in her bed.

Hinanya's reaction time, stymied by the drug, kicked in full gear as she readied herself to pounce on the intruder. She would dominate the other and overcome them. She was more than willing to kill if the struggle demanded it of her. But as she charged and apprehended, she realized it wasn't a stranger.

She shouted to wake the person up, who to her astonishment was Kurt. "Get up! Hello!?"

Kurt stirred, at first languishing then flashing his open eyes to her.

"What are you doing in my apartment, Kurt?"

"Huh? Oh. You said I could sleep here tonight? I told you my place was being fumigated, and you'd be out of town?"

"Oh, no. You cannot be here... how are you here?" Hinanya was out of her mind in exasperation trying to piece things together. When had she ever told Kurt he was able to be in her place? In her bed. He was practically naked. "I have to be alone right now."

Kurt did not contest, only nod. The boy hadn't been here when she'd left earlier that night, and she was not able to call to mind when she could have possibly let him be here while she was away. But then again, she was high. At that point, her own name might have eluded her. Still, had he ever even been to her apartment?

Kurt and Sasha believed in angels. Consorting back and forth, Hinanya wished they could pray away their need to pester her.

He'd ingested too much alcohol one night, she finally remembered, and she offered him to stay over once. He had slept on the floor though. But that had not happened tonight! When was that?

"I don't get it," he'd said. "We have a lot of fun together, don't we?"

"I thought we'd be over this, Kurt. I'm not interested in a relationship with anybody."

"Right, we have. Over and over. I know. But what you don't know, because we haven't discussed it, is I'm in love with you."

"Thank you, but to be honest, I don't care."

"Gee, thanks."

Just the sounds of the words, in blackness. Where were they? This was *her* apartment. His biological imperative was manifesting lies.

"Kurt," Hinanya began, "we met in your school, not mine."

"So you've been lying," Kurt said, twisting his lips as he rose from the bed. The longer she dragged this chat with Kurt out, the further from the truth she felt. "What do you actually do then?"

Normally, Hinanya would have fortifications, verbal dams. But subterfuge escaped her. Hinanya said, "Well, uh—"

Kurt's hand rose in the air to stop whatever answer they both knew *wasn't* coming. "Better yet, what will you do? Is this going to be the rest of your life, Hinanya?"

The implication did not affect her. So she started a nod. Then she paused, narrowing her eyelids to say, "If I want, yes."

"But don't you ever get lonely?"

"Yes. That doesn't mean I want a relationship, though."

"Maybe you do. For fuck's sake. I know you must. Sasha and I talked about this—"

"Not *this*. Me. You talk about me."

"Look, forget about me if you want, but what if you're missing out an all these amazing experiences, Hinanya? I'm not saying be my girlfriend, but think about these things as you do everything else. You're depriving yourself of a great thing!"

"You are disturbing me in the comfort of my own home. In order to preserve my happiness at this time, I must be alone."

"I'm sorry," Kurt muttered. "Here's the key you lent me. Sorry for the confusion. I just wanted you to know what it was like for once. How I feel about you. It's the greatest feeling in the world. You make me so happy. And I know I could make you happy."

"No," Hinanya said. The burden continued to bear down on her, so all she could do was to point to the door while looking at Kurt. "Out there, my friend. How it really is. Mmm. You have an infatuation for me, but really, any girl who gave you sufficient time and care, as you believe I have, would do. It's

131

just that I'm me, and you happened to have met me while I was right in the middle of finding something, by the way, and so, for now, you must show yourself out. What you seek isn't here."

Kurt left in a pathetic parade, just another man with a deflated ego. He contributed nothing more to the conversation, understanding the two of them would not be together the way he wanted. Whatever she opted out of was none of his business.

After the encounter, Hinanya wished to be purged of her gender. The long line of disingenuous monsters who'd thought sexual things of her, all those years. But now she was alone. With the 8IL, she was now, at last, alone.

Shakily, she consumed the damp blue sand from the second circle, sipping it between her chapped lips as per the instructions. 8IL was all about synergy.

14. BE (II)

Where must I go if I am to find myself?

When faculty has been decommissioned by the effects of a substance such as 8IL, words are worthless. No words could ever possibly hope to contain the full experience of any drug trip. Experiences can be recounted, but those only occurred within the framework of any retrospective thought. The memory. And memory, even in the most optimistic sense, is highly unreliable.

Still, no matter how limiting language can be, no matter how unreliable memory can be... we are not yet allowed to be apart from them. And so then drugs serve the function of trying. The futile and perilous bid for transcendence.

And while some horrors are unspeakable, but none are unthinkable. Such horrors subsume language and morph into delirious emotion. It is at that point that humanity is bypassed and life itself is isolated in a place where it could not be at all times.

In the purest sense, Hinanya was alone to fend for herself, left with only one reservation: to verify the fact that what she had inside of her was 8IL.

Minutes passed like days in realms of her thoughts. Her scalp seemed to peel back when she heard the first whispers of the supposed autonomous entities found in trips of this magnitude. As she fought against their stature, those beings of higher intelligence. She slashed away at their malevolence with her blade of rationality, in a boundless chamber of radiant stones, only to see she was only harming herself. Those other entities were maybe her self.

The chamber she was in was no longer there.

Gradually, the high rose to the point of climax but reaching it felt untenable to Hinanya. That point of leaving herself was something she didn't want after all. The sensation was too much. But she'd taken the 8IL, and there was no off switch. There was only riding it out, no matter how much she wanted to end it in the process. After devoting her life to the obtainment of it, she found herself in a penitent state. 8IL was perhaps not manufactured for her. Her fractured mind that, even without the use of illicit substances, should have been institutionalized by now.

No matter how much she used her thoughts to cast away the notion that she was surrounded by other entities, that it was merely a sophisticated reflection of her subconscious, she couldn't verify she was alone in that room. Kurt had disturbed her process. Her mind brought that to her attention, but wasn't she her mind? Could she just ask herself?

Hinanya vomited shortly after that, as those two questions yielded dozens of others, ones she asked to the entities only to be laughed at in some alien sibilance.

Then times past where she felt good for accomplishing something that had mattered so much to her at the time, even if she didn't want to it any longer.

Her eyelids flipped open and closed as if they were the wings of her soul trying to fly out beyond her. And her arms and legs kicked out in front of her as she was lying down in her bed, flinging out to stretch beyond their physical reach. She'd made Kurt leave, but traces of him remained. Why did her mind mention that? Hinanya had made him leave in order to do the thing she was doing, the thing she was ready to do.

Another—something Hinanya perceived as others laughed—then translated its otherworldly tongue: *YOUOR NAWTREADDIEY*, dug deep into the foundation of her mind's eyes. It spread out into an abyss. Her perception's translation. Was she being barred access from leaving her body? Or was there no way out of it?

There was no response to that. And Hinanya wrestled for a few minutes to be okay with that. She realized she was still high, higher than most people out there. Her mind would get back to her when it had the chance. But wait, had it left her? Was it beyond now, having left her behind?

Hinanya, I am your mind, and you're talking to yourself. You can't really have a conversation with yourself like this. You can only... you understand?

Her hands rushed to her cheeks and rubbed them. The lights that went into her eyes ceased.

There is no schism. Yes, it can be said that you are not your thoughts, but you're only with yourself. You are you and have been you, even when you change.

Hinanya surrendered to a rather violent incarnation of the awful rush. In her room, she saw melting prisms producing tintinnabulations. Hinanya knew the truth. The juiciness of her eyes. It was no worries for a little while.

Hinanya would not have to worry about whether or not to commit suicide or if her soul could exist—because she was dying, surely! She would leave her body but only to fade into nothingness. 8IL was a diabolical potion, only a bit like whiskey, lethal and legal, for slow-motion suicide. How sickly she was. How could she believe she was dying?

It would only be fitting. Why should she fear getting something she wanted?

Unknown.

In opening her eyes, she still saw objects around her from outside spilling in from the streets. Blackout. They held her fancy as her things. The pot on the counter, the books on the floor. Each had its own molecules that were not hers but their own.

Sometimes she thought she discovered the answer to her problems, and then it would slip her mind, and she figured it was a trick all along. She hadn't learned anything because maybe learning itself was a trick. Maybe people knew it all already, that they came from somewhere else, a mystical realm of—

No.

Felix came to her in a fuzzy vision with his hoodie up and a gas mask on, trying to spray paint adoration with her thoughts, but it didn't work. Those thoughts were caustic. Spray paint was caustic. Is that why Hinanya fancied the Felix representation? Was he trying to tag her thoughts all along? No wonder she was so devoted to his craft. Layers emerged from two-dimensional surfaces on the colors, and speaking of the colors, the colors ate each other when they became different. There was no blending or mixing—it was an utter takeover. Her bad thoughts ate her good thoughts all the time. Might is right. It wasn't pretty, but it was the world.

Hinanya admitted she'd grown quite fat lately, which was funny, as she hadn't really been eating. She'd been so hungry her body went into starvation mode! And that was miserable but there had to be some happiness there for someone who'd committed, no matter how foul the activity.

Out of shape. Kurt thought she was beautiful. Not as beautiful as she was when they'd first met. *Huh?* Hinanya thought. *What's going on, Hinanya?*

Why should she take care of herself? After the trip was over, she would still want to die. Her soul didn't appear to her. She was nowhere near out of her body, and so there was nothingness waiting.

It'll be an ambitious suicide. She wanted to die in order not to suffer. Her mind attacked her regularly, but she *was* her mind! How could she ATTACK herself?

When she wrote it went away. As a writer, she was soothed. But it was conditional. In conjunction with searching for this 8IL, she found that the creation of graffiti was so cool. Hinanya didn't like it anymore. It had served its purpose and was stupid. *Why not die now?*

Well, no way. No, wait!

The gun is...

Why look. It's right there.

Hinanya understood but didn't believe until she looked on the floor. In getting up for the first time in (time was relative, wasn't it?) she wasn't sure how long, there it was. Stefan's gun, no holster, on the floor of her pitch-black apartment. For months, it had been missing. She'd looked everywhere. But the floor, apparently?

Hinanya didn't want to die like this. She didn't want to be killed under the influence of 8IL. No, she had to survive it. Challenges. If the climax was still to come, she was not yet done.

What does it matter when you die if you will anyway?

Maybe she wouldn't. Or maybe the 8IL was slowly killing her now and shooting herself would save her from dying in a way she'd already told herself was unacceptable. That's right. That's so right!

Right, ego death, right. The dark night of the sole. Sole operator, body, body, brain, and bind. Hinanya touched the sheets on her bed with irreverent strokes. No, she wasn't alone. No way. Tons of organisms were composing her surroundings and her body. Roaches in her apartment. She fed them, keeping them alive just by living here, inadvertently dropping food particles and dead skin the parasites would eat. How motherly of her. To have a host of bacteria amount to a few pounds of her own weight in her gut, nurturing them as they helped keep her alive. It was just like the ocean.

And Hinanya was so deep the sun would never touch her.

She knew, though, she only had one love, and that love was a danger. What greater danger was there than being suicidal? It was constantly risky! So what if her wanting to kill herself was just a contrived way to always have that stimulation, to have that love close?

It was a horrible, abusive love, if so. But so what? Hinanya had experienced no other kind.

Wow. She mused to herself as the gun gained more pressure against her temple, and her index finger was wrapped around the trigger and off again with an amusing routine.

Felix... she wanted to talk to him and tell him who she thought he was and how he must not even be that really. But even if she escaped, she'd never reach him.

Why not? Pray to him. If there were any time for an angel to appear magically to you, it'd be now!

Even as messed up as she was, Hinanya would not directly communicate with Felix for fear of not reaching him. Without trying, the outcome was guaranteed.

Instead, she came across what she felt was the solution to the mess that was New Orleans. All that ignorance, poverty, and sin abolished.

Her mind projected the voice of an aged Caso. *Wait. What if he is an angel? He helped you, didn't he? Like angels are supposed to. Suppose. He is. Jus' say thank you. Don't expect nothin' in return. Jus' cast out your gratitude. Show me that grace, girl. I was just feelin' your spirit. It used to buy holy things as sure as the theory of gravity itself. It seeks them out again, but it had 'em before. God. Imagine some homey who does things for you when he can't possibly get nothin' back. Then imagine doing that very thing, even once.*

No! Hinanya was there to debunk that nonsense.

But hadn't she yet? Before the trip? She'd always been grounded in her body, spiritually vacant. The church was fallacious. No evidence or credit. Only that singular noise.

Click.

A lost gun. A found gun. It wasn't unloaded. But it had to be if it was, by definition, a gun.

Tingling, vibrations, sensations. All common symptoms of people who have claimed to leave their bodies. It was said to be achievable through coarse and patient practice. Hinanya didn't think so.

Hinanya knew drugs would help her sort that soul business out. Not even 8IL could open the door to a higher reality. A place where she can know and soar through the heavens timelessly. It would have been nice, though. Sure would have.

Click.

As the climax of the 8IL transpired, Hinanya was consistently scared, and she discarded the gun to face a heart-racing nightmare environment she was unable to stand up in. Behind her were good memories. Now it was changing.

She never did relent to her dearest desire, the attempt to pray to Felix.

The journey back took some time, but Hinanya slowly gained a hold of herself. Her thoughts, fears, and high all subsided. The illusion of it all was revealed right before her eyes. To have the truth is not to touch the truth. Looking upon it was a sordid thing, but at least you could look away from time to time. But to embrace the truth, there was no way to diminish its effect.

Once more, she contemplated suicide, only to wonder something new. To rise up from the floor to ask why she was so hard on herself, especially after learning the answer to her question. There was no longer any question about wanting to die. But that complexity dismantled itself in another brief lapse toward lucidity as she stood over a spot on the floor. Hinanya's pants were down to her ankles, she still had on her underwear, but there were feces on the hardwood floor. Feces on the floor, but no stains on her pants or her underwear. Hinanya had remembered vomiting, but there was no vomit on the floor, only this foul excretion she was only just now smelling. Hinanya cleaned without shame.

"How will I know it's really 8IL?" Hinanya had once asked Uncle Rawls.

"You will know why it's called 8IL. It will come to you at some point after the climax. After you've been to beyond the observable universe and back. You'll get a few new things. And when you're ready... when you're ready, you'll go outside."

It was morning, and so after a dreadful time of cleaning her floor and herself, Hinanya fumbled to unlock the door and made sure seven times that she'd locked it and no one was inside. She was ready.

15. BE (III)

Though most of the 8IL had passed through Hinanya's system, she was still rather high. She could walk, albeit with a zombified air befitting any New Orleanian forced to shuffle off to their various obligations at such an early hour. Surfacing from her stupor three blocks past her house, Hinanya saw she was outside Stevenson's, a convenience store. Hinanya was famished, and for once, she was going to eat. But not there.

As she turned away from Stevenson's, Hinanya accidentally bumped into a tall man. "Oh, I'm sorry."

"It's hard turning into a person, isn't it?" the man said quizzically.

The man walked on, and so did she. Her mind and her feet set themselves apart, so much so that when she returned to the present, she had strayed away from anything familiar. She didn't know where she was. Some street or neighborhood near Stevenson's, but where? Hinanya was left in her own city. With a farce of attentiveness, Hinanya tried backtracking, and then checked if she was dressed, and yes, she was. Still, she felt a kind of paranoia in parading around the city still high. Eventually, she found St. Anthony, a street she recognized, and headed down it. Crossing one of the blocks, Hinanya spotted a young man with light blond hair. The young man had just been walking out of a bar, and he had a beer in his hand. Hinanya nodded to him as a profound desire to pull the Glock from her jacket and shoot him came. Just to shoot him once. That kept happening, an inane desire to pull it out, to use it for what it was meant for. Destruction. Why else did she hang onto it?

It all came down to the choice between creation and destruction. Hinanya felt affirmed in her bizarre desire as the male looked as if he wanted her. But he'd never. She was a woman. Designed for creation, bent on destruction. And he walked on unknowing, not at all aware of how close he'd come to her penetrating him.

The comedown was taking too long. It wasn't fair! All she wanted was to be at the end, to stay down for the duration of her life (however long that would be), but 8IL rolled around in bits still, indefatigable. Just like Uncle Rawls had told her it would be.

Ultimately, it had failed to produce the anticipated results. Whatever Uncle Rawls metaphysical state had experienced on the 8IL, Hinanya had not.

The Crescent City Connection was the forefront of the horizon, a bridge bringing travelers to the lands south of New Orleans. Hinanya made her way down to Decatur Street, it was scattered with fast food wrappers and plastic cups. Unbearably hungry, she remembered the single pickle she'd had at some point during the earlier part of the 8IL. Most of the time, Hinanya suffered through an empty stomach by choice, but her recent decisions left her feeling especially weak. So she sought out a breakfast place until she found one in the French Market. Sunrise had turned the temperature up. Most of all, she needed water. 8IL was a rather powerful thing to have lost her in New Orleans.

Sitting down on one of the stools at the end of a row, Hinanya offered a greeting to the server at the counter. "I want a black coffee. And pancakes. But no butter. Instead of butter, ice cream. Ice cream, is that okay? I hope that's okay."

"I suppose, yeah okay," said the middle-aged woman. Hinanya despised the reaction. So what if she wanted ice cream instead of butter on her pancakes? They were both just as odd and nasty, both milk derivatives. Hinanya adored ice cream.

The meal came, and she ate without incident, the ice cream had melted by the time the plate hit the counter. The pancakes drowning in a pool of vanilla. It had been her father who'd taught her the value of melted ice cream. She played with the lumps. He'd told her then to savor the flavor of ice cream even if it was melted, for some children would never know the taste of ice cream. And she'd smiled, that girl of nine, unable to comprehend death or anything.

It came to Hinanya then amid the dense air of that dawning New Orleans day. She *did* know why it was called 8IL.

16. DEEP SHIT

Shaun hadn't left his house for much lately, but when he'd been invited to a crawfish boil up the street by his homey Caso, he had to go. Crawfish was just too delicious to pass up. On top of that, the boil would host a modest amount of dealers far and wide. Shaun was sure if Ciara had still been alive, she would have been there too. In truth, he hoped to meet with a Wenin liaison there. Without any definitive link to Wenin, he felt liberated, but he was most curious as to what that meant. He'd done a great service to Wenin. But then there was Ciara. Was he next? Or was he next to be granted the 8IL?

So he went in hopes of following up on that, though the crawfish certainly sweetened the deal. It had only been a few days since that strange girl got her dosage and he'd heard nothing new—which Shaun was not feeling too hot about.

Working by day at Buckland's, he was gradually digging himself out of the game. It was challenging adapting, but Shaun was motivated. Using pot, he'd gone from the streets to his own apartment. From there he moved up to selling cocaine, which ended up furnishing the place. But addiction came and made him sloppy. From then on, he was in nothing but trouble. One night, he was robbed at gunpoint after his apartment was broken into. They'd stolen $2,356 and even more than that in cocaine. That and the one hit of ketamine he had been trying to get at least a hundred for. In the hole, Shaun hounded every connection he had until Ciara came through. Just as things were looking up again, some homeys ratted him out one night, and he was nabbed with possession with intent to distribute.

In jail, he'd met Caso as the guy took steps and squats picking up playing cards in his cell. "My dude," Caso had said to Shaun after he'd told Caso how he'd ended up there, "one thing I don't be followin' it's like this. Aite, so you got your ass robbed, you tellin' me you have an idea who did you in that dirty, but you don't retaliate?"

"Caso, I'm a lot of things. But I ain't no snitch."

Shaun swallowed a second Valium as he approached the house on Piety. The sound of the pot was inescapable. The scent of onion, garlic, and pepper flirting with the boiling crawfish. Making his way to the backyard, the volume of the bounce music was as heart-warming as the scent coming from the two giant pots alongside the house. To his amusement, he saw a moon bounce with jubilant children knocking around inside of it.

A chorus of *'ey's* and *yo's* arose from the people in lawn chairs. Shaun wondered why his world couldn't be this chill all the time. All the people at the party just wanted to make ends meet and have a good time. They were street

141

smart and handled their business. Those racist fucks at the top just how to keep keeping them down though.

"My man!" Caso called out. He was in a circle with some of his friends.

"Sup, Caso?" Shaun asked, giving him dap.

"You gotta get you some of this, kid," Caso said, pointing down to his tray of crawfish, potatoes, and corn.

"Oh, trust me, dawg, I'm on it."

"Glad you're here. We got a few things on our minds, I hear."

"As always."

"But damn, hold up. You jus' got here! Take a seat. Pussy'll be right over."

"You mean there's still pussy left?" Shaun said, mockingly looking around at Caso and his boys.

"You know we sharin'," said Avery. "No one thinks about it, but there's a lotta pussy on the planet. I get mad confused whenever I hear two dudes battlin' over a bitch."

"True," said Shaun. "You gotta take 'em as often as you gotta give 'em up."

"They be tryna to hoard a bitch," said Derek. "It's like, bro, you really about to marry some thot who'll be a piece of shit like you? I mean even if you somethin' special, which nobody is, it's not like you taking that pussy with you after you dead. Why worship one pussy all your life? People on that level freak me the fuck out."

"Yeah, but bitches be on that one dick shit all the time," countered Shaun.

"They just posin'," Avery said.

"Y'all, shut the fuck up, y'all dumb," Caso said with a chuckle.

Shaun made a beeline for the crawfish and served himself a tray of the season's first crawfish. As much as he wouldn't mind getting his dip on, Shaun was more interested as to what Caso wanted. The two soon made for the front porch for privacy, and they sat beside one another. Caso patted Shaun on the back.

"You doin' good for yourself? Son, I heard you passed off that Wenin shit."

"Damn, Caso. Not for nothin', but that's hush-hush type shit."

"Fair enough," Caso said. "But you gonna tell me anyway, right?"

"If you wanna know bad enough, I may know. But first, is there any other Wenin liaison here?"

"Yeah," Caso said flatly.

"Is he lookin' me for?"

"Nah," Caso said.

Shaun's shoulders sank, and he inhaled to let out a great sigh. Downtrodden, he said, "Fuck."

"He ain't lookin' for you 'cause he already found you," Caso said, winking.

"Quit being sly. You being serious? The thing is, if you're fuckin' with me, I trust you, and if I start poppin' off about this shit—"

"Wenin told me you're next for the 8IL."

Shaun looked over to Caso, their eyes locking. "How long you been a liaison?"

"You a fool. You know that, right? Shaun, how do you think you got in with these people in the first place?"

"You— You recommended me," Shaun said in bewilderment.

"Y'eard it here first."

"Sorry. Aite, what choo wanna talk about?"

Caso reached into his pocket. "This first." Caso revealed a baggie of cocaine. "Bump with me."

"Out here?" Shaun said, looking around the neighborhood.

"Shaun, this trap is my kingdom. This white shit is my currency. Don't nobody in this vicinity have it in 'em to fuck with me."

Shaun wanted to contradict Caso, to ask him if that was really the case, then how had he ended up in prison just like Shaun. Instead, he took Caso's offering into his nose to speed the conversation along.

"Now we cookin'," said Caso, wiggling to a stifled groove in the background. "Nah, so Wenin says you next. But first I need to know who you gave the shit to."

"Oh, nah, Caso. If you actually a liaison, you're higher up than me. Like the fuck happened with Ciara?"

"Shaun," Caso said, his tone one of admonishment. "Ciara fucked up, forget her. Here's the situation. Wenin said we got to rein this one in. Ya dig?"

"I ain't no snitch."

"That's fine. I already know who it is, see. I just want to be certain. We can't just go hitting anybody, 'cause that ain't right. And I already know it was some fat bitch."

Shaun knew all too well the dangers of silence. Still, he said nothing.

"That one. Mhm. The one you knew I been after. Bro, she got my gun."

"I *ain't* no snitch," Shaun reiterated.

"That's all right, though. I ain't trippin'. I already know."

"Isn't this a kind of... conflict of interest for you?"

"Huh?" Caso inquired.

"You been trying to bust this bitch that duped you a couple of times now. After I gave her the shit, now Wenin wants her?"

"It's all one thing, Shaun. He tryin' somethin' The gun she jacked from Diggy that night. Where do you think I got that from?"

"I don't know. Some dirty cops?" Shaun questioned, unable to hide his consternation. "Like I could give a fuck where you get your shit from."

"Wenin has many separate enterprises other than 8IL. It's hardly market-ready. Man's got to make his money somehow."

"So he's a man?"

"To be straight wit' choo, I don't know, Shaun."

"Look, all due respect, I've been thinking. That bitch broke your arm. I don't want a part of this. "

"But you want the 8IL."

A few doors down, Caso and Shaun began to hear a nasty argument between a man and his girl.

"Yeah."

The shouts erupted into pleas. Caso and Shaun looked over to see the girl pointing a gun at the man. The man shoved her and pulled out his own piece. People near them either took cover or joined the fray. Shaun saw four shooters by the time the firing started. Caso pulled tight against Shaun's shirt to get up, and they ran for the backyard. The sounds of the party were punctured by a flurry of gunshots. Caso, behind Shaun, tackled his friend to the ground amid the shattering velocity of the bullets flinging through the air. Shoving Shaun under a minivan, Caso crawled under with him. Shaun realized Caso'd been hit when Caso's leg slapped against Shaun's knee and the rear tire. Blood burst out of a wound on Caso's ankle.

"Fuck, fuck, fuck!" Caso cried out, bending his body as best as he could to staunch the blood flow. "It's those fuckin' 5th Ward whack-offs creepin' onto my turf. I fuckin' told them not to fire shots on this block. They fuckin' dead!"

Shaun was in shock at how Caso wasn't afraid. All he could think of was retaliation. The gunfire subsided and several cars peeled off down the street.

Shaun looked at Caso. "You need to get to a hospital!"

"I know. Call a ambulance. This fuckin' hurts like a bitch, brah. Where were we?"

"Huh?"

"I need somethin' to distract me, Shaun. I been shot. What was we talkin' about?"

Shaun tried to recall. All he could think about was Caso's blood on him. "You saved my ass."

"You ain't no snitch," Caso said through gritted teeth. "I already know her. Her name's Hinanya."

"What are you proposing?" Shaun asked with a flash of nerves surfacing above his Valium high.

"She'll be coming to us pretty soon. It's pretty fuckin' lonely after 8IL, I'm told. Look, I just need that gun. I tried to get it without Wenin. Now he's stepped in, so there's no room to fuck around. You don't have to help out with this. You can do whatever you doin' from now on. We'll still be chill. But then see, like that, you don't get the 8IL, and personally, for all the time you've

144

clocked in to earn it, stepping out on it would be... it'd be dumb, Shaun. Fuck I hate bein' shot. But you can be dumb if you want. Maybe you don't see it as dumb. And I am down to respect that. I don't live your life, fuck. You can do this with me and still not be a snitch."

"I guess you're right..."

"GOD FUCKING DAMN!" Caso shouted as loud as he could. The sirens soon drown out the sounds of Caso's hollering.

17. The Purpose of Meaninglessness

Days after the 8IL had been through her system, an enormous emotional toll set in for Hinanya. After a time, she finally got out of bed to wash her sweat-soaked sheets and tidying up her disheveled room. Each step she took felt as if felt echoed disjointed moments of her experience.

If the autonomous entities were real, they had once more faded into an indecipherable background, as Hinanya couldn't commune with them.

Hinanya was crippled with malaise, for she didn't feel very much changed from back to how it was before she'd obtained the drug. The night had been poetic in nature, a useless metaphor to Hinanya. 8IL was powerful, but it did not provide her the answers she'd wanted.

If nothing else, the gun was back.

A few people had come knocking at the door. Two had been unknown, and one of them had knocked at 3:17AM, seconds after the freight train honked its horn in the distance. The third had been Sasha.

"Hinanya? Are you home? I talked to Kurt. I talked to your family. What's going on with you? Your phone doesn't ring anymore. Your sister needs to speak with you about something very important. I'm really worried. I know I shouldn't be. You're so independent. In case you are listening, write me a letter, would you? You don't even have to send it. Just... write one. You know? Maybe it'll help whatever you're going through. I do that a lot. If you need help finding a job, I know some people. Okay, I'm going to go. Unless you want to let me in?" Sasha didn't say anything for an entire minute. "Yep, I'm going to go."

There was only one possible way to get out. Wherever Hinanya had gone was inside of her head, within the space of her mind.

In light of the failed experiment to know the metaphysical, her suffering was only bound to intensify. And each moment that passed by seemed to be uniformly drained of meaning. Yet together, when she was dead, would the totality of that life taken as a whole have meaning? That if there was some after, and death was the only method of seeing it, life was only a distraction. Some whimpering and superfluous prelude.

At any rate, Hinanya would be done philosophizing anyway. That would be solace in itself. It didn't matter to her if there was only nothingness after her death. It was a purely practical matter: she had fought many foes and others in her time, but she couldn't win against herself.

Hinanya was alone, and for once, she wished not to be. But she didn't want to see anyone in particular. She'd sustained a terrible wound at the hands of reality. It spurred her on to some final inquiries, closing thoughts. Could this be the fate of every 8IL user to find the utmost rationality in suicide?

Maybe that's what she'd been failing to understand.

First, Hinanya would seek out Wenin and other 8IL users. Hinanya had come to this conclusion while handling Stefan's gun. Then she would find out what unspeakable thing was happening with her body and her mind. Things hadn't been adding up to her as of late, and whatever was happening was only compounding, ever since she had arrived in New Orleans. Irregular periods, unquenchable thirst, the lapse in consciousness, each demanded medical attention. Tests would be conducted, and the only thing Hinanya would omit was that she was suicidal. After all that... that was when she would do it. Hinanya would finally take her own life.

18. ' Hood Plague

The street lamp illuminated Hinanya's rolling shadow as she walked on to Shaun's apartment. Once more, she passed the Rally's, and in light of her preparations to end her life, she fancied herself some fries. As she waited in line, a woman behind her asked, "Excuse me, ma'am, but are you all right?"

"What?" Hinanya asked with incredulity.

"Are you all right?"

"Yes." What had given her away? In truth, though she was nervous, she didn't feel as if she was projecting anything too telling.

Out of the corner of her eye, Hinanya saw the woman nod. "Stay safe." Then the woman exited the line and walked away. Hinanya subsequently decided against the french fries, against any food at all. It coincided with the arrival of the awful rush. It urged her to sit while her existence seemed bent on ripping itself from the present into the worst parts of her 8IL trip. Still, she walked on, determined.

Before Hinanya crossed the intersection which Shaun lived, Hinanya noticed a hole in the wall of the cemetery by his house. It bore into the other side of the wall, but Hinanya had no idea how since it did not look like a car had collided with it. The pore was centered between the ground and the top of the wall. Shrugging off the curiosity, Hinanya saw Shaun's roommate, Frank, standing at the front door. As Hinanya approached, the man stiffened as if in anticipation of a drill sergeant's inspection.

"Who are you?" he asked before a radical cough overcame his body.

Hinanya, tired of people asking her, said only, "Shaun knows I'm coming."

Frank's eyes darted back and forth. "Look, you can't go in right now. You oughta leave. Come back later, I mean."

Behind her, Hinanya heard a car engine idling. "Shaun told me to come right in."

"No."

"That's what he said. So that's what I'm going to do."

"To be real with you, I wouldn't." It was when Hinanya tried to pass Frank that she knew something was off. Hinanya let Frank try to lay a hand on her first before scooping the man up and slamming him against the steps. People rushed out of the car as Frank moaned. Wasting no time, Hinanya rushed for the screen door, ripping it open. She locked the screen and then the door itself before the people reached the door. Though the lights were off, Hinanya could see the room was trashed. A Drake song played, blasting through Frank's stereo system. Hinanya crept forward, deeper into the apartment. She could just barely make out voices coming from Shaun's room.

She waited, poised, and took her chance while she could.

Her gun was out and ready to fire before she spotted the blood on the floor and who had made it.

19. CITIES OF THE FUTURE

When Shaun was going through sentencing for his drug bust, it had been Frank who'd made sure he'd still have a place to stay after he got out. And then, as for Caso, well, Caso had practically taken a bullet for him.

So Shaun thought it was a real bummer the two had joined forces to take him out.

Shaun had been smoking a bowl, waiting for Hinanya. Just as Caso had predicted, she was coming to them. In no time flat, Shaun arranged a time for Hinanya to swing by and got with Caso after to sort out the details. It was all tough shit for Hinanya, but Shaun figured it was him or her.

Shaun was oblivious as to what was really going on. Even after Caso barged in, hobbling on one leg, and panicking about trouble outside. He'd begged Shaun for his Magnum. It was behind the toilet of all places, and Shaun had given the gun up without a second thought. Caso pistol-whipped him with it after saying something about how in the future there would cities in the sky and the sea. No more crime or poverty or risk or love. No more racism or gods.

It hadn't been that hard, so Shaun thought the guy was playing. "Dude, you tryna get me hyped or wha—"

Caso did it again with a dreadful swing sufficient to topple Shaun over. Shaun spit up blood onto the floor as he got to his knees. When Shaun looked, his own gun was pointed at him. "Caso—"

"Into your room, Shaun. No floating cities for you."

As Shaun was paraded into his room, he said, "I'm not a threat. Fuck. Caso! What's going on?"

"Shaun, I got about enough time to tell you we been playin' you, but not enough to tell you why. So shut the fuck up, please."

Caso's eyes drew up and saw the door into the kitchen move a little. With three shots of Shaun's gun (Caso had screwed on a suppressor with experienced finesse), Shaun's other roommate Alanna, who'd be hiding on the other side of the door, began crying out in agony.

"I thought she might be doin' the deer in the headlights thing," Caso noted dispassionately. "I gotta quiet her down, don't bother trying to run for it. Frank'll pop you."

"Frank?"

"He's helpin' me here. Bummer of a job." Caso said this as he finished off Alanna with a few more bullets. He then reloaded.

"Nah, fuck dude, why you gotta get me like this?" Shaun asked, feeling a hundred steps behind. "I never turned anything in on Wenin."

"Oh, we know that," Caso said. "You've been a good boy. This is your reward."

"I was supposed to get the 8IL!" Shaun said. "I don't want to fuckin' die."

"They amount to the same thing, good boy."

20. THE MESS

Hinanya burst into the scene, shocked to see Shaun unharmed on his floor and hysterical. She'd thought her one connection to Wenin was almost gone. That's why she'd gone charging in. There was no eye contact or words until it was already settled. Hinanya aimed and pulled her trigger twice, sending Caso against the wall as he almost finished reloading his gun. Each round roared out, the air around her seeming to crunch in Hinanya's skull. This was the first time she'd actually used this gun on someone. She had always used earplugs when shooting

She'd imagined so many times who, if anyone, she would actually need to fire at. As much as she'd wished it was Caso, who represented a source of her life's confusions, she never thought she'd actually be forced to use a gun on someone else. But there it was. Caso was down.

It was not lost on Shaun following those moments where the gunfire's bite continued to echo and bore into his ears, that the girl he'd betrayed had just saved his life. Shaun saw Caso, his body gnarled and looking up at Hinanya.

"Still want the gun back?" Hinanya asked the dying Caso contemptuously. "Kind of dangerous, don't you think?"

Shaun hesitated to rise up, to thank her for the gift of life. He thought about the other's present psychology and found himself uncertain of her intentions. He didn't know one thing about her besides the fact that she was cold.

"What are you doing?" Hinanya questioned Shaun sharply, her gun aimed toward the kitchen. "Look, whatever's going on isn't over yet. We need to fight!"

"Fight?" Shaun stared at Caso as the man peeled off the wall and sank to the floor. His white shirt was soaking up the spilled blood. Saturation occurred, causing it to push through the pores in the fabric onto the hardwood floor generously.

"Pick up that gun!"

Shaun didn't budge. He didn't want to pick up a hot gun and the clip Caso had been feeding, even if it was his own. Then he realized he had no choice if he wanted to live. He reached out for it, trembling as he nabbed it from the floor. Shaun resisted the urge to fire into his would-be killer. Partly due to fear, partly due to Hinanya's words.

"Didn't think you were watchin' my back like that," Shaun said.

"He's an evil bastard."

"Same," Shaun said, too embarrassed to admit his betrayal.

"A loose end," Hinanya said. "I saw Caso sell his own brother out."

"But he'd saved my life before."

"Back to square one," Hinanya said. "Hey Shaun, you ever tag? You look familiar. I've been looking for somebody... really talent. But I've never actually seen their face."

"I tag, but I'm not talented," Shaun said.

They heard a noise from outside.

"Later," said Hinanya. "We need to get out of here."

Before they were in the kitchen, more shots went off, one after another shattering the glass of Shaun's closed window. Since Hinanya was next to Shaun, she witnessed each round as it pierced the man's jacket and skin to hit the wall just beyond him. His chest, his thigh, above his hip, the small of his back, his neck, his jaw, the last belting into the base of his skull behind his right ear.

Shaun couldn't tell just how many times he'd been shot. A part of him (the same one that had trusted Frank and Caso) figured it had been Hinanya who'd done it, but no.

That wasn't it.

"Too late though," he muttered to himself.

Hinanya went to his side.

"Hinanya, you're open."

"Let them kill me!" she shouted.

"They told me I was next."

Standing over the dying man, this link to Bluebell, Hinanya wanted to ask Shaun who they were. Instead, she comforted him. Whoever *they* were, they only wanted Shaun dead. The shooter from outside had unloaded his entire clip just on Shaun.

Shaun spoke up once more, struggling to speak. "For the 8IL, I mean. Hinanya, I ain't no snitch."

Hinanya didn't see how that mattered. "It wasn't all it was cracked up to be, Shaun. I was told it was supposed to take me away. Into the unknown. I thought I'd fly off as a soul and laugh at the things I'd faced as a human. Here I am though."

Shaun listened. And bled. Her words went into him as his blood went onto her. All the types of bleeding he'd learned about. Capillary. Arterial. Venous. He'd been a boy scout. He'd learned to patch all three kinds up. What a jip. He couldn't staunch his own bleeding or muster the force needed to instruct Hinanya.

"I thought it was a way to leave this plane to behold one higher," she was saying. "But no. There's only one way. And I hope you find what the 8IL couldn't give me."

His mom was right. Damn. But to him, Alabama had been wrong. He still felt that. Yet. How he wished he was a fish. He was cold, so that was a start. "This really ain't a comfortable flight."

He was dying. Crap.

Shaun convulsed, and he was pissed because all the shaking was going to wring him out that much faster.

Hinanya waited for him to expire and for the possibility that she was wrong. She knew they would like a chance to kill her, if for nothing else than that she'd gotten Caso. But as she suspected, the others of Caso's posse were long gone. Before Shaun was gone, he sputtered some words. One of them sounded hauntingly to Hinanya like the word angel.

20. DEPRIVATION

Hinanya made for the aperture into the cemetery. She didn't ask herself if it was a terrible idea, she was reacting purely on instinct. Shaun was gone. There was no point in blaming herself for his death. She felt no guilt about how she could have done things differently. If anything, she'd given Shaun a few more minutes to live. And speaking of life, she'd been too shaken to make sure Caso was taken care of. Now there was no possibility of going back.

Down the alleys of graves, she hobbled, desperately searching for a place to hide. Tombs in New Orleans were largely housed above ground, one on top of the other, row after row. The arrays of family plots soon brought Hinanya to a place she had no idea she had been looking for.

Hinanya looked up at the statue of a feminine angel set in prayer. The statue's eyes were closed. A mausoleum was erected below it with another aperture. Looking at the steps to the tomb, Hinanya saw several broken fragments where pieces of rubble had fallen. Taking out her gun once more, she slipped inside. She was alone. Alone as the blaring sirens came, followed by scant flashes of red and blue light. Hinanya leaned back out of the tomb in an attempt to find something that could convincingly cover the hole.

First, she'd played executioner, then she'd violated a space for the dead. Laying back onto the floor as best as she could, Hinanya reflected on Shaun's fate and what it could mean.

Hinanya felt he hadn't been out to hurt anyone. It didn't seem to be in his nature. Shaun had been a victim. Maybe Caso too.

The War on Drugs never waged a battle against the drugs themselves. No, the War on Drugs made enemies out of people like Shaun. There was little hope for rehabilitation or recovery through imprisonment. It only hardened an individual.

But as the world had mistreated Shaun, so had Hinanya. She'd used and valued him only insofar as he would give her the 8IL.

Like the angel above her, eventually, Hinanya shut her eyes to sleep despite the cramped and hard space. Nobody came into the cemetery after her, and Hinanya remained inside that tomb for almost two days before emerging filthy, sick, and dehydrated.

21. FINAL CREATION

Stefan's gun needed cleaning.

Then, because she missed Felix and wanted to try one more time to reach out to Wenin, she went to the garden neighborhood she'd found that night when she'd jumped off the freight train for one last tag. If Felix had been Shaun, he was now elsewhere. Gone.

All she did with herself for a week after escaping Shaun's place was tag, not wanting that to be so Felix. And though she would not pray to Felix, she was also unable to discount him as an angel, even if only in the sense Sasha had put it. If he had gone from her, it meant she no longer needed him. Wasn't that how angels worked? He'd set her up to write, and she'd taken it as far as she could.

A few minutes into a tag and the fumes from the spray paint made her feel dizzy. It began to burn in her lungs.

The freight train passed her by as she tagged the side of a warehouse's roof.

The police were probably searching for her.

New Orleans—our lady of perpetual sirens, Hinanya thought, remembering Shaun's words.

Kurt understood that the entire time he'd known her, there was something wrong, something so warped that she herself didn't understand and so couldn't be spared from it. Kurt was useless to his angel. That's why she'd cast him away. Hinanya was afflicted with a disease. Then maybe Felix had cast her away? Surely, if he was a writer, he had the same reasons as she had. And who was Felix's angel? That was easy. He tagged in the code of Wenin. A hierarchy of another irrational divinity.

No human should be merely *just* surviving. Survival was for microbes. Humans had to be more. That was all Shaun or Hinanya or Caso ever wanted.

Hinanya looked over her last creation. It was complete.

22. BECOMING

A long cloth sheet did its best to cover the whole of Hinanya as she sat up anxiously in the physician's room. She was inside of a walk-in clinic not far from her house, where she'd decided she wanted to end things.

She had sought out medical attention finally to know why her body was so out of sorts.

In the meantime, her thoughts lay exclusively in the realm of how she would best ensure death from shooting herself in the head. Hinanya didn't want to botch that up. The police would find her, the gun, tie Caso to it, and hopefully, trace how the damn thing got from Stefan's dead hand to Caso's.

It was early in the morning, and Hinanya had stumbled in straight from her last tag. She barely slept since exiting the tomb a few days prior. The room she found herself in was frigid. Not like the waiting room, where the A/C had refused to flow. Hinanya flipped through one of her sketch notebooks. The pen in her hands clicked, but she didn't click it. She only remembered having clicked it just a few seconds before, returning like an echo.

On one page were the words CREATION/DESTRUCTION spread the width of the page, clearly separated but equal.

Hinanya shut her notebook at that. The world peddled the value of creation as it destroyed all it could have of itself.

But creation was not finished with her yet.

The door to the room swung open, and a broad woman with neutral features stepped it. Her hair was pale blonde and in a ponytail.

"Hello. I'm Dr. Sierpiński." There was some kind of European accent at the forefront of her speech. The doctor didn't hold it back, not like Hinanya's mother who strangled her Indonesian accent even amongst her closest relatives after mastering English. The doctor looked away from Hinanya as she put on her glasses to see what was written on the clipboard. Her flabby dimples twitched but her face looked as if she were years away from a smile.

Dr. Sierpiński rose from the clipboard, and the two women made eye contact for the first time. "Ms. Ven, we need not conduct any further tests to confirm— do you honestly not realize that you're seven months pregnant?"

There was no awful rush. No feeling of being ripped from reality. Only a series of wide-eyed blinks. "Doctor. I'm not sexually active. I'm a virgin."

Dr. Sierpiński did not yield. "Ma'am, be that as it may... it's the truth."

And after a lifetime of hiding her true self from people dampened reactions and silence where a war boiled within, Hinanya protested. Her knuckles smashed against the wall. "Lie. You must be—I'm not crazy. Misdiagnosis. I don't—" Hinanya saw through the window of the building and saw a discrete cross-section of New Orleans.

The doctor nodded sternly, gaining no sympathy or emotion in her cadence. "I know this is hard, but you need to understand."

"There's something else wrong with me!" Hinanya exclaimed.

It seemed Hinanya's frantic movements didn't put the doctor on guard. In an almost antagonistic fashion, Dr. Sierpiński assured Hinanya, "You're going to be a mother."

EPILOGUE

Before the French explorers, led by Bienville, had decided to erect a city at the natural levee crescent, there was much debate over the permanent settlement of the Louisiana colony. To begin with, they had not been prepared for the barely charted land, its harsh weather, or life-threatening wildlife. It was Bienville who pushed his vision upon the skeptical explorers to build there. From the untamed swamplands, they erected a city, only to face flooding and fires that consistently chipped away at the population. Between those disasters, there was also malaria and confrontations from the Native Americans. Despite all of that, the thriving port city eventually came to be one that rivaled the grandeur of Paris itself, made of the toil of slaves sourced from Africa.

New Orleans was not an especially large city by modern definition, due in part to how it came to be. Its dimensions and shape were formed by the ebb and flow of the Mississippi River itself. It was crowded northward by Lake Pontchartrain. New Orleans sized itself up as modest, only what it needed to be.

The wild around it persisted for some time. In fact, it could be argued that nature, not humans, still dominated the region. Still, generation after generation insisted on living there, bringing refugees from across the globe.

Its rich history had always been of great interest to Peb. While most other subjects bored him, the stories of his ancestors fascinated him.

After the situation with that dumb psycho bitch, he'd been sold down the river by his grandmother after narrowly avoiding a juvenile detention center. No one would believe that he didn't set that building on fire. Peb didn't even know how to start a fire. He had not spoken to Caso since that night nor did he want to.

Peb was walking with invigorated steps down a forest path. It was early in the morning, and he paced faster in hopes of evading the many mosquitoes that followed after him.

To the northeast of New Orleans some ways, close to the border between Louisiana and Mississippi, there was a city known as Slidell. Those who lived in Slidell lived along the bayou. When the sun went down, the swamps took over. He hated it here. There was nothing going on, the people were racist as fuck, and there was no telling when he'd be able to go back to New Orleans.

The only thing Peb had found to do was to explore, and this time, he was expecting to hit the motherlode. Some kids in school had told him about a secret bunker built by the military on the outskirts of Slidell. They had left Peb behind, and he was trying to find them.

They'd set off for the bunker almost eight hours ago. His new friends teased him by not telling him the name of the place. There was no telling why Peb trusted them at face value, but he had.

They said they had been there before and that it was haunted by violent spirits. It had been a long time since the road had ended in palm trees and thickets. Peb had packed diligently, wearing hard boots to protect from snakes and a goofy garden hat that belonged to his cousin's wife to ward off the sun. Peb was thankful it wasn't too severe as he looked up to see the cloudy spring sky.

Peb soon saw what looked like a huge igloo of grass punctuated by a concrete lining near its base and a short black rectangular aperture that led beneath the ground. Going to it, he took a flashlight clipped to his side and saw the rectangle was mostly concrete. Looking down it, he saw it lead to bare blackness, darkness which Peb stuck his hand into. A chilly air engulfed his fingers. Peb, knowing he'd found something. Angling his flashlight to make sure it wasn't a deep hole he'd become trapped in, he saw a floor not too far down. A floor and pallets, which would allow him to manufacture a way back.

"Yo, guys, stop fuckin' around. You down there?"

It took some time to slide his way in through the opening, but for once, his tiny stature paid off. He saw a small room with a low ceiling that even he had to crouch down for. There didn't seem to be anything of interest here so he pressed on. On the end other there was a glass window in the center of one of the sidewalls. He busted the glass without reservation.

"What the fuck?" he muttered to himself as he traversed the dingy space, fearless until after about five minutes of crawling he saw a light at the end. Hadn't the boys said the space was abandoned? Shutting off his light, Peb advanced to follow the light into another room—one of which made him consider turning around. What Peb had been told was that bunker was a dark and dead fortress where soldiers trained and scientists quarreled, but that was long ago. The room he found was like the nursery of some hospital. It had pink walls and a dresser. Peb's head hovered over it all and saw a crib with adornments of stars hanging above it. It was like a bunk bed with three separate levels, and on the top one, he could see there was actually a baby, a slumbering white infant wrapped in a blue wool blanket. A wooden door was shut just beyond the stacked cribs.

Whatever was going on inside that place, Peb didn't care. With a cautious air, he descended from the opening in the wall and his boots touched a fuzzy red rug. Then he hopped up through the shaft once more and heard what sounded like an A/C kick on. Peb wanted to leave the bunker and never go back. Fuck whatever it was.

He was almost all the way through the opening when he heard the door open. Before Peb could get any further, he felt a hand wrap and constrict itself around his shin. Unable to pull away, he kicked at the arm with his other leg and began to wail. The hand did not relent, pulling him from the opening and back into the nursery. Spreading his arms on each side of the tunnel only resulted in terrible scraping as more hands ripped Peb from the wall like an unwanted weed. Peb's face almost slammed into the edge of the tunnel as he fell onto the floor in pain, but he made an X with his arms to shield himself. That done, he whirled onto his back to see an imposing balding man with a goatee standing over him. The man's clothes were reminded Peb of doctor's scrubs, a teal-colored garment with no wrinkles. The man looked as if he might bludgeon Peb if he didn't stop. Then he simply brought a finger to his mouth to mime a silent *shhhh*, gesturing to the babies. Others appeared and surrounded Peb.

One, then two of the babies began crying. The man looked even more upset. As he turned his back to Peb, Peb attempted to rise, but the men bent, one of them getting Peb's shin again and dragged him out of the room. In a move of great stupidity, Peb grasped the door with both hands in hopes of stopping the madness, he never he did help. He was brought into a hallway, which was more like what he'd imagine the bunker to look like, a concrete interior. Yet there were lights installed. Power.

"Please, man," Peb said. "I thought this place was abandoned, dude. I don't want nothin' to do with babies. Let me go. I want to go home."

"Yeah, you do," the man responded eagerly.

The friction of being dragged against the floor was beginning to cause him pain, a burning in the small of his back where his shirt had frayed apart. The skin there began to tear.

Another person appeared. This one was dressed like the man with the goatee, only his uniform was more office, topped with a white lab coat bearing strange symbols above the breast pockets that Peb could have sworn he'd seen on some graffiti in New Orleans.

The man spoke once more. "See, this is the problem. This is the problem right now, right here."

With a pleading, high-pitched timbre, Peb cried out, "Oh God, please don't hurt me. Where the fuck am I?"

The dragging stopped. The two men stood above him. They looked at each other. The man with the goatee shrugged to the other then looked to Peb and said, "Not relevant."

"For real," said the other man. "I mean, I thought you wanted to be let go more than you wanted to know where you are."

"Nah, really. Where am I?" Peb asked. "My friends and I were just tryna chill. What's going on?"

The first man pursed his lips. "Dawg, I think the problem with that question is you already know the answer."

"Huh?"

"You know where you at."

Peb attempted to get to his feet, but the men raised one hand each in a sign to remain where he was. He shook his head and said, "No."

"You in deep shit."

Behind Peb, the babies still cried out.

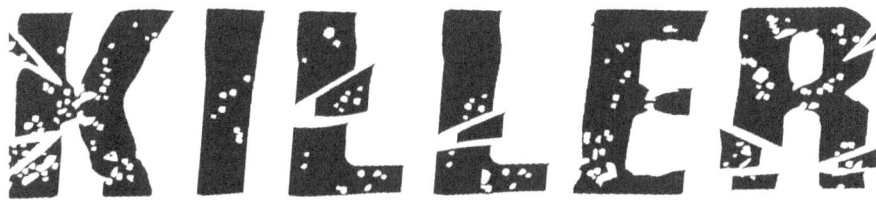

"It's not what you make, it's what you leave"

-Green Day

1. PARASITES

Cockroaches were a silent infestation. Once a single roach was spotted moseying across a kitchen counter, hundreds if not thousands could be swarming unseen beneath the pipes and woodwork. Breeding and germinating. Even a small infestation had a way of making itself known in time. Brown specs appeared on plates or in cupboards. Fecal spots.

In New Orleans over a third of the homes hosted roaches. Humidity was a roach's Eden.

Resilient, it was their role to survive. Any trace of moisture or crumb of food would be assimilated. Roaches could eat paper, the grime off an old coin. They would eat the corpses of their own family and thrive.

A week after Hinanya had learned she was well into her third trimester, she dropped everything she had going on to drive the cockroaches out of her apartment. Admittedly, it was a hopeless gesture to undergo on her own. But that was how Hinanya operated.

Scrubbing on her hands and knees, Hinanya was shoulder-deep into her kitchen sink cabinet sterilizing all surfaces with a mixture of bleach, boric acid, and a household cleaner to neutralize the intruders. She remembered the terrible exchange a few days before with Dr. Sierpiński. The conversation played over and over in her head. Once Hinanya could admit there was no mistake she was pregnant, the next logical step had come to her.

"I want an abortion," she'd said with unflinching resolve, her body rigid but straightening where she sat.

"Ma'am, I'm sorry," Dr. Sierpiński lamented, "but it is rare to move forward on such a late-term abortion. You see, it's a gruesome thing to terminate at this stage. The typical methods would not work. We'd have to induce labor and have the fetus come out stillborn. Many medical professionals consider this homicide. This is because the fetus may have the means to survive outside of the womb, independent of you. Whatever took you so long to see me, well, it was all time. Time for this baby to just become *that*. There's no gray area here. It's not a potential person. Even if you miraculously found someone to do this for you, there are heightened risks to you. No, we have to consider more rational alternatives here."

"I don't care about the risks!" Hinanya spouted vehemently.

"Miss Ven, others do. You have a child inside of you. If you do not want it, you are going to have to seek out an adoption agency."

"You mean I have to give birth?" Hinanya remarked vacantly. She never felt such a lack of control over her circumstances in her entire life. Hinanya despised children. She had come to New Orleans to sever all ties from her family, not begin a new one.

"Yes. We have a lot of work to do."

"No! I want to talk to someone else."

"Dear, you're not a killer. There are would-be parents who would give anything to adopt this baby and give it a life you never could."

Hinanya scowled then, finding Dr. Sierpiński's assessment flawed. Hinanya was a killer. She was killing every roach she found indifferently. In droves. With poison. They would all suffer and die at her hand. Those disgusting parasites that had infiltrated her space and filched off of her.

The purging of the vermin from her living space had been distracting Hinanya. Leaving her dwelling in the past, not facing her present. How could this have even happened?

Since learning she was pregnant, she'd done no research, no follow-up appointments, nothing.

She would not commit suicide either, for she wanted to learn more about the 8IL, she had taken. Hinanya had been among the few chosen for reasons she didn't understand. Her only suspicion was that it was due to a loose affiliation with another claimed user of 8IL, Uncle Rawls. He'd been the one who'd had informed her of the existence of 8IL and its ability to allow the user the option of evacuating his or her body. An experience Hinanya had always felt she needed, for comfort against this progressively inane existence.

When she had gotten her hands on it, it led to a bitter and crushing defeat that left her craving suicide more than ever.

In the course of eradicating the bugs in her apartment, another memory came to her. That of her friend Sasha and a printer she'd set on the floor of her apartment. Soon enough, Sasha had found traces of roaches on her printer paper, realizing they'd found a home there. Half a roach's body or a leg would come out with the page being printed. The thing still worked, so Sasha had to wrestle with the decision to keep the printer, to coexist, or to throw it away, blowing the cost of the printer but eliminating one certain source of her roach problem.

Sasha had had made a decision about the printer. And despite what Dr. Sierpiński had said, Hinanya also had her own decision to make—because there was no way Hinanya would play mother to any parasite. It came from the sight of her bulging belly, the maddening sphere always below her to look down at. A sign of her neglect and a serious indication of outer forces beyond her control. Between the constant internalization and the death drive, Hinanya knew herself to be on the verge of some mental breakdown.

Just because the thing was there feasting on her, didn't mean Hinanya had any intention of being its mother. It was as absurd of a question as who the father was—because Hinanya had never had sex before.

The belly demanded a resolution. As while it provided some explanation of the past seven months of strange bodily incidents, it raised more questions than answers. What virgin such as Hinanya would believe the tremors and symptoms were a pregnancy? Freak accidents like this did occur, but they did require some contact with semen. Such inquiries left her shuddering and violated, but she had to be ruthless. There was a need for the truth. It became another thing subverting her suicidal desire, but by no means did it improve her mood.

Yet at the same time, it seemed that suicide was the only way out of not delivering the baby.

As a rule, primary and sometimes even secondary details of her life were well-guarded secrets to Hinanya. She excelled at shutting people out while making sure they weren't too concerned about her. But this thing was so beyond the magnitude of anything Hinanya had experienced. Every trace or clue of an answer to her pregnancy had to be followed.

The first clue Hinanya had latched onto was the lapse of consciousness she'd experienced that had transported her from her apartment to the abandoned Devon Riley Dixon building she'd later burned down. It came to her in the context of Dr. Sierpiński's conjecture that she'd been raped while unconscious. That, in an extreme case, the memory of a sexual encounter could have been so traumatic for her that she'd suppressed the memory. How could Hinanya truly not remember something like that? She'd been the target of many unscrupulous enemies since she'd arrive in New Orleans (the month of August coincided with her estimated insemination time), but none had got to her, not like that.

She took those dark speculations to the brink, then stalled more, applying the anti-roach solution everywhere. Boric acid was a combination of water and a composition commonly found in the soil known as boron that could attach itself to roaches as they walked over it. As they cleaned themselves, they ingested it, and the substances broke down their internal systems. The killings settled Hinanya in some macabre way. It was a simple maxim of nature: killed or be killed. She'd taken that ethical stance from Uncle Rawls.

Each morning, she'd wake up and survey the floors and the sealant she'd introduced to the cracks in her wall to dispose of the remains of the dead roaches.

When Hinanya spotted a live one fleeing for safety, she'd crush and kill it instantly with the tail end of a Kennedy half-dollar.

Hinanya went on to sweep her apartment, though there were no more particles or dust to be found. Then she mopped an already spotless floor that had been cleaned the day before. The tortured girl lay on her back and instinctively cradled the terrible swelling in her abdomen. She could kill herself—she had in it her. Just not yet, as there were things she needed to attend to. Hinanya needed to end things right. As she took the roach lives, she knew there was some greater force dangling above her, chipping away at her peace of mind. That's why she wanted to soldier on. To find who created all of this suffering in her mind and make them suffer.

Later, despite all her obsessive cleanliness, Hinanya saw a small German cockroach on its back on the drying floor. She watched it struggled there, knowing it wasn't going anywhere. For a time, she neither helped nor harmed it, only observed. Then she deemed the trespass unacceptable.

The small insect never having a chance to escape, Hinanya again used the half-dollar, then lifted it to see the flattened thing. Having come to the sudden acknowledgment of its coming death, the cockroach had expelled her ootheca. Was that how the thing had ended up on its back? An imbalance? The ootheca was an egg case, separated in the hope that the separation would allow the nymphs to be.

Hinanya would permit neither mother nor offspring to live.

2. SURROUNDED

It came. Despite all Hinanya had been, how she felt about things, an undeniable maternal instinct of which she had no control over was making itself known. Perhaps it had been there all along, and she hadn't been able to identify it. Each instance of sympathy and yearning to carry her child to term was tinged with utter disgust fully in line with her personality. The completely alien feeling was one she tried to isolate herself from, as it was only her body carrying out a biological imperative more ancient and more lasting than her singular identity. But as it stood, the baby was a part of herself, not yet a separate entity.

Given a future, it could become something.

Being seven months pregnant also meant she had been pregnant when experimenting with 8IL, whose side-effects upon a developing infant were practically unknowable.

What did any of it matter if she was just going to kill herself? If only she could surrender and dispense with all of the excuses. Giving birth *had* to be worse than suicide in Hinanya's mind.

Hinanya sat with her legs dangling on the roof of an abandoned Medical Center in Mid-City. Fully aware of how easily she could jump.

Had she only gone to the doctor's sooner, they could have performed the abortion, and there would have been no issue. It was all so confusing. At that moment, she slipped back against the pebbles on the surface of the roof, knowing part of her problem was having all of this bottled up inside.

She had to confide in someone.

As she made her way home, a vomiting fit came on. And all of it a consequence of her sex, her gender. The sum of genetic coding forming her anatomy, demanding she reproduce.

If only Hinanya could have been born at some future time where the concepts of gender and sex were considered obsolete. She didn't want to identify with the sex she was, and yet it was the crux of her being. Any such vision was impossible for Hinanya to imagine, her greatest failure.

Hinanya was surrounded by people asking if she was okay. It had been dark when she'd left the roof of the abandoned building. Now it was morning, on the path of the Lafitte Greenway. These were breeders and devourers. It was by their eyes and will that the world was on its way to ruin. And they asked if *she* was okay. Hinanya only nodded, finding herself at eye level with a black Labrador on her way up. Hinanya rose stained in her own puke.

3. MISUNDERSTANDING

Sasha and Kurt sat down on Hinanya's bed, rather close to one another. She told them about the pregnancy. Sasha looked to Kurt, but Kurt remained fixed on Hinanya. Stammering, he managed to let out, "Who? How?"

"I don't know."

"This is... unbelievable, Hinanya," Sasha said. "After everything you've told me."

"It explains an awful lot, though," Kurt mused.

"I'm happy you think so," Hinanya snapped back. "You two must know I don't want this baby. But it's too late to terminate."

Sasha nodded with what seemed to begin with a slight shaking of her head. "Hinanya, you weren't given knowledge of this pregnancy until it was too late to get an abortion. It's a sign."

Unable to restrain herself, Hinanya shot back, her arms spreading out above her, "A sign of what, Sasha?!"

Sasha, recoiling, said, "I don't know. But there is little doubt as to what must be done."

"Especially considering the circumstance," Kurt added.

"Look, guys, I'm having a really hard time of this. I need your help. I think I get what you're trying to say, but I don't what to hear about any Immaculate Conception nonsense. Somehow... even if you're right, and it was God himself, this was... not something I wanted. And I'm not going to be able to care for this thing," Hinanya admitted.

"But the child, it's a special thing. It deserves to exist, like you," Sasha defended.

"Do you know the gender?" Kurt asked.

"No," said Hinanya. "I mean I don't want to know, okay?"

Kurt gazed over to Sasha, "I bet it's a boy!"

"Why are you assuming that?" Hinanya asked, crossing her arms.

Kurt simply shrugged, but Hinanya's dirty look made him feel the need to explain. "If I knew why I assumed that, I'd tell you. Just guessing," Kurt said.

"Look, to be honest, it feels like my mind has been apart from me for a long time. My mood, actions, behavior. Yes, I isolate myself, apparently even from the truth. What I'm getting at is I'm not sure where I stand mentally anymore. I need to ask you both. Do you have any idea as to how this happened to me?" Hinanya wished she was able to ask this to Kurt alone, considering the time she found him in her bed. But considering the way the two sat now, Hinanya didn't think it'd be prudent to bring that up. Especially since she'd been on the 8IL at the time.

"Hinanya," Sasha said, her voice undercut with disappointment, "you've been so secretive all this time. What do you expect us to tell you?"

"Yeah, exactly," Kurt said. "How could we possibly help you now? We want to, but I just don't think there are any clues available to us due to a lack of information. Most of the time with you it's a communication blackout."

"I'm just afraid, okay? And I can't do this alone. Apparently, I'm not a virgin. But I'm so bound in darkness, ignorance. I don't know what to do anymore."

"We can make guesses," said Kurt.

"Yeah, and you'll shut them down," said Sasha. "If you want to be honest with us, we'll be honest with you."

"Exactly. I know how to start. Why don't you tell us exactly who you think you are? Then, oh, that'll be a cinch. We'll compare it to our point of views! It won't be a totally efficient thing to do, as I haven't personally spent that much time with you, but what else do we have?"

"Yeah, okay," Hinanya agreed. "Let's do that."

"Before we do," Sasha interjected. "There's something really important you need to know. See, ever since you shut off your phone, your family has been trying hard to reach you. So have Kurt and me. You know that."

"Yeah, I'm really sorry about that," Hinanya said apathetically.

"Look, Taylor has a message—for you. I've tried to get it to you sooner, but it hasn't worked out. It's a voicemail. So will you listen to it?"

Hinanya frowned. "All right."

Having already had the message cued up, Sasha gestured for Hinanya to take the phone and listen. In the digitized murmurs of her sister's voice, between the static indicative of a busy road, Hinanya learned some shocking news.

"No, no!"

"What's the matter?" Kurt asked.

Surfacing from the message as it was still playing, Hinanya asked Sasha, "Have they found her yet?"

"The latest I've heard is no. Taylor is still heading here."

Letting out an anguished growl, Hinanya hissed, "She can't do that. She can't come *here*. She doesn't even know."

4. RESURRECTION

Nobody wanted to admit it, but without the pantry boy, Buckland's was slowly falling apart. It was an entry-level position at the chicken shack. Simple duties like making desserts and getting items from the walk-in to the line. Buckland's itself was a small place. There was some seating, but most of the orders were takeout.

It was mid-morning, and the staff was getting ready to open. Arie was burdened with the task of doing the dog all by himself, the dog being the machine they used to filter out the deep fryers.

Those at the bottom of the pyramid were sorely underrated, he mused to himself. It was because of a bad decision on the part of Shaun, the deceased pantry boy, that Arie Schorel now suffered this menial task. He only worked there part-time, as much as he could handle.

By all rights, this should have been done at end of last night's shift. But when Arie had come in, it was obvious it had not. Rather than piss and moan, he simply set about completing the task in between his other opening duties.

If Shaun hadn't gone and died, a lot of things would be different. The good news was that pantry boys came and went. There were always desperate folks gnarled by the streets and in need of money. Maybe it was for their baby mammas, or their addictions, or legal fees. Given that fact, doing the dog by himself happened only occasionally, and Arie had no issues about getting his hands greasy.

The rest of the morning-shift workers began piling in to greet Arie. Arie was surprised to see several faces, former employees who'd been fired shortly after the new manager Tim had taken over. It was Buckland, the owner of the chicken shack, who'd attempted to relinquish control of operators and management to Tim, so Buckland didn't have to. Tim's credentials spoke for themselves. In the many restaurants he'd managed, he'd reduced labor costs and increased profit time and again.

The problem was, Tim had never worked in a place like New Orleans. The man had been all business. By the end of his first week, a third of the staff at Buckland's had been fired. Another third became disgruntled but didn't want to lose their jobs so they assimilated into the joyless routine. Long story short, Tim did what he'd set out to do, but the price of the increased profit margin was too much for him. On Tuesday, in the middle of the dinner rush, Tim went out for a cigarette and didn't return. Buckland was forced to seize control of his restaurant once more. Out of sentimentality, he hired back nearly half of those terminated by Tim.

"Arie!" rejoiced Andre. "Don't tell me you survived that mofo?"

Arie nodded.

"Damn, you must be sore."

"Hmm?" Arie wondered what the man meant.

"From bendin' over all these weeks, dude. Shit. You think things gonna go back to how Buckland had 'em?"

Arie's response was vacant. "If I had to venture a guess, I'd have to say definitely."

"It's good to see you, ya hear?"

"You too, Andre. It's nice seeing all you again. Like a family reunion."

"We goan have a long day today but after you know we gotta drain the daiquiri machine."

"You know it," Arie said with a smirk.

Andre chuckled. "Before I get started over here, Arie, I gotsta know. How'd you stay off of that shithead's radar? How he ain't bald?"

"It was annoying, wasn't it? To see an old geezer like him with such a full head of hair."

"Sure was! Man, I ain't even forty-two, and I got the baldness." Andre made his way over to the grill and began prepping the flour baskets.

"I guess... I know what it's like to be in charge, Andre. Not here, obviously. Being in charge here would be like, well—the ass in charge is still an ass. I guess most of the time you have a job to do, and you do it. It seemed like Tim wanted people to do their same thing different and there was resistance to the change. Out of the ordinary things, you all were like, that's not my job. I just did the stuff. No big. I'll be the first to admit it, but I need this job, Andre. This job is important to me. And no matter how bad things got with Tim, I think, in the end, justice was served. You've got guys like you welcomed back with open arms. And then Buckland knows Tim's methods might have been good for business but they were abysmal for the workers."

"You ain't need a job like this, Arie. You a smart one. Even when you get drunk. Still smart. I don't get it. It's like when you can be blackout drunk and recite all the first ladies in order."

Arie let another smirk rise out of his passive expression. "You hear about Shaun, Andre?"

"Mhm."

"That's why I'm stuck doing the dog right now."

"I hear that other boy ain't dead, though."

"Really?" Arie voice lilted in wonderment.

"Yeah. They can't figure out just what went down over on Saint Roch that night."

"Right, the one in a coma now. Apparently, some bad people made their way in. It's only a crappy house in a crappy neighborhood. People don't even realize the locks they use to secure their lives and possessions were designed centuries ago. They only offer the illusion of safety. Morons."

"That jus' fucks my heart from the back to hear shit like that, Arie."

"Sure. But Shaun was running his own little side-hustle. Cocaine at least. They found that, a lot of bills, not the type of money you'd make at Buckland's, mind you. All of that and an unregistered gun."

"He was just a boy. Ain't no one deserves to be shot in the face for nothin'."

"Not even Tim?" Arie asked with levity. This place was so beneath Arie. However, he suffered it in a jovial manner.

"Ah, come on. This Shaun stuff is serious."

In looking down at the tepid grease flowing through the pipe from the deep fryer, Arie knew there was no way he could argue with Andre about that.

5. COVEN

Bourbon Street's residential end began at Esplanade Avenue. It was a quiet area, shockingly so. Hinanya entered in the French Quarter with caution, eyes peeled for any sign of the place she was looking for. Hinanya was frantic, for Taylor could appear at any time. Hinanya would politely turn her little sister away, but it would be much easier if Hinanya wasn't pregnant at the time. Otherwise, there would be far too much explaining the unexplainable.

The houses on either side of Bourbon Street were concealed by high walls and fences, topped broken glass and rusty nails jutting out in all directions to deter intruders. After a period of wandering, Hinanya stood before a three-story building, an edifice of Spanish architecture common to the French Quarter. The building was a desiccated white, splattered with grime. She made for the entrance, but those large red doors were barred. Hinanya surveyed the area anxiously, figuring there had to be a way in. Eventually, she found what the voodoo priestess on Decatur had told her— the small crevasse on the side of the building. Wasting no time, Hinanya slid through, turning her flashlight on to see there was already someone waiting for her inside.

"Good morning," a thick Parisian voice announced.

She pointed her flashlight to the voice. It was a tall man in a top hat, clean-shaven. He wore both a vest and overalls.

"I was told," Hinanya began in a whisper, "about an abortifacient one could take late-stage pregnancies."

She pointed the light away from the man, suddenly wondering what he'd been doing before her arrival. "Yes, they do talk about such things. In stories, child. Magic, wouldn't you know?"

"I don't believe in magic," Hinanya admitted with a hint of condescension. "I'm just here inquiring if this brew is available as I need it. Immediately."

"Ohhh?" the man asked, his curiosity unmistakable. "Suppose I ask of you to believe in magic or it won't work?"

"Then I'll search elsewhere for it."

"Come with me," said the man.

Hinanya pointed the flashlight at the man's shins.

"Lower, please."

Doing as she was told, she followed the man for several minutes as they crested the steps onto the second story of the old building. Light occasionally seeped through, and the man took extra care to step around the beams. He took her from the basement area to a front lobby. Along the way, she noted others. They remained on their side, never getting up. Splayed over in what was no doubt an afterglow. In the lobby, it was easier to see the man than it had been in the basement. His face was acne-ridden. Hinanya wondered how many people lived there.

"By the way, I am Varliot," the man said, introducing himself with a bow. Hinanya took that in without commenting that his accent had altered dramatically with his last sentence, going from a French one to a more Scandinavian inflection.

"I'm a little frustrated, sir. You didn't tell me whether or not you had it."

"What?"

"The abortifacient."

He hissed softly for a moment, then said, "It is interesting. In desperation, people are sent here of all places. Many stay in order that they may lead a new life. Does that notion interest you at all, girl?"

"I'm afraid not."

"Well!" Varliot said, flustered. "Doesn't believe in magic, doesn't introduce herself, can't even name the item she is looking for."

"I know this may be wrong, but I was told to ask for silphium."

Varliot snickered. "Silphium is long extinct. And even if it was available, it was for birth control. Control is the operative word. You, mademoiselle, would have seen better use of that many moons ago."

As determined as Hinanya was to play along with the character and his routine in order to get what she wanted, she was unable to take that statement without some fight. "I don't believe in magic, and I don't think there's such a thing as vampires either. Give me the abortifacient, and I'll give you enough money to get a real apartment."

"Please don't think to send me away," Varliot pleaded. "I'm actually quite happy here. But you're so powerful, you know?"

"What?"

"Mothers are the strongest thing I can think of. They divest their own energy to produce another. It's an exchange, you see. The mother drains herself for the child until it is complete. She does not even think twice about this process, for no obstacle is insurmountable to her in lieu of bringing to bear her seed. I'm sure you can conceive of things without mothers. Or could you? They say life itself was just a fickle something from nothing, the cosmic mixtures dancing to produce some force which yielded life. This is power. See even all mothers must yield to the beginning of them all. Right now, if the world uses the power of its mothers in the right way, we could even challenge whatever space vomit caused us."

"Yeah, that's all great. But that's not my battle, Varliot. I want out. I did not ask for this role, for motherhood. This is not my lot in life. If you do not possess the abortifacient, I will find another way to absolve myself of this situation."

Varliot walked over to the lobby. On the counter was a wooden crate. From it, he took out a small decanter and several items Hinanya associated with the occult: candles, a thin shimmering purple veil, and a small chunk of sandy driftwood. "It shall cost you."

"Whatever it costs me is fine."

"You must let me give you a reading. I sense you are in need of one. You see, I am an empath. An old soul able to outline where you end and your troubles begin."

"Okay."

"Sit," Varliot said, pulling out a folding chair from beside the crate on the counter. Hinanya stepped over in a rush and sat down. He took a seat across from her. Varliot's eye contact was a constant. "Hmmm. I see. Yes. You find yourself seeking still after you had thought you'd found what you needed. Many contractions are common to our reality. Higher up, girl and things will become clearer. But you wonder if there is an above, below, besides, beyond."

"Yes," said Hinanya.

"You have a demon!" the man bemoaned. "I see its leavings, but not its form. Hmm, what demon is it?"

"I have an idea."

"Silence, I'm—" Varliot let out a creaking sibilance that sounded to Hinanya like opening an old door. He threshed for a moment. "Girl, you must be rid of this demon."

"Right."

"Only you can do it! Ancient Egyptians did this thing way back in the day. They call it something different now. I forget... the casting out of a demon... Uhmmm..."

"An exorcism?"

"Yes! The ancient Egyptian method shall do you well. You must hurry. Once this demon, his name is Strilark, has marked you (which he already has), he will proceed to devour you unless you are able to declare autonomy of your existence. He lurches above you, in the astral plane."

"I'll need to get there to take him on, huh? I'm not so sure about that."

"No, you may state in physical form. Another thing you must know: the demon and your baby are completely independent of one another."

"Wasn't expecting that," said Hinanya. "What if I don't believe I have a demon, will that drain it of its power?"

"Not in the slightest! Confrontation is the only way to dispatch evil. I'd help you but—"

"Just give me what I came for already," Hinanya said impatiently.

"But it could just do the opposite of what you'd like, accelerate the pregnancy. Infest you with a demon seed."

"Which is different from the demon itself?"

"Yes."

"I think whatever infesting in question has already taken place, to be honest. Damaged goods, Varliot."

As Varliot approached Hinanya, he looked from her to the decanter. "This potion is known as Johnless. Its maker would have birthed a handsome man named John who discovered the cure for cancer in an alternative timeline."

Hinanya found herself feeling increasingly claustrophobic in the old building. The people along the walls and around them appeared to be closing in around her.

"You will get sick."

"Pregnancy is an illness!" Hinanya declared with rancor.

Somewhere behind her, somebody echoed the word illness.

"Will you truly take this based on everything I've told you?" Varliot asked, seemingly startled.

"If it works, then it works. If it doesn't, then it doesn't."

"I mean, I can tell you think I'm crazy."

"I'm crazy too, Varliot. That's my demon. You don't get rid of demons. You tame them There's no ethereal entity after me. Maybe, just maybe, some autonomous entities, but I'm probably mistaken. We're both crazy, see? That's why I'm willing to try this. That's why I've acquiesced to your so-called price of admission. This child is becoming a huge problem. That's what it is. A person. To be. Unless I intervene somehow." At that, Hinanya snatched up the potion and made her way out of the building.

6. THOUGHTS ARE THINGS

Stefan. Something about the adverse effects from the supposed abortifacient Johnless made Hinanya realize how often her mind now forwarded to thinking Stefan only in terms of his gun, not the boy himself.

Collapsed on top of her toilet bowl, her floor peppered with dead roaches she had yet to pick up, Hinanya threw up again. It seemed that all of the Johnless within her was gone.

Uncle Rawls, Varliot, Wenin. They all knew the same things. Felix and Shaun. Stefan.

From the kitchen, Hinanya heard a broom hit the floor.

"What the fuck," she murmured. She was unable to investigate the noise.

Years after the despair of leaving New Orleans and her final encounter with Uncle Rawls, his many prophecies seemed to come to fruition. Life took on a more sinister quality. The move to Minnesota catalyzed her parents to give birth to Taylor, a development Hinanya resented. Life had changed then settled.

For three years, Stefan had just been another boy in her grade. What changed was a question he'd asked her the day of a school presentation where Hinanya had to go up and read a paper she'd written. The topic was if you could change one thing about your life, what would it be? Hinanya railed against Hurricane Katrina and how it had ruined her life and how she was afraid she'd never see her home again.

Hinanya slammed a fist into the floor. She caught a splinter for the trouble.

They had been friends. Stefan was truly broken, constantly persecuted in school for being gay. Hinanya would stand up for him. They were prime targets, the fag and the fat-ass.

It was all there—the awful rush, the simmering suicidal ideation, the suffering brought on by the unexplained pregnancy.

The splinter was out, and she was bleeding.

Yes, she'd benefited greatly from knowing Stefan. But that initial contact, before she knew him before the friendship that died with him blossomed, it all began with a single question.

"How could I help you get back to New Orleans?" Stefan had asked her.

Hinanya, at the time full of hate, conjured a nastily sarcastic thought she'd never say aloud. She didn't know Stefan, but she hated everything automatically. It was an irrational tick. She had thought to herself then and there: *You can kill yourself.*

7. ANOTHER

Three days after surviving the Johnless, Hinanya sat through a tirade from Dr. Sierpiński in the examining room where they had met.

"Yes, you moron, you're still pregnant, and you have nearly killed yourself! You need to be checked in and hooked up right away!"

"Why?"

"You're clearly malnourished. Dehydrated. I don't even know how you walked over here."

"I enjoy walking," Hinanya said in a serene reverie.

"You're covered in blood."

"It hurts, and I apologized to myself."

After Hinanya was brought into a bed found and given an IV, Dr. Sierpiński continued to scold her."Focus on getting better. You're eight months pregnant."

"Yeah, about that..."

"What?" the woman asked.

"Drugs."

"Huh?"

"I took some."

Dr. Sierpiński's hands rose to her face. "What?"

"I wanted to induce a miscarriage, but obviously, I should have kept my receipt."

"You're not right, Hinanya! Jesus. What was it?"

"I don't know. It was called Johnless. Kind of sickening. Think it was tinged with some psychedelics, you know?"

"You must realize this may have consequences for your baby."

"Duh. I didn't want to be pregnant anymore."

"Reality check, Hinanya—this whole giving birth thing, it's happening."

"But I don't wanna baby, doctor."

"We've already been through this, Hinanya. Give it up, but don't try to kill yourself getting rid of it." Dr. Sierpiński sighed.

"There's more," Hinanya said, feeling uncommonly loose. "Before I knew. Drugs."

"What else...?"

"It's a secret."

"Tell me."

Hinanya put her fingers to her lips. She gave the doctor a comical look and said, "Shhh. So, my sister, she ran away from home for whatever reason. She's coming to visit me. The thing is, I don't even want to see her. At all. I hope she doesn't make it. I don't care how. If she calls me, and I pick up somehow, I'll tell her... you know what I'll tell her? Not the whole truth but enough. I'll tell her there's trouble here. To do what I tell her or else. Or else I'll tell her about the candy water. The candy water, Dr. Sierpiński!"

"Oh no," Dr. Sierpiński spoke with trepidation. "No. You don't mean?"

"Yes!"

"8IL?"

Hinanya was thrust from her tirade against her sister. She regarded Dr. Sierpiński with a stony gaze. "Huh?"

"8IL. The new illicit substances that have been revolving around New Orleans. Did you take that?"

"Not today."

"But you do know what I'm talking about," Dr. Sierpiński said firmly. "When?"

Hinanya found she couldn't dance around Dr. Sierpiński's interrogation, try as she might. "A few months ago. It was only once. Why? How do you know about it? I'm not on it now."

Dr. Sierpiński discontinued scribbling on her clipboard and pulled up the chair next to Hinanya's bed. "Only once goes a long way in explaining your situation."

"What do you mean?"

"Hinanya, 8IL is a highly experimental compound. Almost nothing is known about it... nothing good, anyway. God, this child's in serious peril."

"Doctor, how do you know about the 8IL? That's a very clandestine matter."

Dr. Sierpiński didn't blink for some time. "Because I encountered someone just like you awhile back. A girl who'd taken 8IL two months prior and was eight months pregnant."

Hinanya jolted upright. "What?!"

"Yes."

"You need to help me find her, Dr. Sierpiński. I need to speak with her."

"I can't do that, Hinanya. That would violate her privacy."

"Don't say that. Come on. I need all the help we can get. What's going on, what do you know?"

"Only that this young lady's circumstances were just as yours were. Didn't realize she was pregnant. She was a party girl too."

"I'm not a party girl. I just experimented once. Oh, I mean the Johnless was out of absolute necessity. And what you're trying to say is she gave birth, and the baby came out wrong."

"I'm not saying that."

"Just tell me what happened, no names," pleaded Hinanya.

"I can tell you everything I know."

Hinanya obliged her, feeling light-headed in the process of nodding.

192

"Okay, I'll do it as soon as you're checked out and healthy." Dr. Sierpiński rose to walk out.

"Wait, no!"

"This is how you're getting the information. Are you listening? Get better. Start taking care of yourself. Because I know she'll want to help you. But not if you're like this. Only if you're willing to help yourself."

As Dr. Sierpiński left the room, Hinanya could have sworn she'd heard a woman mutter after they had finished talking, but Hinanya couldn't make the words out. They might as well have been from autonomous entities.

8. THE QUESTION

The day after man managed to overcome mortality, dying would become fashionable. In a universe devoid of meaning, the posh futurist notions he espoused to his class at the university were fantasies of his, nothing he actually bought into. In all actuality, Arie was dying. If man did one day conquer death, it would be long after Arie was already gone.

The tall man was steeped over his office bookshelf, putting away his sculptures. Projects he'd crafted that would outlast him.

He chipped away at them in his garage whenever he could, but there were seventeen of his favorite pieces he had created that were decorations for his office. Those sculptors he was boxing would join his others in the garage, all of them measuring part of his existence, his worth. Summer had come, and Arie would have more time to tinker. He didn't lament the loss of his office. Nothing was ever lost.

"Professor Schorel?" a voice from behind him asked.

Arie turned to see one of his pupils with a few pages stapled together in his hand. "Hello, Max. Please, take a seat. What's on your mind?"

"I wanted to ask you about some things from your last lecture."

"Please do."

"So you said heaven may have been our ancestor's fantasy, but that shouldn't stop us from trying to actually create it."

"We'd have to merge with machines, and then something like that could be possible, yes."

"And that resolves the problem of man's great problem with incompletion. Many authors and scientists leave problems behind, but we could those people back in a sense."

"Sure," Arie said as Max sat down. "Please don't mind me, but if I don't clear this office today, the janitors will just toss my things."

"No problem at all, professor. It's a lot of hopeful speculation to me, this metaphysical stuff we all seem to desire."

"There's a single question, with only five possible answers that I can imagine. The question is, is there an apprehensible metaphysical state of being beyond that of a human? A substructure all things we cannot see?

"The first possible answer is: Yes, there is a metaphysical substructure to the universe, but man, no matter how advanced of body, mind, and spirit he becomes or what tools he uses, can never reach it.

"Second: Yes, there is a metaphysical substructure to the universe, but man can only access it through special circumstances. In this case, access would be provided via a person's soul—meaning he would have to part from his body, whether temporarily or permanently. It is not sufficient that some

195

people claim to have had out-of-body experiences. Those fringe events, if truly possible, should be readily accessible and available to all people who seek out such an experience.

"Third: The question is indeterminate. We are unable to reach a consensus on what consciousness is. That seems to be the stepping stone to answer this other question. But though we might one day all agree on what consciousness is, we could still remain able to furnish a yes or no to the initial question we are asking.

"Fourth: No, there is no reality that exists beyond the confines and conception of humanity's imagination in longing to be more than just a mortal body and brain. So then we ought to regard it as a fantasy best left behind. A waste of time relative to other pursuits and human projects.

"And lastly: No, there is nothing metaphysical that exists beyond the confines of humanity's imagination in longing to be more than just a mortal body and brain, at present awareness. But then we would only need to manufacture an approximation of it through future technology."

"Wow, that's a lot to digest," Max said.

"The light of a man's mortality shines brightest when he does not question it. Me, I'm nearing the end. I'm content. As content as you might expect."

"Yes," Max said. "We still deal with death the same ways our ancestors did. But all this talk about conquering death, it feels very dependent on faith."

"It is. But science is in there too. They weren't always so separate. I think that in the future people will be able to blend then safely again for the most comprehensive picture of the truth."

"Yet if we fail to do as you predict and unite, then what other hope do we have? The damage we caused would be irreversible."

"Once I was dreaming, Max. I was in floating in space. A string was coming out of my forehead, and I was being pulled along. Strange beings approached me. They asked me, what is it you'd like to know? I told them it was a nice offer, but I don't want to know anything. They laughed, amused." Arie added sternly, "And not at me."

"I see," said Max.

"We like you, they said. You're different. What I'm getting at is, sometimes, it's fine to speculate, but ultimately if you're so hell-bent on definitive answers, you'll probably go mad. Enlightenment is not our right. Existence is. For a time. Then, as far as I'm concerned, nothingness is also our right."

9. FINITE BLESSINGS

The horror of Hinanya's condition propelled her to attend church with Sasha and Kurt. And to her surprise, the service wasn't that bad. In fact, Hinanya found herself enjoying it. It was the first time in months she'd dressed up nice, in a maternity dress provided by Sasha. The female preacher began in an unassuming manner with an affable greeting. It was a Unitarian Universalist church, which Hinanya realized made all the difference. A short time into the speech, the preacher made a reference to being gay. There were no guilt trips or threats, only a dialogue infused with humanist elements.

"All of us want to find solace in others before we assess the depths of ourselves. And you know, it's fine to find that solace, it's definitely something we all know we need, but sometimes we need to search within ourselves before we look elsewhere. To accept the consequences of making our own decisions. Maybe there is no higher authority than our own sense of right and wrong.

"Then you might come to ask yourself, what happens to people's motivations when they no longer believe in heaven? That's a lot of unpleasant work to be done without God. You have the government with their laws, but too can clash within one's own moral compass.

"Would you think that was something wrong with murder if your parents or your government hadn't told you you'd be punished? In certain contexts, murder can be something we reward. Step away from both sides and see the need to understand yourself. We do not have a unified global moral system because religions are in constant warfare and disagreement. I urge people to think about these things, because crafting secular morality is a worthwhile chore.

"Now, the motivation is easy to marshal, but it dies so quickly without reinforcement. It may take days, months, years for it to come in a form you can utilize. You may falter in your mission once you've built some momentum... but then you just keep right on going. The present is all we are guaranteed. Glory is not a blessing, but something to be earned. The same goes for grace. You don't just get it. You earn it. Because if you want something, you don't just get it or take it or want it. You earn—blessings are to be counted, earnings are to be achieved."

Hinanya took a look around the congregation. It was not adorned with many idols or statues, but above the pulpit was a reprint of Juche's painting *To Fallen*. Hinanya had seen it a few times before, in Sasha's apartment. But the one in the church seemed different than the one she'd seen at Sasha's. For the rest of her time there, she was tempted to approach the piece.

Shortly after, the church sang hymns. Then each new member of the audience was encouraged to introduce themselves. Hinanya did not flinch. "My name is Hinanya. I'm eight months pregnant. Things have been difficult, and I do not have any idea what I'm doing but—" she paused as her mind went blank. Then she confessed to the crowd. "That's what you're supposed to say, right? Life sucks, but... well, I don't have any *but* to offer up. I'm confused with the way things are, and I think it's all we've got. It seems like you all know better and that's good. I'm going to have a seat now."

The audience clapped. Kurt clapped a hand on her shoulder as she sat down again. Hinanya had the support of the entire room. She looked over each of them. They all looked so familiar... one by one, each of them someone she thought she'd seen around the city before.

Other writers, grocery store cashiers, students from the university. There was Professor Schorel. And... Dr. Sierpiński? So many faces she'd come into direct or indirect contact with. How could this distinct combination of people be gathered here around here?

Hinanya looked at Sasha and Kurt. "I have to go."

"Okay, Hinanya," Sasha said. "We all love you."

"Yeah, see?" Kurt asked. "We're all going to be okay."

"The woman, that woman preaching," Hinanya said, the recognition swallowing her. "It didn't hit me until now. But that... I knew her from before."

"Oh yeah? Do tell."

Hinanya was going to say it was Stefan's mother, but instead she exited the church hyperventilating. Nobody stopped her. They hardly acknowledged the commotion. They only began to sing again.

10. DUALITY

The woman, Mihanna, had dark pupils that seemed to see beyond, into what Hinanya may have supposed was the underlying current of the world. In that look, Hinanya recognized another of her kind, a user of 8IL.

The two didn't smile at one another nor furnish a greeting. Their dead expressions were mutual, and any pretense was obliterated.

"I don't want to talk for long, so I won't," Mihanna said with a brusque tone.

"And I don't want to take up your time."

"Well, shit, you will."

"I'm Hinanya."

"And you already know my name. Let's get this over with. Don't know what you want to know, but I'll tell you anythin' you like that I can say for sure about. Fair?"

"Fair."

"Before we get goin', come inside. It's hot as New Orleans out here."

Hinanya entered the house, into a front room, where she was instructed to take off her shoes.

"And your mask," Mihanna said in front of Hinanya without turning to look at her.

"Huh?"

"Everyone got one, Hinanya. You only comin' around here once, I can promise you that. So whatever you need to talk about, be ready to talk about it."

Hinanya was led to the couch and nearly collapsed onto it. Mihanna sat on an armchair across from her. Between them was a tea set, ready to be served.

"I was hopin' you'd indulge," Mihanna said, eyes cast over the contents of the table.

Mihanna saw the indignation on Hinanya's face and said, "Relax. It's just Chamomile. Sorry, I'm out of Pennyroyal."

"Funny. I'll pass regardless. Look, Mihanna, it was good of you to see me. I need to know what happened to you. Flat out."

"Hinanya, the same thing happened to us both. Found out about the latest drug—oh, how cool, 8IL, out-of-body experience. Spent months seekin' it out because it's so rare and new. Found it. Took it. Come out mostly disappointed to find out that I'm pregnant."

"Is it something in the mixture?" Hinanya wondered.

"No, Hinanya. Or I doubt it, okay? It's pretty impossible to get pregnant that way."

"How did you learn about 8IL?" Hinanya asked.

"I was born just outside of Slidell. It was a stormy night. They say a tree outside of the hospital got struck by lightnin' the very moment I came out. Do you think there's somethin' to that?"

"No." The couch was very comfortable, and she found herself sinking into it more, burdened by her great weight. She then noticed the baby pictures. The life Mihanna was portraying to her through the home. The way Mihanna seemed to accept it all seemed like a threat to Hinanya.

"Maybe not. But the lightnin' could have hit somewhere else, and I would be dead, you know? The timin' there," Mihanna snapped her fingers and then clapped both of her hands together. "I grew up around here. Drugs are popular. I just knew the right people. Or maybe the wrong ones."

"Have you met Wenin?"

"Can't meet someone who ain't real," clarified Mihanna.

"What?"

"Wenin is a concept. Not a person... You don't meet Wenin. You're askin' who when you need to be askin' what."

"Then who makes 8IL? Why hasn't it gone beyond New Orleans?"

"But it has. It wasn't even created entirely here, Hinanya. It just found a place here."

"Who makes it, Mihanna?"

"You're not thinkin' about this the proper way. It's already been made. It's out there, floatin' around."

"Are there more like us?"

"Most don't make it through after... Suicide, you know."

"Do they all get pregnant?"

Mihanna nodded. "Even the men."

Hinanya closed her eyes in frustration. "Don't taunt me. Look, I need to know what's going on."

"Excuse me, no. I did not mean it like that at all. You see, when you say pregnant... it's somewhat open, is all. You and I became pregnant with an actual baby. Yes, a baby. Others came away from it with ideas. Like, instead of bearin' life, they decided to take life away. That's all I meant. Only the universe would be so quick to call it."

"Fine. But how did your baby come out?"

"My baby?" Mihanna asked, nonplussed.

"You decided to have it, I'm guessing. After the unexpected pregnancy. The 8IL. Was the baby okay?"

"Fine, fine. But didn't you know? This—" Mihanna gestured around the room with her hands to the pictures. Hinanya wasn't able to get a good look, but as Mihanna said it, it hit her. "It happened to me twice. My man and I used to pal around all these crazy ones in New Orleans East. Yeah, I had a man. We met in elementary school and started fuckin' by middle. A love like

200

that, you know?"

"Sure," Hinanya said tersely.

"But we always used protection. I mean every time. We started out all right, just blazin' up with weed. Then he suggested other shit. Open your mind, he'd said. I wanted to draw a line somewhere, but that's just how we ended up. Dumb lovers. One day, he brought it. Enough for the both of us in that weird Teeny-shaped container. I loved those things growin' up."

"How long ago was this?"

"2005."

"Were the babies his?"

"The first one was."

"So you two must have made a mistake on 8IL, and you don't remember."

"Hinanya, I remember every second of that high. We didn't fuck. We couldn't have. Unless it gives you false memories."

"I haven't had sex, Mihanna."

"That's what I was gettin' around to. See, the first time around, I had my man and shit. The second time, I was single."

"This is getting me nowhere."

"What did you expect, Hinanya? I don't know what happened to me either. We're like the only two girls who've had this experience. Ain't like we can go to the police about it, right?"

"Yeah," Hinanya said, thinking about the horror the church had become. Maybe she needed to get as far away from New Orleans as possible.

"Mihanna, you need to help me get to this Wenin. Whatever it is. I need to get closer. To know what this is all about."

"I wish I could help you, Hinanya. But the first time around, my man brought the 8IL over. Then he started actin' funny. Disappeared. I had no contact wit' no Wenin people. I had the first kid, tried to make ends meet. After it was over, I was stayin' with my mom for a bit, and one day, a package gets dropped off... I think it was from him. Rawls, that ass."

Hinanya suppressed herself. "That was his name, huh? Rawls?"

"Yeah. His nickname, really. The second dose... I don't know why I took it. I guess I thought I'd see him somehow. But I didn't. I only got pregnant again."

"I... I, uhm, I have to go."

"Already?" Mihanna asked.

"I didn't want to take up your time, and I have," Hinanya said, squirming to get up. "It's clear—" Hinanya was panting. "You can't help me."

"Let me help you up, at least," Mihanna said, also rising.

"No, no. That's okay. I got it. Thank you, Mihanna."

"You're welcome. Now, you know you can't come around here again, right?"

"Yeah, yeah, no problem."

"I don't want nothin' to do with this shit anymore. I don't want to see what kind of trouble you get into from here."

"I understand." Hinanya thrust herself out into the desolate New Orleans street.

11. The Beating

Several minutes after her meeting with Mihanna, Hinanya was more lost than ever. This took her invariably down some alleyway, which seemed to be calm enough until whatever was after her, at last, emerged into a haze without mercy or pathos.

"Hinanya," said slurring voice from deeper into the alleyway.

It was Caso. The man she'd shot and tried to kill. He was on his feet, barely able to walk. He wore red satin pajamas and leaned against crutches.

"Reciprocity, baby." Two men burst from behind a dumpster where Hinanya saw a scooter was parked. But she was ready. She had the Glock. Seeing them all cower, she slammed the butt of it into the first challenger and elbowed his skull.

As she whirled around the second opponent, she knew Caso had an opening to shoot her if he saw fit. There was some failure in her that prevented her from firing on him again. And he seemed to sense it.

"Why did you let me live?" Caso asked.

"Trust me, that was an accident."

"You pretty fat, huh? Damn."

Hinanya had tried to kill Caso that night, but she'd flinched. She hadn't been able to save Shaun. She was just in danger and defending herself. But she was winded, worn down. More of Caso's people came on her, and she felt overwhelmed. Each person she'd knock out made her wonder why they hadn't just shot her yet.

"You can't have this gun, Caso. I need it! It's not yours."

"I don't much care about that these days. It's funny since you shot me, Hinanya. Shifted priorities and all that."

A primordial rage awoke in her. "I'm pregnant!" Hinanya spun around to strike two of her assailants. There was one more still standing, demanding her blood. First Hinanya leaped into him with a head-butt, and then she unfurled the fingers from her right hand and dug them into the man's eye socket, knocking him over.

"Savage!" Caso called out as if it was all in good fun.

At least a dozen people around her writhing on the ground in pain. Exhausted, Hinanya put down her bloody fists for a time and let them do as they pleased to her.

"Beat me," Hinanya muttered through punches to the jaw.

In surrendering, she quickly lost the fight. She fell to the ground, and they began trampling her. They kicked her, and she relished it. The suffering was an ecstasy.

"Stop!" Caso demanded.

She felt the blows subside and heard Caso's crutches smacking against the pavement.

Using the moment for reflection, Hinanya anticipated Caso wanted to land the killing blow. So she lashed out, and the fighting began anew. In standing up, she was terribly off balance but able to fight the others back with brutal aikido locks and precise hits to pressure points. An aisle began to clear between Hinanya and Caso. They saw one another face to face. Hinanya wondered what she'd do to this tireless man, who'd hunted her down like an animal for stealing back what was her friend's property, who'd sold his own brother down the river for a shot at her, and who'd orchestrated the murder of Shaun.

"You are—" Hinanya lost her words as two cars pulled up. At first, Hinanya thought it was more of Caso's people. But then she saw they were SUVs. Cop cars, without their sirens turned on.

"You done now, Hinanya," Caso said.

Cornered, Hinanya threw up her hands, before the officers were out of the vehicle and demanding her to put her hands up, their pistols drawn and ready to fire.

12. FATHERHOOD

In no hurry, Arie made his way down St. Claude Avenue on his way home from another dismal night at Buckland's. The clouds in the sky teased a cooling rain Arie would welcome. No matter what, he planned on stretching out. He was so giddy that he lit his first cigarette in four years. Arie had never been addicted. Addicts were pathetic to him. He'd only been one kind of addict in his life, an alcoholic. But that was a long time ago. He'd effectively killed the man he used to be. The younger incarnation of himself had gone into those drunken years and the idyllic hero only to come out a tragedy, a father not only to his first sculptures but also to his son. He was now overworked, underpaid, and under-appreciated.

Arie got it into his head to call his son. The time was right. They hadn't spoken in a few weeks, but that was because nothing had changed.

In retrieving the phone from his pocket and dialing the number, there was no hesitation. The only delay came when he heard Gregory's voice from the other end.

"Hey, kid, what's going on? Oh yeah? Well, fuck New Orleans, right? No, I was just walking home. I suppose. Will you be back on time? No, I mean you're as always under no obligation. Greg, this is important to me *because* I'm doing it on your behalf!" The conversation continued in a sour manner from there.

Arie deviated from his course home. Sweat accumulated on his palms and the small of his back anew as he increased the pace of his step.

After hanging up on his son, Arie noted the first sign of drizzling from above. The first beckoned the second, and soon, the sky was balling its eyes out.

The sudden downpour coincided with Arie going into a full run, discarding his backpack in the shoulder of the road. He didn't return for it. Instead, he proceeded across the landing dock of a Walgreen's, sighting the telltale flash of wrongdoing—the red and blue hues casting their beams against the walls and buildings stoic against the calamity. The scene Arie saw had its players contained within the perimeter of the two police cars, each diagonally parked to enclose them within. Arie dared to get closer to confirm, slowing down with great care, and then squeezed through the two police cars with his arms up.

Three cops were pointing their guns at the girl—Hinanya Ven. The misfit who'd hijacked his lectures. The tormented one waiting in line for transcendence as if it was deli meat. With his arrival, the cops twisted their heads while keeping their guns aimed squarely at Hinanya. Caso's men were on the ground at the cop's mercy as well.

"Sir, vacate the area immediately or else—" one of the cops, a portly man began to speak. Arie lowered his left arm slightly while curving his wrist to the cop. The hand became a pantomime gun. Any resistance was quickly stripped away as the man's own gun mimicked the motion of Arie's fake one in a parallel line with an endpoint at the left brick wall of the alleyway. Arie pulled his trigger and imitated recoil. The portly man did not fire his gun but dropped it while gazing at his open hand, then fell to the pavement headfirst. But all that happened was his forehead clashed with the ground and split wide open with all the force he was able to muster.

The other two policemen reacted in shock, targeting their weapons at Arie before the portly man slammed onto his face. But Arie had another hand, and with it, he repeated the ritual. Then again with his left hand, still seeming to tremble from the imaginary recoil. All three cops fell the same way, their foreheads expelling blood and gray matter.

For the first time, Arie regarded Hinanya, who was the only one still standing. Arie mimed unloading the imaginary gun then discarded then.

"Hello," Arie said with a shy wave.

Those on the ground fled in all directions as if a mighty gust had blown them away like leaves. Hinanya was not fazed and remained where she was.

"You sure were about to be arrested for the attempted murder of that guy," Arie said with a tinge of amusement, pointing over to the stumbling Caso. He was one of the people who remained.

The girl turned her head to Caso, who nodded, not at all alarmed at Arie's intervention.

The train whistle blew out into the night. Hinanya's cue.

"So I get it," Arie began, "you're speechless. The thing is, you aren't safe just yet. We've got to get out of here—got it?"

"Who are you?" Hinanya asked, peering down at the men who'd almost taken her away.

"Oh please, Hinanya. Let's just go."

13. BOUNDARY UNFURLED

It felt as if Hinanya was about to be ripped from reality. The worst awful rush she could remember took over her body. And though it had come from the answers she'd been after, it was unbearable in the moment of discovery. The injuries on her body from the fight and the illness in her belly were of no sensational consequence as she tried to return into some semblance of stability. She felt each thought as an assailant. Her questions were measured by the raindrops that pelted her. From their position pinned down from the police cars, the mysterious man thrust Hinanya over to the passenger side of the cop car. She knew him.

"You're that professor! From the college, from the church!"

He bolted to the driver's seat and flipped the sirens off. "Please. Sit down. It would be a grave mistake to remain here, considering." The professor rotated his left wrist, gesturing to the unconscious police.

"Them too, professor! They're after me," Hinanya said, referring to Caso and his accomplices.

"Not quite," the professor said as the men stepped off the wall and hopped into the back seat.

"You're saying... they're with you?" Hinanya asked.

"They're under orders as liaisons not to do what they've been trying to do."

"Yes, indeed," Caso said. "We mean you no harm in that way any longer."

Caso's usual vernacular had changed into something far more sophisticated. Hinanya accepted the situation and closed the door to the cop car. The professor—

"Wait, sir. What is your name?" Hinanya asked the driver.

"Arie Schorel."

"Doctor," one of Caso's accomplices amended.

"Yes. But, guys, don't worry about that."

"We don't."

"More than you realize," Arie said with a smile.

Hinanya, having no inclination to do so, smiled in turn. He was a delightful man, an uplifting force. If she had forgotten how to smile, it seemed as though Arie would have been able to show her how. "I greatly appreciated the presentation and content of your lectures, sir."

"Ah, but you were no student of mine. You stole in. I find that sad. Sad that my neurological magic can only work to harm, not help." Arie started rubbing his chin with his free hand, stroking against stubble.

"I don't get why I'm here," Hinanya said. She did feel a sense of relief, but she couldn't say why.

"We're not here, we're going there," Arie said, pointing to the oncoming train tracks. A few blocks later, Arie pulled over, and they all scrambled into the bed of a truck as the train made its nightly journey out of New Orleans. Caso offered a hand to Hinanya, and she hesitated.

"I thought we already settled this," Arie said with a slight grumble. "You've done well, but you've gone as far as you can on your own. That's why you sought out a doctor, why you confided in Kurt and Sasha."

"How the hell do you know all this?"

"You've left quite a pile of creations and destruction in your wake. Not sure how the equation's going to balance. Now the police don't have your name or address, but they will. They'll figure out you were at the murder scene. Caso here set you up as the fall guy, I mean girl, for Shaun."

"I sure have!" Caso said, delighted.

"The only chance you have is to hop on this truck and get out of here. Right now."

"But where are we going?"

"Where we make it," Arie said. "Where you can hear the whole story."

"Basically," said one of Caso's cohorts.

"Shut the fuck up, Anthony!" Arie chastised. "Hinanya, I want to get you away."

"Wenin," Hinanya said, the only affirmation out of her mouth in a long time.

"Ha-ha. Almost, girl. Nearly, that is!"

Hinanya was hoisted into the beat-up truck. It sped up the road adjacent to the train.

14. DEFENSELESS

When Arie indicated they were in a hurry, Hinanya didn't think he meant it was because they were about to miss the train. But that was, in fact, the case. The truck followed alongside the train for a few minutes before the others indicated they would need to hop the train.

"We miss this one, there's no other way to where we're going for a while," Arie said.

"Why didn't you come for me sooner?" Hinanya asked.

"I will be happy to answer most of your questions, but the thing is we need to get on that freight train first. Then we'll have to make an agreement."

Hinanya sighed, looking at the motion between the truck and the train.

"We're going to wait for the right time. It's going to stop very soon," Arie said.

"So are you going to need help?" one of Caso's accomplices asked Hinanya.

"Uhm, if you don't want me to splat onto the road, yes," Hinanya said.

"We definitely wouldn't favor such an outcome. But usually, you are so self-sufficient," countered Caso.

Hinanya shot an ugly look at the man, baffled as to the change in him. For months the man had been after her. Now it seemed he couldn't care less about the weapon she'd taken from it. It still sat on her side in an open-carry fashion.

The time came. They got out of the truck and made it into the train. When Hinanya got on it was rough because the train was still moving a little. It felt as if she had twisted her ankle.

Following a few minutes of assessing the damage to Hinanya's heel, it was determined she was still able to walk.

"At least we're well on our way," said Arie.

"Yeah, but we still gotta get her back out when we get there," Anthony said skeptically.

"What is this place you're all talking about?"

Arie exhaled with a cough. He took a few steps to look out into the passing darkness. "I've already told you. We made the 8IL there. This is what you wanted. I know it."

"Yes. But *how* is what I want to know."

"Listen, we're going to be there in a bit later. I'll permit you to ask me one question right now which I will answer—"

"Where—"

"Halt!" Arie raised his hand to silence her. "I will pick the question. And answer it. It's something you want to know very much, but it's not the primary thing on your mind. I need you to agree to something first. Let's just help each other out here. I will begin by answering a single question, with the assurance that I will continue answering questions of your choosing. But now until we arrive. And provided that you agree that you will not kill yourself prior to the delivery of your child."

Hinanya was unable to take it in stride. "Fuck you!"

"Mhm. Right. Yeah. I see that. But that's the price of admission, Hinanya. You see this baby to term. Let me clarify what this means. You see *this* baby to completion. It doesn't have to be *your* baby. Got me here?"

"I never intended to see this thing born," Hinanya said. "I've never wanted it. How did you do it? What did you do to me?"

"What did I say about questions? Hey, just agree, and maybe that'll be the question I answer for you. You just don't know. Because you deem it necessary to be obstinate. In reality, you have no choice other than compliance here."

"Or suicide, as you so eloquently pointed out."

"Yeah, but you've wanted to off yourself all along, we both know that. What difference does a few more weeks and an infant you have zero investment in the matter?"

Hinanya gritted her teeth. "I will... see this thing to term."

"Okay, but if you pull anything slightly suicidal, even if it's just a fake-in for an attempt to seize control of your enormously fucked-up situation, you're going to be numb and strapped into a hospital bed for the duration of your pregnancy. I've been strapped, Hinanya. It *ain't* fun."

"I agree."

Arie clapped his hands together, and the three others in the room clapped after like an echo. "Groovy! So, the question I select to be answered first is: Whatever became of dear ole' Uncle Rawls?"

Hinanya despised the bargain she had made but was transfixed upon Arie. The man turned from the world passing by outside to look at her. He drew closer and stood above her the entire time he answered the one question.

"He became quite a sad statistic, to be frank. Another sickening statistic. Like many of the victims, he not doing anything remotely illegal. There's just some strange boiling racial impulse. Roland Avery a.k.a. your Uncle Rawls was strolling down North Roman Street several weeks after Hurricane Katrina. Yes, he survived. But the cops heard a transmission to be on the lookout for an African-American. The cruiser pulled up on Rawls, decided he was not the man they were looking for, but during a routine pat-down, he admitted being armed. Now, he had a permit for it. Still, they forced him to the ground, and he was shot. Their claim was that he was reaching for his firearm. Quite a fabrication, I'd say. In the plastic bag he'd been holding there were eggs and baby formula. Oh and the receipt. You want to know the worst of it,

Hinanya? Charges were dropped entirely for your mentor's murder. And it happens like that a lot, doesn't it? Sometimes, the guy isn't even armed. Just black."

Hinanya sat through the account passively, then broke down and began crying.

"Yes, he was defenseless. Like Shaun. But not like Stefan, who chose to die."

This man had been watching her, and there was no telling for how long. This was who had been controlling her actions. She wanted to ask more, but she knew it would do no good.

"Can I ask you some questions, Hinanya?" Arie asked, pulling up a broken milk crate and sliding it close to her. "I'll totally pay you back."

"Fine."

"It bothers you, doesn't it? That the people you care about are taken in an instant, and there is no justice."

"It was him!" Hinanya said, throwing her hands out to Caso. "He was going after me, and Shaun was in the way."

"To be honest, Hinanya, it's much more complicated than that," Caso said with somber tone. "But I mean, if you're at all feeling off about that, why didn't you come forward when you burned down Devon Dixon Riley?"

Hinanya said nothing, unable to counter.

Arie snapped his fingers, and Hinanya felt her attention shift to the man's gaunt face. It felt imperative to her then to watch and listen to the man. "Look, answer my questions. Please. You never know what'll happen; we live in an interesting place."

"It's hard turning into a person, isn't it?" one of Caso's associates mumbled, pretending to shove against Anthony. Hinanya snorted derisively.

"So you don't like it when people who have done nothing wrong are murdered."

"Who does?" Hinanya argued.

"Some people. I ask for clarification because I see you seem to have been willing to kill a person, though you have not entirely gone through with it. But man, have you been close."

"Anytime I've applied lethal measures in a confrontation it was a matter of life and death."

"Oh, is that so, Hinanya?"

"Yes. That's what Uncle Rawls taught me. To only take a life when it's absolutely necessary. When there is no other course of action. When it's them or you."

Arie chuckled to himself. "You are spouting contradiction, though. What have you done wrong that you should take your own life?"

Something about Arie made her drop any pretenses and inhibitions. "This life seems to be the totality of my existence. It is beyond my ability to handle. Any moment of joy is compounded with suffering and confusion that overwhelms any benefit of being alive in the here, and the now I see. So if this is all there is, I don't want any more of it. And hey, if there is some greater beyond, I would like to know. As it has to be better than this."

"So not only are you obsessed with ending your own life, but you constantly put yourself into a position where you are liable to be murdered. In either case, your death drive is the same, apparent, and also does not mesh with what I'm hearing you say now."

"How do you figure?"

"You've willed the death of innocents before."

"Never!" Hinanya said. "NO. I have not. If you've been watching me, you'd know that above all else."

Arie looked at his watch. "It's quite late. Do you know where your sister is, Hinanya?"

"What does Taylor have to do with this?"

Arie spoke on with a new zeal. "I understand you won't want to, but once again, the price of admission must be paid. Sacrificing your ignorance for knowledge is what makes knowledge so valuable. But not useful. Hinanya, I myself already know the truth. But I like to test people and ask like I don't on occasion. I ask them something I already know the answer to. They don't know that I know, see? If they can tell the truth to me, well, I savor them. But if they lie in that instance, I know, and they are exposed from then on. It could be something trivial I set them up with. In your case, it seems you have lied to me about something massive."

"No," Hinanya said.

"Yep. You're a hypocrite. Taylor adores you more than the world, despite how truly ruined you are."

Hinanya swallowed from a dry throat. She assessed her surroundings. Arie, Caso, and the others didn't seem to be surrounding her, but instead, just hovering about. Their eyes and stillness were more threatening than any physical moves to hurt her.

"As a matter of fact, the first truly independent decision Taylor ever made was to run away from home to find you. Because she was worried about you. Now, don't worry. She is fine, and more importantly, ignorant of the fact that you're wanted for the murder of Shaun. No, she just wants to talk to you. Right now. Call Taylor!" Arie shouted to one of the others. "You're going to talk to your sister. Because what about her? If you want to go to the 8IL facility and learn the truth, then you're going to tell your sister what you did. If you can fess up to her, then I will fess up to you."

"It's ringing," said Caso, a cell phone against his ear.

"I can't," Hinanya protested. "This is too much. Please stop. I don't—"

Caso shoved a phone into Hinanya's hand.

"Hello?" Taylor's voice murmured.

Hinanya shut her eyes as not to see the others and brought the phone to her ears.

15. CANDY WATER

"Finally!" Taylor exclaimed. "I've been trying to get a hold of you for months. I ran away from home. I couldn't take Mom and Dad anymore. I'm coming to see you. I'm almost there."

"New Orleans?" Hinanya asked patiently.

"Yes. I'm almost there. I wanted to see you. You disappeared. I know you don't really think of me much, but I love you, and I think we should work together."

"Taylor, you're not even in harmony with yourself. This is insane. How did you get from Mankato to—wherever are you now?"

"Arkansas," Taylor stated with a sense of pride.

"Wow, you got far."

"All for you, sis. What's been going on with you? You move all the way down there, and then say you aren't even in school, and then you shut your phone off... You don't even have any social media! You're a ghost, but it's like I'm more afraid *for* you than I am *of* you."

Hinanya saw Arie and others looking down at her, wanting her to get on with it. "Look, that's not important. I'm pretty sure I'm fine. Been busy with things. What was so bad that you had to leave?"

"It's like, I don't know. See, part of it was how they acted once you were gone. But I managed. Then, when you cut communications with us, Mom and Dad went ballistic. Just completely going after everything I did. If it was wrong, I'd get hell. If it was right, they'd say I only did it for selfish reasons. They talked a lot about selfishness. How I'm like you."

Hinanya felt a kinship with her sister then. "They can be cold. Dim-witted. But they aren't abusive. You have to go back. Bad parents are better than no parents at all. And I'm no parent. I can't nor do I desire to set you straight. It's not for me, Taylor."

"I know. I know you hate me—but Hinanya I'm not a child anymore. I can be an asset to you. Our parents are out of their minds. I'm telling you. It's different. It's been nearly a year. Everything's different."

"You don't understand. Taylor, there's no place for you down here. Especially not right now. Turn back, please. You're not thinking this through. You're thirteen years old."

"I'm fourteen years old!" Taylor corrected. "Look, just put me up until I figure out what needs to happen."

"You don't even have a plan?" Hinanya questioned.

"I'll see you in a few days," Taylor replied.

Hinanya saw the others looking out at the Louisiana landscape. Except for Arie, who was watching her every move. He seemed amused. Caso, on the other hand, seemed to be tense. "I can wire you some money in a day or two. But you need to use it to turn around."

"Hinanya—"

"No, Taylor. I can't deal with you right now. You're family. That doesn't mean the same thing to me as it does to you, I'm sorry. You're chaotic, and I have my own problems you're just going to make them worse. And frankly, even if I didn't, I don't want anything to do with you." Hinanya rubbed the swell of her belly—of the baby, her baby.

"I have nowhere else to go!"

"Taylor, how do you know if I wasn't lying about school, I wasn't also lying about where I was going? I'm not even in New Orleans right now."

"What?" Taylor asked, aggravated. "Don't make shit up, Hinanya. I have the envelope with your address on it. I'm going there!"

Hinanya tilted her head over to Arie, and she nodded as he gestured to do what she needed to do.

"There's danger here. I'm a danger. Taylor?"

"What?"

"I tried to kill you."

Arie smiled. Hinanya noticed for the first time he was missing a few teeth. "Excuse me?"

Hinanya closed her eyes and let out a deep breath. She didn't inhale until her recount was complete. "When you were younger, like three, or maybe four since I'm tripping up on your age, I *hated* you. You're right about that. You took all the attention from me. You know, unless I did something wrong. It felt like our parents were disregarding me entirely. That's how I remember it, but I'm sure that wasn't the case. You were born after we moved away from New Orleans. After Katrina. If it weren't for that storm, you would have never been. I loved New Orleans. I didn't want to leave. I didn't know why but maybe it was because of this. This experience of helplessness when they told me I would have a younger sister. Reality was out of my control. I was an ignorant child contaminated with hatred. I felt excluded. It was cold then, Taylor. Minnesota. Winters I'd never known I'd have to battle. My thoughts turned evil. If you were just... gone, things could be a bit easier. It was just more change than I could handle. Perhaps I was mentally ill, but I wanted you dead. I'd hovered over your crib imagining the seconds of the struggle between my hands and your tiny throat as you choked to death. How quickly it could be done. How they had no idea of the height of my malice. Whatever happened after, I wouldn't care, but it would have been worth it to tell Mom and Dad just how badly I did not want you in my life."

Taylor sounded as if she wanted to say something, but Hinanya didn't allow it. "I need to finish, Taylor. Let me finish! Do not hang up until I am done."

Arie was no longer watching Hinanya. Though she was certain he was still listening, he was preoccupied once more with the night sky.

"Instead of taking you quietly while you slept... like a baby, as they say, one day, I saw you in the kitchen. At one point weeks before I had tried to get under the sink. Mom warned me about it. I had a book in my lap. One of the Narnia ones. Mom and Dad knew I could space out entirely. She hadn't asked me to keep an eye on you that day. She was in the garden, but the garden was far away. I set the book down, and I asked you, in the vein of a loving older sister, if you wanted some candy water. I told you how tasty it was. You didn't really have many words at your disposal then. Not much of a talker. It worked in my favor. I used your little hands to open the cabinet. It was baby-proof. Together we took out the bleach. I made you drink it. Not too much, I needed to make it look like an accident. But you drank plenty. It was nasty. You started choking on your own breath. I ran from you as you were being poisoned, into the den. I waited a few seconds even, then I rushed in and witnessed little Taylor was not surviving her environment. Convulsing and vomiting, I stood over you, and you didn't even notice me. I looked the scene over, satisfied that the evidence would not point to me. My book was upturned in the den. Your suffering took you out of the room. Mom was lazy from the chardonnay and the sun. I wanted you dead, but I didn't try hard enough. I knew this was my only chance to do it surreptitiously. Even as you were writhing there on the linoleum, I found I could handle it. It was a manifestation of who I was. How I felt inside. What I thought I wanted so badly. But hey, you made it through. They saved you at the hospital. I think Mom figured out the truth at some point. She never left you alone again. Nor did she summon the nerve to call me on to watch you.

"I think you should know, I feel differently now. Indifferent to be exact. I don't hate you. I just don't care about you. I don't believe in family. I've taken it out of my life's equation. Your life doesn't matter to me. Don't come any closer to the one who almost killed you, Taylor. Go to the ones who gave you life. I've ignored my own well being. I cannot possibly care for another."

16. THE WHOLE STORY

With that, the pact was made. Arie never supposed Hinanya would falter. He had all of the leverage.

From the freight train, they made for the place known primarily in some people's paranoid imaginations.

They were dropped off along a dirt road, surrounded by swamp, and went off the path for some time until the vivacious thickets did away with the path and gave way to a slope of uneven turf. Arie stood out with open arms, the hump in the ground indicating the Wenin facility. They waited until a concussed blast of pressurized air revealed a curved slit.

"It's been a long night. Would you like to be taken to your room?" Arie asked.

"No. Arie, you told me you'd answer my questions once I got here."

"I stand by that."

"I'll sleep after I know the facts."

"That's certainly your prerogative to think that," Arie said as he stepped from the small entryway. It led to a giant steel hatch. Arie twisted it open.

From there, Arie brought them through a network of thin hallways. Some sections were unfurnished, decrepit. They were forced to wear helmets or crane their necks. Eventually, Caso and the others fell away in one of the twists and turns that became a white hallway with obsidian-shaded tiles. The walls were adorned with folders and papers in plastic bins.

"You'll be given full access to this facility while you are here, Hinanya. I will even hang on to Stefan's gun, a great privilege. We have a cubby there where you can lock it up, and you'll have the only key, I swear. No one will ever try to take that Glock away from you again. We will not harm you, as you know we have an interest in the baby and would like to facilitate its birth—which, yes, will be happening here." Arie stopped in front of a glass door and punched in the thirty-four digit numerical code. The door opened, and he let Hinanya inside. She'd been hounding him with questions all night, despite his insistence that he would not field any of them until they were both settled and seated in the room he now took her in. "So thank you for being so patient with me. I understand this has all been difficult. For everyone involved, trust me."

"You people got me pregnant," Hinanya said with vehemence.

"Yeah, I have a lot of explaining to do. I would think it'd be best to leave you be until you're able to listen with a critical and objective ear to what I have to say. Is that going to be a while, or will you calm down?"

"Fine," Hinanya said.

"Do you want any water?"

"Yes, please."

A few seconds later, a liaison stepped into the room with a tray of a dozen bottled waters. He was short, dressed in a fine suit tailored to his frame. The two immediately recognized each other, but Peb didn't acknowledge her further than that.

"Most of them are warm because we know your preference in that regard," Arie pointed out. "Although sometimes we have seen you vacillate on whether you want your water cold or not."

"So him and Caso were all just part of it?"

"Yes. Peb was actually what you'll understand to be an independent variable. When you witnessed the police carting him off, in reality, we were starting the process of turning him into a liaison."

"I'm a goddamn slave," Peb said.

"Oh, please," Arie said, his head turning to look at Peb out of the corner of his eye. "Would you have preferred to actually have been arrested? We saved your ass and got you out of trouble." Arie looked over at Hinanya as Peb walked over to hand her the water. "He's just got an attitude because he keeps being outsmarted," Arie looked over to Peb, "because he's fucking dumb!" Arie looked back at Hinanya, shrugging. "It's true."

"Take the water so I can get the fuck outta here," Peb said to Hinanya. "It ain't right anywhere in here. Sucks they got you too."

She took a bottle of water and Peb left. Hinanya regained her focus. "Why does it feel as if I've been here before?"

"Oh, great starter. I think I have a whole story to tell, and that will answer the majority of these questions. That might be how we do this... for expedience. But for now, we'll do your way. It feels as if you've been here before because you have, Hinanya."

"I don't even remember."

"That's how it is meant to be. A vague, haunting familiarity. That's how we conditioned you to feel."

"What is this place?"

"We make the 8IL here. It's the only place in the world it is being produced. Some other stuff happens here. We do cool experiments. It was built by the government when they were afraid of nuclear war. It was supposed to be a shelter for the elite, but when the Cold War fizzled out, the place became obsolete, so they gave it to the scientists. From there, some entities collaborated to create a synthetic drug more powerful than any previously created."

"Why?"

"You'll see!" Arie said jovially.

"How long will I be staying?"

"Oh hey, before I get around to answering that one, would you like some

8IL?"

Arie saw Hinanya's face twitch, her forehead creased. "I'll have to decline."

Arie made a note of that.

"What are you writing down?"

"That you are not interested in 8IL. This way the cooks know not to drug your food," he said pleasantly. "You're obligated to stay here at least up until you've delivered our baby to us and are of sound mind and body to leave. We will offer you mental health services and subsequent prescriptions if deemed necessary. Or you can totally leave as you are after you've had the baby. To—as I have already mentioned, kill yourself if that is truly your wish. We're not here to impose upon your free will... although, after I tell you everything, you may be inclined to disagree with me. I would also be remiss if I didn't add that appropriate arrangements will be made with the authorities, and you will not be suspected or identified as having anything to do with the night of Shaun Nichol's murder. Cool?"

"Yeah, great."

"I would like to explain why we intend to let you go. See, we've known about you your entire life. In truth, we've orchestrated many major events throughout it all. I think you'll agree with me that you have quite a suicidal mindset. Society supposes we help our fellow man off the ledge to save him. But, and I know you're with me here," Arie leaned across the table and look deep into Hinanya's eyes, "you have to be worth it. In the case of all other animals and species we know of, if you've truly lost the will to live, there's no helping you. They don't pander. No, they just move on. Suffice it to say, Hinanya, if you want help, we'll do everything we can. That's the human in us. But if you're all set, I don't mind yielding. Although I know you want to answer the question."

"The question?" Hinanya asked.

"Is there a metaphysical substructure to the universe, are you able to feel it?"

"I don't care to comment on that," said Hinanya.

"Oh, I can definitely see how that would make you uneasy." Arie took a sip of water after Hinanya, who'd taken a warm water bottle, as he had anticipated.

"Arie, what is your plan for the baby?"

"Ah, yep. See? I told you. Now, I'm going to tell all here. If you don't mind. I'm sure you're cool with it."

Hinanya nodded with a sour expression.

"Like I alluded to earlier, your life has been almost completely fabricated. To give you a quick example, have you ever seen *The Truman Show*?

"No... But I understand the premise. His entire life was a sham... everyone he met, they were actors on a set. He grew up like that. Then discovered the truth."

"Exactly. The difference is that you're in real life, and so there are a ton of independent variables. About half of all you've interacted with in your life were agents or liaisons of Wenin. Of that, both the people you supposed were your parents are not actually your parents, but liaisons tasked with raising you as their own."

"Great work. Look at me now."

"Yep."

"Who are my real parents?"

"Dad: unknown. Mom: name not important, deceased, just another Uncle Rawls kind of statistic, to be honest. She was a nasty drug addict, and if you think you're bad now, be grateful that she gave you up for a pile of drugs. I mean, she was obligated to leave you in our care due to the fact that she had accidentally got her hands on a precursor to 8IL. See where I'm going with this?"

"Yeah..."

"That you grew up in New Orleans and that 8IL is only there is no coincidence. It's all been carefully calculated. Think what New Orleans is. You've got a history of staunch Catholicism, voodoo culture from the Haitian refugees of a slave revolt, and a population that's perpetually glazed over in some intoxicated oblivion. 8IL could be useful in a place like New Orleans because, if there is a metaphysical region we could possibly perceive, the portal ought to be more accessible here. That's what this Wenin business is all about. Answering the question."

"I did not have an out-of-body experience with it, though," Hinanya objected.

"Right. But Uncle Rawls told you he did. Drugs only hint at the possibility. 8IL is a man-made substance. Humans are trapped in their bodies. But you believed his account, which allowed us to see if your bias there would yield any new results. Look, this is what people don't get. Nothing can give you the truth. It's always seen through some kind of filter. Any truth you got from 8IL was its using parameters. And our own nervous system. Very unsavory. No, you were selected for this entire thing. We gave you a psychological obsession with the question, suicidal tendencies, but also the drive to pursue the deeper meaning of it. We made Uncle Rawls be the first person you encountered who verbalized your thoughts. 8IL was designed by my partner and me. Together, we are perhaps Wenin. An entity composed of a male and female working together. I've spent my life on this thing, and I think it may be a dud, but Hinanya, if you so choose, after you've given birth, I would like to kill you. And bring you back, of course! Pronounce you medically dead. With the help of 8IL, you may have a kind of special preliminary coverage to see something no one else has yet. Not some light at the end of the tunnel mind you, but true transcendence. That's the true function of 8IL—to garner information from people who have gone past the edge. What do you think? Well, before you say anything look at it this way.

"Most people, as you know, operate themselves under basic evolutionary functions: the fight-or-flight response, fighting over territory, and so on. They breathe, but they do not live. After they learn to communicate with others, they breed. That's it. The cycle repeats. Our research seeks to push human consciousness past these primitive programs and become a greater thing, one which can defeat death instead of fear it. While the world's politics go on and on about equality and poverty, we are honing in on the one true equalizer. Research any information we can about how to work with what's after death. If we ever succeed, we could change the way the world views everything.

"The problem is, you have grown to hate how people are operating, because in this world these people are nothing more than animals, but animals with the ability to destroy themselves. We go through these cycles unconsciously, and I for one think it's time for an awakening, hence projects such as you. That's the truth."

"The truth?" Hinanya asked. "You raped me. You made me a person that hates herself. And now you want to kill me? After you tell me it's never something I've really wanted but some attribute you programmed through years of a faked life?"

"Hinanya, don't feel so offended. Most people aren't like you and decide to live fake lives anyway. Besides, like I said, this part is optional, but we did kind of design you to say yes. So revolt if you that's your cup of tea, but we both know what you really want."

"Yes then," Hinanya said. "Take the baby and give do whatever."

Arie anticipated that too, that lack of struggle. That was all he needed to do. Give her the truth. Just enough of a push to set her into oblivion. "Great, it's settled."

"So the baby, it'll be subjected to a manufactured life the same as mine?"

"Mhm," Arie said. "You have to get you're not the only one of the many so-called Trumans out there. But you are special, and we have invested a lot in you. Just think of it as an iterative progress, Hinanya. We can save the world, you know? That's what this is all about. Evolution of man and such. We do this, and someday, no more pissing matches over my god or your god. No more diminishing the value of life. We aim to create a procedure that might give people a lucid vision of what's after life. It may take generations, but we've already begun."

"Okay," said Hinanya. Arie saw tears in her eyes for the first time in the entire night. "One more question, then I'd like to be taken to my quarters. Who is Taylor?"

"Another Truman. Unaware as you were, though I see you've had abstract suspicions you chalked up to drugs. Taylor is actually your biological sister. The only real family you have. The mom you knew faked her pregnancy for months, and then we dropped off the newborn Taylor to y'all with ease."

"What is her purpose in all of this?"

"She has been conditioned to love you no matter how foul you are to her. We didn't have to condition her too much at all. She is your little sister, after all."

17. FAMILY

For two weeks, Hinanya did not see anyone besides Dr. Sierpiński, who would not only be delivering her child but was also the co-creator of 8IL.

Hinanya had her whole identity swept away, but the trauma hadn't landed yet. For days, her thoughts were anchored on her 8IL experience. She'd be taking it again soon. Going to her death. Would she even try to return?

In truth, Hinanya no longer had a grip on things. She'd been undermined. Often, she'd doubt bits and pieces, most of the time the whole thing, although the evidence was available if she looked hard enough. As a child, she'd been here. She couldn't summon specific memories, just feelings or impressions of the walls or the clinical smell of the place. Even though they were inside the facilities, Hinanya could hear the sound of crickets chirping and the train going to New Orleans whistling as it passed by from afar. It sounded as if she were in her apartment. She was forbidden from contacting the outside world, which didn't matter as Arie wouldn't tell her who else in her life was real or a liaison.

Was she even here? What about any of this was real or fake? She had no way of knowing.

Hinanya declined all offers for mental health services. All this time, she'd been pushing people away, and all along, they never genuinely cared for her anyway. She'd never suspected that.

For most of Hinanya's life, she had been criticizing the concept of family. But now hers was gone. All except Taylor.

And the baby. Their baby. That was one thing they refused to tell her, how it was they'd gotten her pregnant. They told her she already knew.

With all of this Hinanya had no idea what she wanted any longer. She feared finding out, as that too may be the wrong thing for her. One morning, during an examination, she asked Dr. Sierpiński if, after she was able to leave the facility, she'd be able to live a normal life.

"Hard to say, Hinanya. You've been made aware of your situation. We'll always be simultaneously gathering data and ensuring your continued existence. Unless, as Arie said you want to end things. It's the least we can do. To that effect, there will be people that aren't liaisons you'll meet, but you'll be constantly paranoid and unable to determine if they are being sent to forward our own ends with you or if it's just a random stranger independent of us. We will bind you to the agreement that you do not tell anyone about Wenin, 8IL, or the Trumans. I think you realize what happens if you do that."

Hinanya nodded. "You'll bring me back here."

"Once you've relinquished the child over to us, you may never see it again. Or attempt to seek it out for that matter."

"Right," Hinanya said.

"We have a deal."

"I know. I know. Dr. Sierpiński. I... lost who I was. I'll never get it back."

"Yeah, but that person was never designed to make it in the first place. We can effectively kill Hinanya and make you whatever you want, to a certain degree. You just have to be willing to start over and follow our rules. We have put you through a lot, and it's not a pretty thing to admit. You've been wronged, but we've always intended to fix it if that's what you want. It will take time, but we have advanced methods that can help you. Many Trumans live fulfilling lives after we have finished with that. We can set you up to get pregnant again without the 8IL. You never cared about family before, but if it's important to you now, you can have one."

"But not Taylor."

"No. She is an active Truman. You are to be relieved. As far as she knows, you will have committed suicide."

"This is all so comforting."

Dr. Sierpiński dropped the polite facade. "I'm trying my best here, Hinanya. It's not like we're building bombs or trying to take over the world. We've deemed that what we're doing has much more costs than benefits. You don't have to agree or disagree with us. Just don't think you are able to pull one over on us."

"Have I ever?" Hinanya asked seriously.

226

18. WORSE THAN HERE

Hinanya battled fatigue to make it out of bed. She went down to the cafeteria and ordered pancakes a la mode. Those at the facility cooked her anything she wanted, so long as she consumed the prenatal and supplementary pills had given to her. Hinanya did eat three meals a day, as she wanted to be as compliant as possible. The scientists and technicians all looked uncomfortably at one another as she sat down at a round table with them.

"What are you all working on today?" she asked them.

Bemused, an elderly female with curly auburn hair cleared his throat and said, "Oh, we can't share our work with you."

"But Arie said I was to have full access to this facility," Hinanya challenged.

"So you do," said a pale man. "You can roam as you please, but that doesn't mean we can tell you about our work."

"I see. Look, I'm just feeling really disenchanted with everything. Dr. Sierpiński and Arie tell me this place is, ultimately, doing good. Your whole mission is so ambiguous to me. In my life, I've seen the few friends I had destroyed by this place's noble intentions."

"I know Arie must have told you we are trying to objectively determine if it is possible to vacate the human body, to—"

"Sir, yes. Please, you don't need to explain your objectives, I get it. But what will the pending results of your projects do to prevent people like Stefan from killing themselves? People like Uncle Rawls from being slaughtered in the street by the police? People like Shaun from being murdered over... What? Did he die for drugs?"

"Nothing," said a cold voice from behind her. Arie. "There will continue to be victims in this world no matter our findings."

Hinanya flung out of her seat and stopped short of hitting Arie.

"Ow," Arie said with a chuckle, knocking a fist timidly against his sternum. "That would have hurt."

"I don't want to volunteer my life to your research anyway, Arie. I think I know what I want my life to be—I want to really help people. It's about wealth. And greed. I want to see the world's wealth redistributed."

He looked down as Peb approached and began sweeping. "Let's do take a walk outside when you're done eating."

It was the first time they'd let her leave the facility since she'd arrived.

The cafeteria was the central component of the subterranean place. Arie took them above, and they walked around the parabolic outline of the facility. Clouds dominated the sky, but Hinanya could see blues slices of the atmosphere occasionally appearing through the gray.

Arie cleared his throat and began. "My aim here is somewhat paradoxical. Since the beginning, man has ingested substances which have no nutritive value for purposes that run the gambit of curiosity, boredom, desire. To experience something beyond them. But the more stable something is, the higher it is actually able to go. Yet to make a person with too stable a foundation is to leave them devoid of curiosity. They languish and do not question.

"On the other end of things, you have the perpetually dissatisfied who press upon what they can't know. It may be drugs or the promise of a better world. The ability to ask why we're never satisfied promises the consequence of never truly being satisfied with an answer. Hinanya, when you were given the 8IL, did you deduct that there were actually two components, two doses? That it was intended for use in a ritual of two people?"

"Huh?" Hinanya asked.

"We knew you wouldn't have shared it with Shaun. Still, it was interesting to beg the question. But part of you finding us held clues to that effect. Like I was saying, you were conditioned to our specifications. So in some sense, you are our failure for not realizing the answer was a willingness to be venerable. You are only echoes of yourself. You found the 8IL to be disappointing because you wanted it to give you transcendence, an answer to the question."

"Stefan... I nearly gave him everything. Did you take him from me?"

"You blame yourself, no?"

Hinanya nodded.

"And why not? It could have been up to you. What did you see, I wonder? That night on 8IL. "

Hinanya went into great detail.

"Right. The post-trip of any drug is as important as the trip itself. And you were unchanged! You still wallow against the shadow of the ineffable. No one, as far as you knew, had any idea what you were up to but Shaun. And you saw fit to refuse him even the spoils of your journey. You regarded him as your enemies. Just an object in the world for your satisfaction—a drug dealer. Not a person, but a stain. An inconvenience. You didn't care what happened to him until he was gone. That's what sealed Shaun's fate. You were so interested in those phantoms chattering in your mind you set them upon Shaun."

"But if I had known—you are manipulating me. What is this all for? I don't want to talk to you. You've poisoned my whole life."

"Hinanya, there's this tribe. The Pomo. They tell of a portal, what they call *dua*. It leads to the spirit world. Whatever I do I do to see it open, to see it open for everyone. For all living beings to look and see within, and be able to return if they'd like. Like I said, nature can provide us a bit of that experience.

But it's not enough. Human belief is fractured over cultures and borders. When LSD was first created, it held so much potential. 8IL is the next step in synthetic drugs because it brings us one step closer to accepting our lot. It is more potent. It is holy. It beckons our coming together."

"Once it gets out to the public, it'll be prohibited," said Hinanya. "They'll make it a crime."

"A crime to salvage the world's people, then."

"The War on Drugs was a failure, but you're just doubling down on something that may never pay off."

"The government is violating people's civil liberties," said Arie. "Research has shown time and again that the proper application of hallucinogens can do a real number on depression. It's as simple as that."

"Yes!" said Hinanya. "There needs to be a policy that favors rehabilitation over criminalization for non-violent offenders. Treatment. If they are not culpable for any violent act, they should still be penalized, but too often they're buried by a heartless system. If we used just a fraction of the funding that went into the War on Drugs into helping addicts, things would improve so much."

"You can have your vision, I'll stick with my own thing," said Arie. "We use Trumans to change the world."

Hinanya thought she understood. "Are you saying... you take people... from a young age. You take them, don't you? Give them something they love and then turn it into something they hate? You drive them to the depths of their limits then turn them around. It's that what's this is all matter?"

Arie smirked. "You know it's interesting to see you perk up like this. Such a manic mess you are. You want to do so much than before. You want to stop us. You want to redistribute the world's wealth. You even have a vested interest in the baby."

"No... you take the baby. I just, I want for it to be spared what I've been through."

The two walked on for a time, then Arie asked, "Hinanya, do you know why the effort to redistribute the world's wealth wouldn't work, even if it was implemented?"

"I'm sure you know."

"Yep, I do. The problems we face in the world today, they demonstrate a stuckness. Cultural imprints. Greed. Even if, as you say, we find some way of putting all this money where it would do the most good, it wouldn't change human nature. Emphasis on rehabilitation for non-violent offenders won't sate people's desire to feel superior. Before money, there was ritual sacrifice. There was still debt, torture, slavery. Our issue is that we can't distinguish between values that need to be held fast to or let go. But where do those values of life stem from? No matter what is going on in the world, or who we are we all must contend with death. Some are just unfortunate enough to have it thrust upon them for reasons outside of their control. It's a hierarchy. And you just happened to come across a lot of people on the bottom. People clamor for justice for the black man who is murdered by a cop. But they are not equipped to accept the facts. Reality is not a place for justice. They say down with the system they support with their lifestyles. Their greed."

"I don't believe any of this. We can stop it," Hinanya said deftly. "We can change it. We are making so much progress every century and—"

"Fine," Arie interrupted. "Say we find a way to equal rights. There's still going to be an unstoppable excess consumption. Where do you think that road leads? There's still going to be people on the bottom. Are these people on the bottom greedier because they struggle for life? No matter what class you are in, there are criminals. There's either not enough money or always more to make. It's now tied to survival. Survival. That's what we do things for. There's value in life, but we now are programmed to feel it with green paper. We fortify our time with distractions and things to push away our last moment.

"Greed means you believe that these things, distractions will matter. But they won't. Meanwhile, our society unfolds all these vanities over that truth. My work, no matter what kind of damage it creates, will create an irrevocable wiring within the self. That's where the change will happen. My team and I work to stomp out dogmatism using these tools. From there we may root out greed. If we cannot do it with 8IL, we will pioneer a procedure to do it neurologically. Scientists, philosophers, religious leaders, all throughout time have sought an answer to the question. None seem to have succeeded. They have claims, but they haven't been able to truly manufacture the experience. To provide an answer to the question. That is why you suffered so, Hinanya. To usher in an age of secular morality."

They crested the hill above the underground facility. "Arie, have you ever wondered if, when you die, wherever you end up might be worse than here?"

230

19. LABOR

Whatever circumstances had led Hinanya back to the facility, it made her realize something important: she wasn't alone in the world. There were others like her, unaware of Wenin's full machinations. That included her baby. For all the losses she'd sustained over the weeks, the encroaching loss of the baby made her wish she could unite all the Trumans like her. There would be a great strength in their solidarity. But would it be enough to topple Wenin? Most likely not. In any case, Hinanya first had to give birth.

The time came. In great pain, they wheeled her from her room on a gurney, Arie watching over her until she was set to deliver the baby. Hinanya's lower back felt like it was being crushed by the force of her own flexing.

"Try to imagine stepping out of yourself and talking on one of our little walks," Arie suggested.

"The cramps are kind of keeping me here," Hinanya said.

She was in one of the facility's delivery rooms. This had all happened before. Her mother had been brought to a place like this to deliver her. And someday maybe her this children would be brought here. Unless—

I bet it's a boy!

Kurt. He'd said that.

She hadn't seen Kurt or Sasha at the facility. There was no use asking if they were liaisons all along. Arie could just lie.

By the time she was given an epidural, her pain was unbearable.

About an hour after the contractions had begun, Dr. Sierpiński gave her a piece of candy to suck on. "Pretty soon, you'll be out of here. Are you eager to leave?" she asked as a swarm of doctors and nurses rotated around Hinanya.

"Somewhat. I'll appreciate the weight loss."

"That's the spirit! So I heard you are backing out of the induced death after all?"

"Yes."

"Afraid of not coming back?"

"Something like that," said Hinanya alongside a sharp pain in her abdomen.

"It's pretty routine. We get better at the process each time. We've never lost anybody."

"Regardless. I've had enough of you people."

Dr. Sierpiński looked quizzically at her. "This arrangement isn't becoming an issue, is it?"

Hinanya looked away from Dr. Sierpiński.

"For God's sake, Hinanya. You were trying to induce a miscarriage."

"It's powerful. That's all. You're right. What do you want me to say? At least let me see my baby, that's all."

"That's our baby," corrected Dr. Sierpiński. "And we will."

"Right. But my sister."

"I don't understand."

Hinanya groaned as her insides seem to stir with nausea. "I know I couldn't give this child the care it requires. I feel woozy."

"They're trying to take care of that for you. What would you have done without us? Delivered the baby yourself?"

That was true. All the same, Hinanya asked Dr. Sierpiński to leave her alone.

Hinanya recognized the sensation of being lifted and tousled around gently. She forgot what was happening for a moment and was spooked. Her breathing got away from her. She thought then of the gift of life. She was woefully present.

"No one ever told me. Is the baby going to be okay? With the drugs, I mean?"

"Hinanya, I think it would be best if you tried to find some pleasant memories to focus on your breathing," Dr. Sierpiński said. "Did you spend some time with some monks in Indonesia a few years ago? I know you did, breathe. Every thing's going to be taken care of."

"They had dedicated their lives to asceticism, limiting their physical experience to beckon a metaphysical or spiritual one. Where are they now?"

"Still at it, Hinanya."

"I'd like to go back there. I hope I don't accidentally go at the same time you send the baby."

"Quit dwelling on the future," Dr. Sierpiński.

"Where's Arie?"

"He's arranging your affairs. Going to painstaking lengths for your future so you don't have to."

"What a guy." Hinanya sighed as she felt another contraction. "I want the blankets," she said, resisting the nurses who were taking the blankets away.

"We will restrain you if you aren't cooperative, Hinanya," Dr. Sierpiński warned her. The woman moved out from Hinanya's sight, under her, examining her parts. "She still isn't completely dilated."

"Wow, this baby is an asshole," said Hinanya. "Cool." Hinanya babbled on.

"We've got it, Hinanya," said one of the nurses. She couldn't tell which one. "Just keep listening to Angel."

"Who?"

"Me," said Dr. Sierpiński.

"Of course that's your name."

Eventually, they commanded Hinanya to push. This is exactly what she didn't want. Ever. But all suffering was supposed to be paid for in the end. The joy of motherhood. The gift of continuity. This whole thing wasn't about her anymore. It couldn't always be. Did they know that?

Hinanya imagined writing in a dream trance against the feeling of her organs being pulled out of her.

"Hinanya, are you still with us?" Dr. Sierpiński. "It's almost over, but you've got to listen to us, hon!"

If she could be willing to die for Shaun, she could die for Taylor, wherever she was. Taylor. She was in danger. Hinanya had to do something for her.

For the one in her arms.

"It's a boy," said Dr. Sierpiński.

"I'm holding it," Hinanya observed.

"Only so you can willingly let it go."

"Like what I wanted," said Hinanya with a weak grimace. No name dared come to her. She saw him, and it was amazing. His complexion was like hers almost, just a little bit lighter. He was smeared with bodily fluids. Hinanya would have, one day earlier, regarded the whole scene as disgusting. Now there was bliss.

20. Programming Intact

At 5:07PM on July 10th, four hours after the baby was extracted from her, Hinanya Ven was pronounced dead. As they steadily pumped her with the necessary drugs to slow her heart to fail, she whimpered of promises broken. They hadn't even taken out of the room she'd given birth in.

"You'll come back in a few minutes," Arie told her. "Or stay there for all I care."

"I don't want you to kill me," she begged.

"It's done, Hinanya."

"I don't agree to this. I never did, or I changed my mind. I trusted you. Don't do this."

"You've judged your existence as worthless. What's the difference now? Have we cured you of your death fetish?"

"Don't kill me!"

Those were Hinanya's last decipherable words.

She'd been a most interesting case study. Taking her family and existence for granted then clinging to both when they were shown to be counterfeit. Arie only wished he could make those vanities true in her head once more. It was all funny to him. That she riled against being killed yet she was so insistent on having an abortion. What a hypocrite.

After she was gone, Angel sidled up next to Arie. "Is there anything to be gained in bringing her back? Why do it? I mean, we've already broken our word to her. What's the value here?"

Arie stretched his arms above his head. "I hate it when you act like the questions you ask me are mine to figure out. Angel, there's the value of our word then there's the irrational rationality of love."

"Let this one lay, Arie. She's going to ruin everything when she wakes up."

"Look at that," said Arie, pointing down at the Glock holstered at her side. "We gave her the gun, and she didn't shoot anyone, not even herself. She really went on about being the only one who should be able to end her life."

"Take it away," Angel demanded. "Keeping a loaded gun in her hands is the same thing as giving her life back to waste."

"Twenty years on this one. And she'll finally think she knows freedom. But we know exactly what she'll do when she's awake."

Angel shuddered. "Hinanya only wants the baby because we took it away."

Before Hinanya was revived, she dreamed. Dreams she knew she would never remember. There was no light at the end of the tunnel. There was only an accumulating nothingness enveloping her. Each movement she made, no matter how heroic or fervent, depleted the remainder of what she could do. So much like falling asleep. Thoughts of love were disregarded as she faced the end in a way she had never wanted. That had been constant—she would die by her own hands if she had a choice. But the choice had been taken from her, as had her life.

"I just want something to be known before we do this," Arie told Angel.
"What?"
"I love what we do here. I see the need for it. But my son doesn't."
"Arie, Stefan wasn't a Truman."
"No," Arie said morosely. "And neither was Felix." He regarded some charts on the wall of the room. "Do you remember when the two of them used to sneak off during lunch?"
"The high school," Angel said. "Of course."
"He'd smoke two and a half cigarettes then let Hinanya have what was left."
"It wasn't until then that her figure really began to upset her."
"Right, right. Because of him handing it over to her, she probably figured he wanted her to smoke so she could be thinner. I guess, even if you do it for a long time, the body does a wonderful job of recouping if you manage to quit."
"There's not much else like that," Angel said with a flash of despair.
They stood over Hinanya, terrified at their own deaths, doing everything they could to prolong the tormented girl's awakening.

Alive, Hinanya rustled in her bed. The first thing she saw when returning from being pronounced dead was Arie. He wore a black Hawaiian shirt with a diagonal pattern of white flowers.
"You're back," Arie said. "Any luck?"
"No," Hinanya said. "You told me that part was optional, and then you went ahead and did it anyway after I begged you not to."
"I betrayed you," Arie said.
"Yes."
"You hate me."

"Yes."

"But you also find me fascinating." Arie twirled his fingers around, and his left hand became a gun. "What do you say we duel?"

"What?" Hinanya asked.

"My gun against your gun. Right now."

Hinanya recalled the gun was at her side as they had killed her. Why hadn't she used it to stop them?

"You can kill me for what I did to you. Is that how you see the universe? You would kill to preserve your own life or to preserve Shaun's life. Would you kill someone who has already killed you to offer balance? My life is over, Hinanya. I'm ready to be as disappointed as you are."

"You would win the duel," Hinanya assured him. "You're bluffing me. You have some kind of ability or tick you put into me. I saw what you did to those cops."

"Hard to forget, huh? What I've done to you already." Arie pretended to cock his gun. "Isn't it so telling about the psychology of guns?"

Hinanya had just been brought back to life. She was weary. "Shoot me if you will, I'm not playing your games anymore."

Arie reinforced the imaginary gun and brought it to Hinanya's temple. "I could kill you again."

"You're boring me." But Hinanya slowly lifted the Glock from her side and pointed it at him.

They were deadlocked, with Hinanya having no idea what Arie's fake gun would do to her.

"You want to know what really caused Stefan to do it?"

"I don't care anymore."

They glared at one another, cursing each blink they had to make. Hinanya saw this as another test.

Arie sighed. He couldn't help but surrender. "Fine." The man loosened the pressure against her temple. His imaginary gun became fingers that undid the bonds that had been attached to her since she was in labor. "Because no one gets to know that. I don't care what a suicide note says. We never get to know."

"That seems to be bothering you more than it does me," said Hinanya."

"We're finished with you, Hinanya. You can go. Fight your little crusade out there in the world."

Hinanya tried to get up, but she was unable. "Didn't you do that to me so I could report my experience back to you? I must have left my body if I died, right?"

"Maybe so. Your life from here on out will tell us what we need to know."

"I don't remember leaving my body. There was no essence that I left. I didn't *go* anywhere. I just discontinued being until you brought me back."

"That's... relatively disappointing," Arie said. "But how could you go from being to non-being and back to being again?"

"There had to have been some residual being somewhere."

"But not a soul that transcended your body."

"No."

"Now, that's really disappointing. But like I said, you're a free girl now."

As soon as Hinanya was alone, she tried to walk. It was challenging, but she was able to cling to the wall for support. After a few steps, her knees buckled involuntarily, and she fell. Her arms were barely reactive to it, so she hit the floor with a thud that made contact with the side of her head at her left ear. Determined, Hinanya rolled and scraped at the wall. On her way, she only saw one person. Peb.

"I'll help you, Hinanya," he said as she panted against the wall.

21. CONVALESCENT

Two days later, they still wouldn't let Hinanya leave. One's of Arie's accumulating lies. Peb brought her lunch, and she asked him, "Do you want to help me or do you have to?"

"You been through a lot. I still think you an ugly bitch, but I ain't much myself if all I do is serve you."

"What's up with the crickets?"

"They won't tell me."

"Let's get out of here," Hinanya said.

"Fuck no."

"You and me, Peb. And the baby."

"Fuck that. It wouldn't work."

"They left me the gun. That's all we need."

"You dumber than me."

"That's just what Arie wants you to think. It's a trick of his. All we need to do is find a road, get back to New Orleans. I think... he's implying that's what he wants me to do."

"And what? You sayin' you wanna keep the baby now?"

Hinanya avoided the question by getting her things together. Then she divulged to him part of the truth. "That's not the point. I can't let them do this again."

"Yours isn't the only baby," Peb pointed out. "I saw others when I first came here. We can't get 'em all. Plus we are so far out from anything. It's fuckin' wild beyond this place. Nothin' but swamps."

"The highway has to be near here. Some road. Come on, Peb. You said you felt like a slave here."

"I fuckin' am!"

"I imagine they're listening or will hear this conversation soon. We need to go now. Last chance. If you're not in this with me, then I hope you'll stand aside, so I don't have to hurt you again." Hinanya pointed down at the Glock.

"I'm sick of this. You people always pullin' me in every direction."

"What would you want to do if you had a choice?"

"Get the fuck outta here. But that ain't exactly an option."

"Maybe not. But why not try?"

"What if someone tries to stop us?"

"How bad do you want to get out of here?"

"Bad," said Peb.

"If someone tries to stop us, you'll have to hold me steady, and help me aim, so I can get a shot at them."

"That's heavy, Hinanya," he said, seeming to reconsider. "Fuck it, I'm in.

Lemme find your baby."

"Attaboy."

"Shit, why not just give the gun to me?"

"Because it's mine," Hinanya said, making her way out of the room. Peb took the lead. It only took two minutes for the alarms all over the facility to go off. Hinanya could no longer hear the crickets.

"It's him," Hinanya said then fired out a single round of her gun, sending shattered glass all over the nursery. Peb threw a blanket over the crib and tried his best to cover the baby's ears. "They'll probably stop shooting once we get him out. Will you hold him?"

"I guess."

"Look, now that's how I got in," Peb said, pointing at the hole between the ceiling and the wall in the room over from where they'd found the baby. There had been others, all labeled by date of birth. Each one was crying out due to the commotion.

"I'm barely going to fit."

"It'll work. You go first, and I'll back you up."

"With whose gun?"

"Damn, Hinanya, hand it over."

Hinanya reluctantly took the gun out of her hands, giving it to Peb, and she cradled her baby with both hands. He seemed very irate. Hinanya was unable to comfort him.

Peb had to help Hinanya squeeze out of the aperture that led outside. They were free, but as soon as Peb started running with her, he stopped. "Ah, no. I'm fuckin' done."

"What?" Hinanya asked.

"I'm going back. Let them do what they want to me. I think they let us leave. It's all part of it. That was too easy, Hinanya."

"No," protested Hinanya. "We need to find help." She tried shoving him back into a run. "He controls people! Fight it! He's done some kind of conditioning on it."

Peb looked up into the night. "Stop. Somethin' ain't right. They let you keep the gun. They... no, this is fucked. I'm stayin' put."

"Peb, I can't hold a baby and escape. I can't get very far without your help. *Please*." She grabbed his shoulder. "Don't abandon me."

Peb scoffed. "Isn't your whole thing you don't ask for help? I wish you the best of luck. I've fucked with these people enough already. I mean, we ain't even need to think about this. The police still be lookin' for you. You

240

can't go to them."

"Not alone. That's why you need to come with me. Alone, I look crazy."

"Hinanya, you are crazy. Arie told me so."

"Stop being afraid! We've made it out, Peb. We might as well see how far we can go." Hinanya snatched the Glock from Peb's hand. It was a challenge since she had the baby in the crook of one arm. Stepping back, Hinanya pointed the gun at him.

"You dumb bitch, you ain't goin' shoot me."

"How do you figure?"

"Arie said so."

"What?"

"He said you don't have the killer instinct."

"Arie anticipated this?"

"Yeah, see what I'm saying?!"

"But you're not a liaison!"

"Not like Caso, no. Nah, just doing what I want. Arie said that's a big thing for you too. I don't know. It's like I see my brother, he seem to know how to fix this life. I know he burned me before, but I gotta figure his game out. Shouldn't you get goin'?"

"Did he ask you to help me?"

Peb frowned. "Not in words."

"What does he think I'm going to do?"

"Get the baby away. Try at least."

Hinanya squeezed her eyes shut. There was no time, but still, she asked, "What's your real name, kid?"

"Start running. I'll tell you when I know you getting away."

Hinanya did as he said.

She liked Steven a lot better than Peb.

22. OPEN EYES

Through it all, the baby seemed fine to Hinanya. Using the memory of her arrival, she was able to backtrack until she found a country road. Then she was led back to the train tracks. She considered hopping on the next freight train to New Orleans, but she wasn't able to justify the risk of jumping with the baby, so she walked several more hours until her devastated body couldn't take the pressure on her feet any longer. On top of that, something about the train made Hinanya feel as if Arie was counting on her using it to escape.

The veins on her feet beat roughly. After a brief nap, she was able to forge ahead a bit further until she, at last, heard bustling activity—I-10. It didn't feel as if she was being pursued.

She had to find a place safe from Wenin. Then she could worry about the rest. Hinanya was loathed to realize her actions were a manifestation of love. To push her way out of the facility and to make it this far, that drive came from a need to see the child spare of the course her own life had taken. The blisters and cuts on her feet didn't matter. What mattered were his eyes. They were beautiful. Hinanya didn't recognize them at all. It made sense. Lifting the baby's brow to her nostrils, she breathed him in.

The baby would need to eat soon. She decided to hitchhike instead of stopping to feed him. There were many cars passing down the highway.

The third car she flagged down, a station wagon, pulled over for her.

The driver met Hinanya's eyes while turning down the dial of his radio, some popular folk singer. The driver wore a cowboy hat and spoke as if straight from the bayou. "Hun. You look downright halfway to your deathbed. Where the hell you comin' from?"

"I'm in danger. Please take me to New Orleans."

"Miss, all due respect, I don't want to know anythin' about danger. Just want to give you sanctuary."

"Can you get me there?"

"Is that a baby?"

"It's mine."

"Fair enough. Get in."

The driver informed Hinanya that his name was George, and they'd be in New Orleans in about a half-hour. Hinanya had no idea what time it was, George's clock radio wasn't working. The music was still playing from the car speakers, however. A droning drum beat with a sonorous chord progression accompanied by harmonica and violin. Hinanya still thought she'd heard it somewhere before, but she couldn't place it.

Without the clock, the only clue as to the time was the expansive night sky that she peeked at as they sped on.

George talked at length, eventually mentioning that he owned a chain of chicken shacks out in New Orleans, and he'd recently lost a pantry boy. The track was on repeat, and Hinanya felt closer to identifying it and in doing so, she began catching the lyrics from the man and woman singing a reflective duet.

"Yeah, good guy he was. Then there was another guy, disappeared recently. Worked part-time on the weekend to help pay for his son's college. Smart as hell on top of that. Knew all sorts of little tricks for cooking and cleaning. I'd have promoted him, but I think then he'd replaced me as the owner. I get insecure like that sometimes. See, he was a professor himself. Too bad, huh?"

Hinanya had taken a gamble and it hadn't paid off. She sat in the backseat of Buckland's car. Arie had worked at Buckland's as a guise. She identified the song, as well. It was "Oh Sister" by Bob Dylan.

"Let me out!" Hinanya said.

Buckland murmured a negation. "You can't do the right thing. But I suppose that's all right. The guilt will make you better..." He trailed off and then sang a line along with the recording: "And you must realize... the dangggger!" Buckland cackled.

"What?"

"Is there something you wanna tell me, girl?"

Hinanya braced herself. "You caught me on your camera. Offered that reward for free chicken. But someone else was accused in my stead. It was all part of Wenin's plans anyway."

"Yep. In all fairness, I didn't give a damn about tacklin' the graffiti problem. I just wanted to look good and get some publicity. Also, I'm just following orders, sorry to say."

Hinanya felt a sinking feeling within. The baby tousled against her breast, stretching. Hinanya's counterfeit parents often played this song in the background of their family activities. It was on a loop.

"To be honest with you, Hinanya, you nearly got away."

"Why did he let me leave in the first place? I don't understand."

"Free will or somethin'. Arie's tryin' new things all the time. So remember what I said about not bein' able to do the right thing?"

"What about it?"

"Since Arie told you everythin', you've cultivated a familial sense of duty to at least two people—your sister Taylor and the baby."

"Yes."

"He went back on his word in a sense, so you felt right in doin' that same, no?"

"I would have taken the baby in any case."

"Of course. The life of a Truman is such a mind-fuckin'. I get that. But,

244

and I'm sorry to have to be the one to inform you of this, but you've got a choice to make."

"You're not getting the baby while I'm alive, Buckland."

"Okay, well, your mind's made up, but I haven't laid out your options yet. You always this irrational? You ever listen to these words?" He whipped his right hand to gesture to the radio. "Don't create sorrow, Hinanya."

"What do you want me to do? I've always hated this song so... Seriously, what do you want?"

"No, it's what do *you* want? See, right now, as you sit with that baby, you demonstrate a greater love and tenacity than your own mother did for you. And your sister. Your sister, who right now is pinned against a real killer." Buckland thudded harshly on the dashboard, and a thud from behind her erupted in a sporadic rhythm. "You got like, what? One bullet left in your gun? Which you can use to shoot me and escape, but I'm drivin' real slow-like, and now you know why. If you fire that shot and this car starts careening, my fuckin' nasty swamp boy will kill her in a prolonged and slow fashion."

"What do you want?" Hinanya asked in desperation. She turned the volume knob down on the song, but the song continued to play at the same volume through the speakers.

"The score is that if you give up that there baby that you never wanted in the first place, you get Taylor intact. Okay, maybe a bit traumatized 'cause my guy may have tongued her ear canal a little, just a consequence that accompanies those tight quarters. Refuse to give us the baby, and we kill Taylor anyway, and the last thing she'll know is it was your call. Where the fuck do you think you'll go anyway? We've been tracking you all along."

"I thought I'd visit my old tags and show the baby... my other creations. But I guess I can't do that now."

"No. You can't do nothin'. We tried to warn you, lady. You can't pull one over on us."

"I still don't understand," Hinanya mused. "Why did he even let me leave in the first place?"

"You're a human experiment. We don't get reliable data controllin' *all* the variables."

They didn't speak for a time. Buckland only added several minutes later, "You could always just off yourself. That'd save Taylor and the baby. We only puttin' her in peril because you are being so contrary."

Hinanya remained contrary in the dissonant thundering of a train off in the distance.

23. EXTRACTOR

There are but two things every person, regardless of circumstance, ought to be given in unconditional abundance. Time and love. For neither is eternal. They go from mother to child, man to woman. But sometimes, the love needed is not bestowed. Or it is not felt. When this happens, time becomes more hollow. Time is needed to cultivate love and love gives meaning to time. That is how love and time are entirely codependent. As a result, when one is deprived of the other after a period of union, the results can be startling. Sorrowful animals whose words do not constitute speech but a primitive longing which admits their time in love had been callously squandered. Or ones who never assimilated the feelings or facts they believed could save them.

This is why the world is not as it ought to be. People are too often not genuinely concerned with time or love. These two things tend to be perceived as habits instead of responsibilities. Hinanya understood this as there wasn't a lot of love or time left in her. At some point during her own programmed upbringing, she'd been made to scrutinize the value of time and love. Now she found herself with a love that she would not have ample time to express.

Along an empty road, still the person she was, Hinanya divested what she could to the sight of her sister and the dead man who'd done harm to her. It seemed her sister was tranquilized. Alive but unresponsive. She'd unleashed her full primal fury upon those who tried to deprive her of her baby. Hinanya had found two objects in the back seat of that vehicle a baby's car seat and a sniper rifle.

As much as she wished to protect her sister, she could not wake up her. The feeling of being cornered pervaded Hinanya. She had dead bodies of Wenin liaisons. It had been out of her control. But Arie knew exactly where she was.

It was morning, and the light from the sky felt like it was boring into her eyes. Sleep-deprived, she tried to think of a plan. But all she could do was recall Stefan's final moments.

Which she had not been there for.

Liaisons were surely coming for her. But she would not yield. Arie was feeding her options, but each one limited the next. The only person she could trust was knocked out. She had to settle the matter alone. Because she could not trust Arie's words. Well, she was not alone, strictly speaking. It was hard for her to realize what not being alone was really like.

All she could do for her sister was leave her near a police station. It was all she could think to do. Wenin couldn't control all of the police, could they? This would be it. How could Hinanya tell Taylor of Wenin? The truth was, she could not. It was beyond her willpower to. She left Taylor there on a sideway, with scribbles torn from her notebook. They'd all call Hinanya crazy, but there might be enough there for Taylor to be spared. She would never know. Hinanya, she would never know. What happened to Stefan. And Taylor would never know what happened to Hinanya. That was all Hinanya wanted.

It had to be better not to know sometimes. What Hinanya knew now left her beyond recognition. Why did her mind keep thinking of Stefan pointing the gun at himself? She found herself mirroring the scene.

Hinanya made a stop at the CVS to purchase baby supplies, enough for a many days, and some flats for her pulverized heels. The clerk seemed not to consider her disheveled appearance out of the ordinary.

Certain she had not deluded herself into buying clothing, toys, and a stroller for the baby, Hinanya parked the car as close to her apartment building as she could get. She shuffled up and down the steps until everything was outside of her studio. For some reason, she saw the broken window by her door as a good sign. The hidden key was still in the crevasse she'd left it in.

No one was inside. Hinanya made sure of it, and then she got everything she'd brought upstairs inside. The baby was asleep. It had pooped, but Hinanya handled both well.

Hinanya barricaded herself and the baby within her apartment. Every object that was not bolted to the ground was piled against the door. Hinanya unscrewed the closet and bathroom door and positioned them against the windows. She found a box of bullets and reloaded her Glock. Then she leaned the rifle against one of the windows. There was much more to be done, but Hinanya wanted to lie down and sleep with her child just one last time before the end, to cue up her dreams to ask what he would become if they'd just let him. Anything. Even if the baby was not hers.

They would stay in here. If anyone came, Hinanya would shoot them. She'd shoot them until there was only one bullet left.

But time stretched out and no one did. No one came to help her or harm her.

She constantly looked out into her neighborhood, hearing but not seeing sirens.

The visions of Stefan had entirely subsided. But Hinanya was so uptight she did not feel any sense of relief.

How odd it was that the baby didn't understand what a gun was. As Hinanya caressed his face with the barrel of the Glock, he thought it was some silly game and seemed overjoyed.

Hinanya knew of certain moral calculations which could justify suicide. But hers would not be rational. It was never meant to be. She was to lash out at the remaining sum of time her love had been.

That was Arie's plan. To see how far she'd go to see they didn't recover the baby.

Her deepest desire was to have them ambush her, knock a hole in the ceiling and come in as if on a mission for the baby. The tumult would attract the authorities. Communication would at least be possible then. A chance. No, Hinanya realized, Arie had no interest in having police summoned. This was a conflict between Arie and herself. She respected that. If she just started shooting outside, the police would come no matter what. But it wasn't that simple. Arie had provided her with that rifle. If she ended her life, no one would be able to breach her barricade in time before the authorities showed up to assess the scene. That was assuming Arie's connections were not that deep. Hinanya had no way of knowing.

Hinanya wished all she could call up to her angels, Felix, Shaun, Stefan. If they were there, all they would do now was close their eyes to her and have faith in her coming act. They would guide her, tell her this might be a mistake.

In her delirium, she thought she heard a knock at the door. But when she asked, "Who is it?" no one replied. She tore away at the stack that blocked any chance of exit. Her words echoed. Was she really here? Was Wenin after her? Did that exist? Of course there was. And this was the only way to stop them. So she remained. And fed her baby.

Ten minutes went by, and still, no one. She would write an abstract piece. Someday, someone would know. Everyone would know.

Know what this was like.

She twisted her wrist with the Glock in her hands as it circled the around and under her nose, then to the baby. Hinanya began sobbing. It was the only certain way to spare the child of her fate.

The baby did not sob. Did not object. Hinanya put the Glock down and pressed her hands against his cheeks. "Don't worry. I love you. As long as I am, I love you. Weighed against what could be... that would be more. So much more, love. And I don't know for sure, but everything may be fine."

Hinanya wished there was some great conflict that would take place. A grand battle against an enemy she could attack and batter until it was on the ground, pitiful and bleeding, confronted and defeated. That she could handle. That she had been trained for. Not for this. Not for the ultimate battle to be the weight of her own decision. If she was gone, it could allow someone to spare the baby from Wenin. From herself. Take him away. She could take him away herself. What was she thinking?

"You know I never knew I was one that wanted to be loved," she said to her baby. "I just thought if I suffered enough, suicide would be rational. But I have no right. But you know what's left then..."

It was decided. The gun was back in her hands. She moved from a prayer position to standing up over the baby wriggling on the floor.

Hinanya Ven closed her eyes to her act before the target of Stefan's gun was aligned. And a single shot burst out to deafening proportion, ceding time and love.

Thank you so much for reading!

Please, if you have a minute I have a huge favor to ask of you.

Leave a review on this title's Amazon page. Reviews don't have to be long, just a sentence or two relaying how you felt about what you've just read. I'm at the beginning of my career as an indie author and it helps me a lot to grow and continue creating even better stories that I can share with you.

& if you thought *Writer, Seeker, Killer* was great, spread the word by sharing it on social media or telling your friends about it!

I have a lot of interesting stuff coming soon.

I tend to write in different genres, but I am constantly writing.

My next book will be the first installment of sci-fi series telling the story of the first group of humans to leave Earth on a permanent basis. Thematically it follows up on many things discussed in "Writer, Seeker, Killer".

Interested?

Sign up at:
Ryansleavitt.com

Check out my YouTube channel!

In addition to writing book, I also make videos on consciousness expansion and philosophy. It's a great way to see what I'm up to week to week. Search Ryan S. Leavitt on YouTube.

About the Author

Ryan S. Leavitt is a fiction author, primarily writing thrillers and science fiction with philosophical undertones. His books have been featured on BookBub and he has also appeared on the briefly televised reality sitcom *Quiet Desperation*. He currently lives in New Orleans.